THE
LONELY
WALK

THE
LONELY
WALK

You Can't Escape Your Past

Jonathan Shaw

To order additional copies of this book, contact:
Xlibris Corporation
1-888-795-4274
www.Xlibris.com
Orders@Xlibris.com
51943

FACT

The island of Gunkanjima does exist but has not been used since the 1940s and travel to this island is forbidden to this day. There are no plans to occupy it again or transform it in any way. The building of man-made islands is physically possible, with example to Kansai International Airport, ten miles offshore west of Japan; yet no Western country has attempted such a task, yet. The existence of Frontiera Island is completely fictitious.

The company Lime.Inc does not exist, and the British embassy in Washington is not connected to any external businesses or weapons dealers. However, the American government does use public offices and fake companies to front secretive activities.

ACKNOWLEDGMENTS

A million thanks to my parents when writing this book. To Ian Schilabeer for his constant nagging to get me to see most of England. Ben Swan and Paul Stannett, the best mates anyone can have, for keeping me going since school. A debt of gratitude to the Japanese anime artists of *Love Hina* and *Metropolis*, who gave me inspiration to my characters. John Prescott, who ran my country for ten years when Tony Blair wasn't around, very precariously, giving us a good laugh and tearing up the English dictionary—the inspiration behind Jif Kitchen. All the staff at Xlibris, you showed the first interest in my work. And not forgetting, Thomas Nordanstad, whose short film *Hashima, Island of Grief* provided the research for the scenes, and the people of *www.schemamag.ca* who led me to the island of Gunkanjima.

PREFACE

September 13th 2003, as Jif remembered it.

A rapid change from the council estates of Humberside. Jif could only remember the plane landing. A heavy thud and rattle as the wheels slammed into the runway. Everything was going great; he was treated like royalty and enjoyed every minute of it. He sat in first class, a comfortable reclining chair in deep ocean blue and mini-TV on his armrest. He sat in the far right window seat with two empty spaces next to him.

The plane was half empty. It only had Asian passengers and stewardesses and no Western faces, making him feel both connected and outside. But they all welcomed him with traditional hospitality and heavily accented English. He was wearing a brand-new gunmetal grey pin-striped suit he'd bought the previous day, for his new job.

The pilot called out on his intercom in Japanese, which sounded metallic through the speakers. Then he spoke in English.

"Ladies and gentlemen. Thank you for flying with us today. Please remain seated until we have stopped."

Jif peered through his window, hugging the cream plastic wall of the plane. The airport was a huge metropolis of glass and steels, shining white from the metallic sky. As the plane trundled and slowed, he could see more Jumbos parked up to a huge dark grey sprouting things which appeared to be the terminal walkways. Jif guessed that was where he'd find his pickup.

Suddenly the plane turned left, and the airport disappeared from his view. He pondered if a set of steps would be used instead. His answer came when an articulated stair truck bounced in front of his window. But just behind the truck followed two black jeeps with tinted windows. And a black-and-white police saloon with red light bar on the roof, flashing.

Jif's heart started to race. He'd never been in trouble before, but he'd seen the brutality of the Japanese police on TV, and Washington was at loggerheads with Tokyo for the selling of military equipment to rogue states.

There was another blast of words through the speakers, and a few seconds later, the plane stopped completely. There was a light bar above each seat with a picture of a belt being closed. It had been on since the start of the flight, and it went out. And with that, everybody on the plane stood up to the noise of sliding metal from the belts.

The door took a further five minutes to open, so Jif stayed seated while the rest of the passengers stood in line on the deck, holding their briefcases and trying to look reserved. The door opened with a chuff, out of sight. A cold breeze wafted in with the smell of aviation fuel. The line of suits marched forward as gossip filled the air, and a female voice repeated the same words over again in the distance.

Once the gangway was clear, Jif heaved himself out of his seat and realised his bottom was sweaty as it gradually got cold as the outside air breezed through his suit. He gazed down at his massive stomach and pulled his belt up over his fat self to make sure the whites of his pants weren't showing.

Jif didn't hold anything. He didn't even have a suitcase or any luggage. He was going to buy new clothes in the new city. He casually wobbled down the dark blue carpet of the gangway, his shoes clubbing the hard surface and creaking unnervingly under his weight. Ahead of him, a bald Asian man promptly paced along, under a plastic archway, and turned left to the exit, ignoring the smiling stewardess standing by.

Jif tucked in his arms, being cautious as his fatness could have trapped him in the doorway. The stewardess was wearing a white blouse, blue skirt, and blue epaulettes with a blue bowler hat as part of the uniform. She was the one who kept repeating "Thank you for flying" in Japanese. But all he could understand was the thank you as *arigato*. So that's how he replied.

"Arigato," he said back, really meaning it.

He stepped over the lip of the doorway and stepped onto the set of shiny steel steps. He held his arms over his eyes. Even with the cloud, the sun was still brighter than he was used to in Humberside.

"Mr. Kitchen," called a masculine Far East voice. His *i*'s sounded more like *e*'s. Jif glanced around the tarmac of the runway, looking through a dozen airport staff in blue overall suits and hi-visibility vests, along with several Japanese men in suits standing around with A4 pieces of white card with names of passengers written in black felt. Among the suits, one in a cheap grey suit held his name in proud capitals.

"I AM!" yelled Jif as he skipped down the metal stairs. It was empty since he hesitated at the door of the plane. He waltzed around several fellow passengers mingling with their pickups to greet the grey suit, who pulled a corky smile below his evil-looking slit eyes and a mop of slick black hair.

"Hello," said the suit, lowering the huge card in his left hand and grabbing Jif's hand with his right, giving a firm shake. "Ohayo, we say in Japan," he went on, dropping the card with slap on the tarmac.

"Could I see some ID?" questioned Jif. He had every right to be cautious. There were uncomforted reports that the yakuza had infiltrated the island, and a company executive could have been a tasty ransom.

The suit nodded and reached into his internal pocket. He pulled out a shiny new brown leather wallet. He opened it with a finger and displayed a card with a picture of a younger version of himself. Writing on the card was scribbled in Japanese hieroglyphs, and the other section of the wallet had a simple badge made of shiny gold.

"Kensuka Kemachi, Japanese interior ministry. I am here to show you to you're new home." He closed the wallet up and slid it back in the breast pocket of his suit. "Welcome to Frontiera Island."

ONE

His ears were still ringing from the blast. He thought he was dead. He had to be. How could a guy so close miss, with a gun so big! But he was still breathing. He could feel his heart pumping. Blood rushing through his forehead! And the dead silence that was before erupted into panicky screams from voices he vividly knew.

Jif Kitchen opened his eyes, feeling a little sticky, expecting to see a heaven or hell. He saw neither, at first. He was still on the roof garden on top of Lime.Inc. Burnt cordite filled the air, making the place smell like a bonfire. And his vision was engulfed by the back ends of a pair of smart men's shoes flying in midair. The cuff of a pair of black pants over a man's ankle completed the picture. Iffy, the bodyguard, must have taken the bullet for him.

As the shoes flew out of his sight, Jif found himself facing straight into the eyes of the disfigured Japanese man that no one had taken notice of before. A six feet tall Asian male, black suit, white shirt, and funeral tie. *Fitting*, Jif thought, when he first realised who he was. The man's face had skin peeling and blistering in a reddish colour on his left cheek. A section of his head, from the eye socket to the left ear, was completely bald, in spite of his spiky black hair. His aviator sunglasses completely concealed his eyes.

The black shotgun he was holding was still smoking. But he was no longer grimaced and primed to kill as Jif had first seen. The man's look now was that of surprise.

Bits of tiny black plastic spun in the air. They looked freshly broken. Almost lifelike. The plastic flew into Jif's face, causing him to blink.

Jif couldn't move. It was as if the weight of his body was now on his shoulders. It felt as though his 239 pounds of fat was holding him in place. He couldn't even glance over to see where the shoes had gone or come from. He knew this day would come, and he was ready to accept it, but the Jap wasn't making his move.

Then, another bang broke his concentration. This time it was followed by a splatter. And a man's scream. And it was not in front of him, but from his right.

Jif didn't break eye contact. He wanted to be sure it would be over. The Jap's face contorted into a look of pain, mouth open, eyes wide, skin pale! There was a two-inch wide hole in the place of his heart, leaking with blood down his white shirt, beneath the black suit jacket he was wearing. The shiny black shotgun was still in his right hand, yet held loosely, as if it was going to fall from his grip.

Two more blasts rang out, and the man's chest exploded again before he fell sideways, like liquid. Jif looked to his right and saw IFFY! Black skinned, black pants, and yellow hi-visibility jacket, holding a black automatic pistol, still smoking. Iffy's expression was one of rage: eyes narrow, teeth exposed, his short thinning black hair revealing a brow of sweat, his tash and goatee almost obscuring his mouth. The Japanese man was facedown on the beige tiled floor, and a pool of shiny red blood flooded its way from under his chest.

Jif looked around, bewildered, trying to make sense of the situation. If Iffy was next to him, who took the dive? He spun his head, shaking his ponytail off his shoulders. Near a set of couches, he found the shoes. The shoes were connected to the feet of a young man in formal black trousers and a dark grey pin-striped jacket, his arms still straight out. He recognised the haircut. It was Charles Ronshoe, the boy he had hired that day to act as his second bodyguard.

It was only now he realised that everyone was screaming and shouting. He heard American shouts of "Man down. Man down. Call an ambulance." He staggered forward with shaking hands, panting, stepping around the dead Jap as Iffy kicked the gun away. Jif wobbled his way over, eyes focused at Charles Ronshoe, still lying where he fell. Jif could see that the glasses he'd been wearing that day were missing. In the dull light, he could make out a gouge on the side on his right eye. It was leaking blood! Jif's heart sank.

He ran over to the man's body. Kneeling down at an angle over the man's chest, Jif was greeted by a five-inch gouge on the boy's right temple. Torn flaps of skin hanging like paper. Ridges of exposed flesh. Red blood leaking, filling tiny gaps in the skin around the wound. It was then Jif noticed that the fat stomach of his tuxedo and his white shirt was coated in dots of red blood. How could he have not noticed before?

With a shaky hand, Jif pushed the head to the left so that he could face Charlie's eyes. Charlie's face sparkled like glitter. Tiny fragments of glass that were once his lenses lay embedded in his face. A black plastic earpiece from what used to be his glasses lay hooked into the collar of Charlie's white shirt. Charlie's skin seemed to go a little paler. Jif's head started to heat up.

And Jif suddenly realised, that the gouge near the boy's right eye was nothing because he had no EYE! The right eye was now a wet red hole. Fresh blood reflected the light from the sky in a series of ripples; the blood swayed back and forth like waves on a pond. Jif suddenly felt his body shiver in coldness. He placed shaky fingers on the man's throat; he knew it was futile, but he had to be sure. No pulse!

Jif's eyes began to water; his breathing became erratic. Feet ran up to him; women's voices began to cry and shriek in despair. He felt a girl's arm become wrapped around his right shoulder. A sky blue cotton jumper against his tuxedo jacket. Smells of intoxicating perfume. Hot pants of breath against his cheek.

"Jif," whispered the girl, "I'm sorry."

He knew who it was, and he didn't care. He wanted to be alone with his friend. He placed his right palm flat on Charlie's chest, his left over his right, and thrust his palm down into the boy's heart in an attempt to resuscitate him.

"He's been shot, he's been shot," cried a girl's voice out of nowhere. After three thrusts, Jif's arms lost their strength. He wanted to shout, "Wake up! Wake up!"

He pulled at the perils of Charles's brand-new pin-striped jacket, shaking the body feebly. The girl released her grip and pulled her arm away. His eyes were blurring, and he could barely see. Grimacing, he slapped the head with his right hand; no reaction. He couldn't hold it anymore!

"Fuck!" he yelled with a shaky breath.

Sitting up on his knees, he threw the palms of his hands over his eyes, panting, mouth wide open, lips stretched back. His body jerked back and forth several times as he struggled to breathe. Finally, he threw his palms away from his face into the air and looked up into the grey sky as tears streamed from his reddening eyes.

"AAAAHHHHHHGGGGGG!" His eyes rolled into the back of his head, his mouth relaxed, and his torso fell forward, lying flat over the boy he so loved, as more and more people gathered round.

May 9, 2006, 1409 EST

The arm that had held Jif Kitchen before he screamed was that of his wife. Dressed in a blue jumper and blue jeans, the blonde girl seemed out of place next to the fat man with a ponytail in a black tuxedo.

In the reception area of Lime.Inc, Jif gripped his wife's hand tightly. Even sitting on the awful red school chair, his legs were still shaking. Every breath he took sounded like a car exhaust spluttering.

He knew he was lucky to be alive. Lucky to be here! And not fighting for the British, or the US, in Iraq or Afghanistan. He'd seen the news this morning; another British soldier had been slaughtered by a roadside bomb in Basra today. If he'd been just a little more desperate to escape from a dad who'd graduated from slaps to punches, he'd have joined the army himself.

No. It was Charlie who got the short end of the stick! And Jif put him there. The very thought was tearing him up inside.

He sat silently, going over the events in his head. How did it happen so fast?

May 9, 2006, 1331 EST

"'Ello, Mr. Kart!" welcomed Jif to the old suit. He was standing next to a food table that overlooked the terrific views of Boston Common where a fifty-year-old man was loading cocktail sausages and egg sandwiches onto a flimsy paper plate. Kart was a considerable customer, having paid $100,000 for weapons last year. He ran a security company that ran worldwide, including Iraq, Afghanistan, and Brazil.

"Man, you're like school in the summertime!" replied Mr. Kart in a husky Colorado accent. He was asking for trouble, but it was worth it. There was even more money to be had since he'd brought all his friends with him today. That was Jif's job today: get more customers and investors.

All around were suits, businesswomen, naval personnel, army uniforms, and even arms dealers who wanted to sell to Lime.Inc, even though it was making enough stock as it was. Everyone here on this cold garden party knew what Lime. Inc was about; they wouldn't have come here otherwise if they didn't intend to spend something. Vincent, his boss, was after some nice, juicy contracts to finish off the two year anniversary of the opening of Lime.Inc.

"School in summertime?" asked Jif with his best grin. He felt Charlie pace up next to him as two bald black men in shirts were grinning drunkenly and sipping champagne glasses behind the old man.

"Yep, you fuckin' piss me off! Lose some weight!" Kart said with a throaty cough. Jif was used to this and, in some respects, enjoyed it.

"Here, Yank. I lose weight when I want to bitch!" He was mimicking a black guy. "Shut ya bitch ass!" The two black guys bent over in a fleet of giggles.

The flat rooftop of Lime.Inc covered about thirty by twenty meters and would normally be covered in felt, but today it had the red carpet. The perimeter of the roof was fenced off by a four-feet-high barricade of ugly black bars to stop anyone falling off the building. Pot plants of some sort had been placed in each corner. In the middle of one side was the elevator, a big steel shed to accommodate the car, with silver door to allow access. It was the only way on and off the roof, except for the fire exit in the apartment block next door, which was only accessible from the outside, this side.

Streamers hung from one fence to another, and placards with the Lime. Inc symbol were decked out here and there. A picnic table in the middle of the commotion was full of Lime.Inc brochures and catalogues and advertisements saying how good a company it was. On each side of the roof were tables draped in green tablecloths, lined up with trays of food and drink.

"God, I love coming here," said Kart, recovering from his giggle.

"Just let us know when you need more stock," Jif went on. "And ya mates—we ain't been introduced." He wobbled about, offered his hand to the black in a blue shirt.

"MATE!" exclaimed the Negro. "I ain't gay, man."

"Never said you were!" replied a grinning Jif. Humour was part for the job. He took the man's hand and gave it a quick shake. "You know who I am."

"Sure do." The man was spluttering a hiding giggle.

"I'm neglecting my other guests." Jif started eyeballing a Japanese-looking man who was staring out through the bars on the east wall. He had a black suit and spiky black hair. He wasn't interacting with anyone. Perhaps he had money to spend. Or needed ejecting. "Enjoy what we have. I'm sure find out catalogue some stimulating company."

"WHAT?" exclaimed the black before laughing uncontrollably again. Jif took a few steps before turning around. Charlie was still behind him.

"Mate, you sure you don't wanna chat to some of these girls?" asked Jif.

"Aw, come on," whined Charlie. He looked like a business executive in his new clothes. Jif was also pleased to see his hair was flat. "They're too rich for me!"

"No harm tra-in," Jif said. "You took on a bunch of girl and became their manager."

"Apartment manager," corrected Charlie with an embarrassed grin.

"Seriously, mate, following me around is quite borin'," Jif coaxed, waving his arms and pointing at the food tables. "I didn't hire you to get bored to death."

"What about Iffy?" asked Charlie. The other bodyguard had vanished. Jif didn't care.

"He'll come back. And I'll be all right. Come on, man, enjoy yourself, have some free food." Jif's accent could be so pleasing at times. Charlie smiled.

"Only 'coz you asked me nicely," said the Boston boy. His glasses had suddenly reflected the depressing grey sky that day.

"At a boy, you'll get into MIT in no time," yapped Jif as Charlie turned away to the tables. Then he realised the music had stopped. It needed sorting again; the stereo had been dumped under one of the food tables.

"Let's put some feeder on." Jif shuffled off, swaying his belly with each step as he wormed his way around two gossiping Arab men, a suit trying to pull a lady, and an old man stooping with a walking stick. He got within a few feet of the Jap next to where the stereo was set up.

"Hello, sir," called Jif. No reaction. Jif was still pacing up to him. "Can I interest you in our new—"

The man spun round, whipping something out of his pants. He had aviator sunglasses on. And the left side of his face was burnt. In his hands was a pump action shotgun. Lethal. He was going to die.

Even then Jif could feel his stomach burn. He felt his smile shrink to a frown. His skin went cold. Sweaty. He'd been running for so long, and now it had caught up with him. History had repeated itself. There was no point in stopping it now. He had to die. To finish this off. He closed his eye and bowed his head.

"JIF?"

May 9, 2006, 1411 EST

"Uh . . . ," Jif exclaimed. Yuzuyu was holding Jif's shoulder, stroking it lovingly. He could feel her breath against his skin. His face burnt from the tears and from rubbing his face with his hanky. He gazed down at his soggy handkerchief, crushed into a ball in his palm, before brutally shoving it into his jacket pocket.

He gazed around the reception. It was a lot smaller than the roof because a white brick wall had been built forward to recess the elevator. Two wooden doors either side of the silver elevator doors held a storage cupboard.

The pine-curved desk covered most of the length of the room, with Lime.Inc on the wall below the desk and on a banner above in case someone forgot where they were. Shiffs and Mitzvah normally sat behind there but had disappeared since the commotion. Beyond the desk was a doorway which led to a small kitchen and a toilet. All this furnishing left a tiny seating area with a leather couch and two red plastic, which Jif and Yuzuyu were sitting on. He breathed and staggered. Then he gazed at his wife, again.

"I'm sorry you 'ave to see this, Yuzuyu," he said to her. His English accent was peppered with croaks and mutilated words. The *h*'s were silent in his speech, and his words followed a continuous rhythm, like most Yorkshire folk. The girl, with fluffy short blonde hair that went no further than the tops of her ears, pulled her lips down to expose her bottom gums. Her face was also shiny with tears.

"How can you say that?" she replied in her childlike voice. Her accent was impossible to place: American-sounding *a*'s, English-sounding *o*'s, Japanese-sounding *u*'s. Her skin was pale, and her brown eyes reflected Jif's own sadness. He was still wondering how and when they had gotten down to the reception; he couldn't remember going. And then the elevator pinged.

On the opposite sidewall where the couple sat was the silver doors of the elevator. The orange light above was on as the doors slid open with a slight scraping sound. There were two ambulance men in green uniforms. One was standing against the corner of the elevator car, the other was squatting down. The elevator was so narrow; they had to prop up the body at an angle. They were practically standing him up.

Jif threw his head down in disgust; how could Charlie be subjected to such inhuman treatment! Even if he was dead. He was just glad he didn't see his face; it had been covered with cloth of some sort. As the sounds of footsteps squeaked along the tiled floor in front of him, Jif drew his head up again and proceeded to stand.

Charles's body was laid on a flimsy cloth stretcher. They had draped a dirty pale blue blanket over his body and head, but it was too short, and his feet were exposed. Jif felt his face go cold as he gazed at the boy's shoes. He took a step to keep up with the crew, and Yuzuyu stood alongside him.

On shaky legs, he still had to crouch down to speak to his wife. She was less than five feet tall and looked so fragile. Jif thought she would break under his weight as he placed his palm on her shoulder.

"I have to see him goodbye," croaked Jif in his north English accent. The ponytail on his black hair had flown up over his shoulder again, but he didn't bother moving it.

"I know," replied Yuzuyu, a little tearfully, with slit eyes. "Dakishimetal no ni," she said without turning to face him. Jif felt a mix of euphoria, and guilt filled his heart. She meant "I just want to hold you."

Jif let go of her hand and paced along the floor to the opening of the building where the medics were turning right. He stepped out into the Boston daylight, and his heart sank again. In spite of the bright sun, it was bitterly cold. Jif's breath hung in front of his eyes. Yuzuyu's fingers reconnected with Jif's right hand, and he acknowledged the pandemonium in front of him.

People were leaving the three-story building in droves, queuing up in an untidy line at the gate. Lime.Inc was surrounded by a ten-foot-high black steel fence. The only way out was through the single gate that was only letting one person out at a time to maintain security. But the ambulance had been allowed into the delivery entrance and was parked up, facing the huge sliding gate that was now closed to avoid a sudden robbery, and was two metres away from the garage entrance where delivery vans would go down into the basement to unload their cargo.

At any rate, the park bay, the pathway, and indeed this block of Federal Street had turned into a disco of flashing blue and red lights from police cars and ambulances. Jif could make out a blue-and-white Boston police car through the bars of the fence less than a yard away from him, along with a cop pacing around with yellow cordon tape.

The ambulance crew made their way over the footpath and the small patch of grass to the ambulance. Its rear doors were still open. As the front man boarded the steps, Charlie's feet shook unnervingly. Jif followed unnerved and began to pant as he too entered the ambulance.

"Pardon me," said one of the crew in a deep Northern American voice as he backward walked off the ambulance. Darting aside, Jif let him pass. He turned his head as the medic disappeared around the side of the ambulance. Jif looked back at Lime.Inc, the yellow brick seeming to glow in the dull sunlight, the tired-looking green-lettered company logo hanging below the guttering of the roof, almost begging to come down. Then, the other medic started talking: slim face, short grey hair, wrinkled face, his hand pointing to the interior of the van. He spoke in a New York accent.

"You can sit on the bench over there, but please don't touch the body," he twanged.

Jif nodded obediently and sat down on the red-padded bench that the ambulance man had been talking about. His enormous bottom plumped down like a pig, pushing out all the air in the seat making a short lavatorial noise. His stomach stuck out its white-clad shirt, covering his crotch. Yuzuyu crept and sat down next to him with plastic rustle that came from under her clothes. She kept looking up at Jif with curiosity and sorrow. Why they were using an ambulance instead of a coroner's car bothered Jif. And he was surprised too about being allowed to ride with a cadaver. But he didn't want to think about it.

"Have good ride," said the Bostonian medic as the doors slammed shut and the engine started. Seconds later, the vehicle moved off gradually and turned multiple times. Jif looked down at Charles; the left hand was sticking out. He was till holding an orange that he hadn't yet eaten. It was the orange Jif recommended he eat. Jif placed his elbow on his knees and buried his face into his hands again. His wife sitting next to him looked around the ambulance and at her husband. She looked back at Charles and exhaled a pant of sadness; she too was at breaking point.

"Jif," she began, placing a palm on his shoulder. He unearthed his face and faced her. She leaned forward to an embrace, and they buried each other into their shoulders. "Jif, I'm sorry," she wept. "I'm so sorry!"

"No! I'm sorry!" replied Jif weakly. They hugged lengthily, kissing, telling each other how they loved each other. Charlie's hand slipped from the stretcher, dropping the orange. It rolled along the floor as the ambulance turned yet another corner.

"Sorry!" How Jif had heard that word so often! Sorry! He clenched his eyes shut as he searched through the fragments of his dreams to remember that time. And it came back.

September 13, 2003, 0019 JST

His knees and hands burned from being scraped along the road. The girl had already crawled her way out from under him. The legs of his pants felt damp as he stood to his feet, staggering over broken bricks and wet cracked road tarmac in a place he was unfamiliar with. He had a massive weight on his back from a parachute he had just ejected. He struggled to get the backpack off.

He was in the place that nobody knew existed. Frontiera Island. Though it did not exist anymore! The buildings around him looked straight out of New York! And yet everything was made in Japan. The pale blonde girl in front of him rose to her feet. She was wearing oversized green trousers and a dirty white man's shirt. She looked like a penguin with the sleeves over her hands. And this girl was to be his future wife!

"Keitaro!" called Yuzuyu. She didn't get a reply. But Jif did!

"Jif!" screamed an Asian man's voice from nowhere. Jif turned around in the direction he'd heard it from, peering through the visor of his motorcycle helmet. Atlas, the man who'd helped him, was standing on the window frame of a shattered man-sized window in a glass-and-steel building at least two yards away. "TSUNAMI!" screamed Atlas. And Jif didn't need to think twice.

He scooped up Yuzuyu into his thick arms and thrust her stomach against his chest. He gripped her bottom tightly and broke into a run. Grinding his teeth, his ankles were sore from where he'd scraped them from landing less than a minute ago.

"Ya, ya!" the girl cried in Japanese, trying to struggle from Jif's grip. He poked his head around Yuzuyu's, watching out for obstacles in the road, dodging abandoned cars and holes in the tarmac. He pondered to himself; maybe he should leave the girl with the boy she had befriended. But he had got through a lot of stuff to get her here. The only thing on his mind was to get out of here with this little girl alive!

He looked behind to catch a glimpse of the tsunami. It was massive, as tall as the skyscrapers around him. He'd survived a fall, an earthquake, and dozens of men with guns; and now he was going to drown.

"KEITARO!" screamed Yuzuyu. Jif made a sharp turn and dived into a vacant building. It was an office block with its windows blasted out from the earthquake. Amazingly, the lights were still on, probably from an emergency generator. He found a flight of stairs and charged for it.

"Ya!" yelled the girl. "Vata stashina Keitaro wetascetaberabeni!" Even though he barely learnt Japanese, he knew what she was saying. "We have to help Keitaro."

"We can't help him anymore!" Jif screamed back in Yorkshire English as he cornered the first flight with Yuzuyu grunting with every turn, pushing her further into Jif. He turned to the next set of steps when the remaining glass windows shattered from his left. He caught a glimpse and saw water begin to gush through the open gaps of the building. The tsunami was here.

Man and girl were panting as they turned to run up step after step. She pulled her lips back in fright, looking over his shoulder. He could only imagine the fear for this girl, seeing the water gushing after them like that gun-toting Jap had been doing all day. His feet made eerie stomps on steel steps, echoing through the deserted building. Twelve steps for every flight; it was never ending. Thirty-six steps already! He was wheezing; his helmet was obscuring his airways. He felt hot and sleepy; he wanted to stop. Yuzuyu continued to struggle, but Jif held on to her butt. Her smell added to his determination. She released her hold of Jif's neck and smacked the helmet at its right temple; Jif raced even faster.

Fifty steps! The building began to flood, and the water level rose unbelievably fast. The lights flickered and eventually went out completely, plunging the stairwell into a grey darkness, the only illumination coming from the outside moonlight.

"Jif," whined the girl on a hysterical note, "I don't like the dark." As she said that, Jif tripped on one of the many steps ahead of him in the darkness.

Dropping onto his left palm and gripping the girl tightly with his right, he let out a short yelp before picking himself up and running off again. It took him a while to realise that his shoe was wet and even longer to see that the water level had stopped rising. *Stomp! Stomp! Stomp!*

Having climbed what must have been twelve flights of steps, they made it to a walkway which held a fire exit. Pushing down the horizontal bar to open the door, the building's fire alarm began ringing idly. Jif and Yuzuyu were on the rooftop. A huge *H* in the tarmac told him it was a helipad. The cold air breezed into his jacket; tiny droplets of cold, sharp water stabbed into his wrists. He placed Yuzuyu down, and she immediately ran to the edge of the roof.

"Keitaro!" she screamed yet again. Jif could see tears rolling down her face. But after ten seconds, her panting subsided. She was concentrating. She held up her arm vertically; she was signalling. Jif tried to follow what was grabbing her attention. In the distance was the building Jif had jumped from. On the broken balcony, gradually filling up with water, Jif could make out a figure.

Red sweatshirt, grey trouser, black hair, Japanese skin. It was Keitaro. And his arm was extended upwards. He was waving. Yuzuyu waved back. Jif did the same. The water level rose; it began to invade the boy's feet. He didn't move. He stopped waving, but Yuzuyu continued. Jif saw him look down at his feet, the rising water. It came up to his knees. No reaction. Jif realised then that he was going to die, and he sighed in disbelief. The water kept on rising, past his waist, up his chest, to his neck, over his face, over his head. Nothing.

"Vatashina munbreNaomi," said Yuzuyu tearfully. It would take a day for Jif to know that she had said "I'm sorry." She felt guilty for getting Keitaro into this mess and leaving him behind. But even so, Jif could tell, and he felt his intestines disappear with her sadness.

As she panted, a loud booming could be heard in the sky. He looked up. In the dark grey sky, an orange helicopter appeared, swaying up to the building where they were standing. It hovered overhead, blasting a downwash of air. A string ladder rolled out, its ends slamming into the tarmac of the roof.

Yuzuyu turned to face Jif. Bewildered face: her mouth open, her eyes bloodshot, her cheeks a little paler than before. He sighed. What else could he do?

He held out his hand. She stepped forward and took it. He hoisted her up to his waist as he pulled himself up the string ladder.

May 9, 2006, 1414 EST

Jif's eyes stung terribly as he opened them. Behind his red eyelids, his brain played a little game of spinning white cogs to let his eyes get adjusted to the sunlight outside. He had witnessed this phenomenon since childhood.

The ambulance had stopped, and the paramedics had opened the doors, flooding the interior with the golden sun.

"Pardon me," the paramedic said again. His smart leather shoes made a *conk* noise on the ambulance step. He didn't take notice of Jif or Yuzuyu as he boarded the cab and shuffled past the couple to where Charlie's head was covered with the blanket. His hands hovered the wooden handles of the stretcher.

Jif released his hold of Yuzuyu, and the pale-faced blonde girl turned around to see what was happening.

The ambulance man squatted down with a crack of his knees, his blue shirt escaping from the back of his grey pants and exposing the small of his hairy back. As medic no. 2 appeared at the doors, the first man took hold of the stretcher. Charlie was heaved yet again upwards. Both medics marched out of the ambulance, turning left towards an ugly grey bunker building, out of sight. Jif petted his wife's knee, struggling to find words to say.

"I've got to follow them!" he croaked.

"OK," Yuzuyu said. "You're my husband. You should do as you want." The words created a sensation of pain in Jif's chest. He bowed his head in shame and ground his teeth.

"Don't say that," he whimpered.

"Why?" replied Yuzuyu in a high pitch of surprise.

"If I order you around, you'd be a prisoner! I don't want that," he croaked again.

"Jif," began Yuzuyu, placing a palm on Jif's chin, trying to make him face her, "girls are supposed to listen and work for their husbands!"

"But that's what bad guys do!" he replied.

"You're not bad," sighed Yuzuyu. Another tear streamed from Jif's eye. He'd received real affection. He struggled to his feet, bowing his head from the low roof of the ambulance. His smart enormous leather shoe "chinged" the hollow steel step of the ambulance, before he made connection with the black tarmac of the coroner's car park.

"I need you to come with me," Jif spluttered, his voice shaking, and his wife followed her hand in his. "I can't do it alone!"

The couple walked slowly with a rustle inside Yuzuyu clothes. Jif looked up and saw Boston Coroner in gold letters on a black plastic board above the doorway. The sign disappeared above him as he stepped up some concrete steps and entered the glass building.

The floor was tiled in a colour of faded limes, like the green mile. They found themselves in a narrow corridor and immediately faced a white plaster wall two meters high with a white plastic information sign stuck up to it. The sign had letters of black that read Reception and a white arrow on a sky blue background pointing right next to the word. Jif moved cautiously forward, gazing to the right wall, and found a recess at the end with a set of old brown double wood doors. The doors were scuffed and chipped around every edge. In the top half were panes of glass with wire mesh squares to stop the glass from shattering. Each door had a silver extended vertical pull bar, curved at the edges to give it a natural look. They both had a tiny silver plaque on top with the letters Pull engraved on.

Jif reached out and pulled one of the doors open. He stepped forward and found himself in the reception area. Walls were all faded blue, and the room was about the size of the embassy ballroom: six metres wide by seven metres long. Iffy had told him that. He turned back to look at Yuzuyu.

"Do . . . do you need to change?" asked Jif. He'd bent his head back to look behind Yuzuyu. Her blue jumper had crept up slightly, and her white trousers were falling down a little, exposing the waistband of her diaper. She walked forward as Jif looked back to view the surroundings.

A huge pine desk sat opposite of where Jif was standing. It occupied the whole width of the room. Reception was painted high above on the wall behind the desk, in white. Two women in white jackets sat there, one was eyes down at a newspaper, another was gossiping on the phone. Jif could see two office chairs sitting vacant on either side of the receptionists. Ahead of the desk were dozens of expensive-looking black leather armchairs, set in four rows, two against each wall lengthways and two back-to-back in the centre of the room. Most of them were empty, and those occupied had old men in suits, smoking cigarettes and coughing noisily.

"No, I'm OK. But thank for asking," replied Yuzuyu as she clutched Jif's right hand again and led him to a vacant row of leather seats. They sat down, the leather and wood board creaking beneath them. Jif leaned forward, dazed, stared at the row of seat opposite. As she sat down next to him, she massaged his hand and faced his left side. "I haven't said this for a while, Jif. You're great!"

"Thank you," he replied, his eyes watering again.

"Not many men would stay with a girl who wets herself and has to wear a diaper," she said softly, her hand moving away from his hand and creeping up to his shoulder.

"I know," he said back, bringing the back of his right hand to wipe his eyes.

"You've done so much!" she said, beginning to get tearful. "You've taught me from scratch! You've always changed my diaper! I'm happy with you, Jif!"

Jif began to pant. His heart was racing. Words that Yuzuyu said were triggering searches in his mind for the time she was talking about.

"So don't let these bad guys get to you!" she whispered. Her hands were starting to shake. "I need you, Jif!" He covered his eyes with his hands again as he bowed over and began crying again.

"They've already got to me!" he blubbered. "Every time I close my eyes, all I ever see is him lying there!" In the darkness of his own hands, he wanted desperately to be alone, but it was coming back. Charlie, flat on his back with a hole in his head. A hole he may as well have put there himself.

How he hated himself. Jif knew it was his fault because he had employed Charlie, and he didn't tell him the dangers. Charlie was also inexperienced and hadn't worked for anything before in his life; why did Jif let him do the job?

It wasn't just that he'd employed Charlie that had got him killed! He had started this ball rolling three years ago: the meeting of his wife, his marriage, forgiveness. It hadn't worked. What he thought was behind him was not. It had caught up with him, and Charlie paid the price for what was Jif's fault.

"How did I get here?" he said to himself. He covered his eyes with his hands, plunging his sight into darkness.

How had I gotten here? wondered Jif. He screwed his eyes shut, racking his brain to remember that day when it all started. All those years ago! In fact, three years seemed almost like yesterday. But he wouldn't get that far.

TWO

Jif woke up to find himself in a room he didn't recognise. He'd been sleeping, sitting on an uncomfortable seat, bent over a hard, cold surface, both his arms folded out, acting as a pillow for his forehead. He raised his head, still feeling groggy, and examined his surroundings. Felt grey tiles surrounded him. Plastic white ceiling panels above him. Beneath him was a red plastic chair, like the sort there was in his school days, along with a grey stone floor with scratch marks from the chair legs. And in front of him was a pine desk, tea brown, with terrible scratches in dozens of places.

A wooden door on his right flew open. Two white men in suits walked in. An older man, pin-striped blue suit, bald head, wrinkled lumps of skin around his eyes, sat down directly in front of Jif, on the opposite side of the desk. A slightly younger man, with a full mop of black hair, thick-rimmed glasses, and horrible-looking nose, shuffled on the left corner of the desk. Jif stared into them, trying to recognise their faces, but he ended up staring at the plastic tags on the perils of their jackets.

"Mr. Kitchen," began the older man. He spoke with a thick New York accent that could cut through cheese. "I trust you got enough rest."

"You're not in any trouble!" the younger man quickly said, shaking his mop of hair at Jif.

"Then, what is it you want me to do?" asked Jif as calmly as he could. He tried to use his words carefully. He knew from the hostility in the air that he was in trouble. So much hostility he could almost taste it. And there was no point in asking where he was because there was no way they would tell him. He also knew it was futile to ask to leave or demand his rights; it was two against one. Why was he here? And what had happened to Yuzuyu? All he could remember was sitting at the coroner's office with her. Was this all about Charlie being inexperienced? Was it the fact Jif didn't have a degree or the shambolic way he'd ran the building? He sat and waited for the demand to be read.

"We'd like to talk about your wife!" said the older man. There! He said it! The game was up. Jif took his arms from the desk and hid them underneath, bowing his head in shame.

"All I ask," he began, avoiding eye contact and trying to hold back tears yet again, "is that she gets treated fairly."

"Where did you meet your wife?" the older man asked immediately. He clutched both hands together on the edge of the desk, in front of his chest. Jif drew a breath. He couldn't say Frontiera Island because it didn't exist anymore. And he'd been ordered not to disclose any details about the island because all parties involved wanted it covered up.

"Japan," Jif replied, gazing down at the scratch marks in the desk. Although he wasn't looking, out of the corner of his eye, he saw the younger man move his head sideways and nod. At which point, the wooden door was opened again. Into the room stepped a man in a green military uniform. He was black, heavy build, midfifties, wearing a white peaked cap with a gold symbol in the middle, his jacket decked with medals everywhere and reeking of cheap aftershave. He waltzed in the room and stood behind the two other men before looking straight into Jif. The door noisily closed itself again.

"We know your wife did not come from Japan!" boomed the uniform in an African American voice. It was then that Jif noticed small patches of stubble on the black man's face. Jif drew a breath and realised that they wanted to know about the island itself!

"I ask again," said the older suit. "Where did you meet your wife?"

"Frontiera Island," replied Jif truthfully and looking at them this time.

"Very good," said the uniform. "We knew that this island was being made by the Japanese and the Chinese in partnership."

The bald man cut in. "We also know it got destroyed by an earthquake and obliterated by a tsunami!" Jif couldn't continue with eye contact and broke off, now staring at a dent in a felt tile on the left of the room. "What we don't know is what was happening before the earthquake. And we think, YOU might!"

"How old is your wife?" asked the younger man.

"She's fifteen!" replied Jif, his face turning red and still not making eye contact. The younger suit took his glasses off with his right hand and rested them on the desk.

"Records show you married in August last year. That would make her fourteen back then. She's a minor!" The suit then picked up his glasses and angrily jabbed them in Jif's direction as he emphasised his next speech. "Do you realise how much trouble you could get into?"

"Yea," croaked Jif. He couldn't hold anymore. A tear ran down his burning cheek.

"You love her. That's good. But the public won't see it that way!"

"So tell us what her connection was!" interrupted the older suit. Jif covered his eyes with his hand as he searched his brain yet again for that time three years ago. How could he explain? He closed his eyes and tried to summarize the details, in his head.

In 1810, in a small reef off the westernmost coast of Japan, there was a chance discovery of coal. Coal mining began; the reef grew into an artificial island of one kilometre in perimeter, and people came to live there. It was named Gunkanjima, or Battleship Island, due to the structure of the high-rise buildings. But when the Second World War broke out, it was abandoned. The natural resources dried up, and once the military left, it was deemed inhabitable.

In the 1990s, however, Japan decided to branch out and use the island as a business opportunity. Off-the-record meetings were held with British and American officials. The plan was to make Gunkanjima a habitable place for secret companies to operate. The businesses were largely military: the manufacturing of weapons, animal-testing laboratories, etc. The chief fund-raiser for this project was a man named Kensuki Kenjiku. His angle on the project was to hold a base for cryogenic experiments.

Building work began soon after celebrations of the new millennium. The island would still belong to Japan, but the British and Americans could stay as long as they wanted and could participate in the construction. The island was renamed Frontiera Island, to make it sound more friendly to Westerners.

Even by 2003, three years after building work began, construction was not finished. But the businesses began setting up anyway.

The island had been increased to four times its original size using an experimental method that had not been done before, and it proved groundbreaking. The advanced construction methods were below the cost and time span associated with other methods of construction at its time. It was no wonder then that a great deal of attention was given to this man-made island whilst held in secrecy.

Vincent ordered Jif to sign an official denial, a no-whistle-blowing policy. Jif wasn't allowed to speak of Frontiera or of the company, anywhere, except in the island itself. He was also kept in the dark about the company. Jif's "company" was simply a front to store weapons for the UK military. It would be off international laws, so they could stockpile all the controversial weapons: cluster bombs, nerve gas, poisons. Jif would only ensure the stock went in and out again and that the right money came through.

At least, that was the plan.

Jif woke up from his "dream" and found himself at the table again, his hand over his eyes. He pulled his hands away and swiftly delivered his answer.

"Yuzuyu was the daughter of Kensuki Kenjiku," Jif began, sniffing a blocked nose.

"Go on," said the black man, shaking a finger.

"Kensuki Kenjiku was a politician, in charge of running Frontiera Island! I don't know if he WAS the mayor!"

"But . . . ," interrupted the younger man, leaning forward as he spoke.

"Yuzuyu died several years before, and she was cryogenically frozen. She'd been resurrected when the earthquake struck. That's how we met her."

"Yea," said the military man. "This wasn't out of love." The man bowed down to Jif's eye level, trying to be friendlier. "He had a sinister reason for all this, right?"

"Did you know him?" asked Jif.

"Just carry on talking!" said the older suit. Jif wiped his eyes with the right sleeve of his suit jacket.

"He . . . he wanted for her to rule the island," replied Jif. The men looked at each other, failing to understand.

"How?" asked the younger suit. His glasses were back on again. "She didn't know how to run a city!"

"They were going to . . . take away her emotions . . ." Jif began to splutter at this point. Every time he took a breath, he struggled; his throat clenched up, his body shook. "She was going to be a soulless lump of meat!"

"And you didn't want her to be like that!" said the bald man coldly. Jif's eyes burnt as tears became stored behind his eyelids. He paused before nodding in agreement.

"How did you get her out?" rasped the black man, leaning over his two colleagues, his shadow from the fluorescent lights creeping over their heads and onto the table, making the other two men appear darker, their eyes like black holes.

"I was helped!" yelped Jif, managing to stare straight into the domineering glare of the inquisitionists.

"You had help!" repeated the black man. "And you didn't finish the job!"

Jif finally made eye contact with the man, simply because he didn't understand what he meant. Openmouthed, he was about to ask what he meant, when a sharp pain suddenly appeared in his left shoulder.

"Uh," he groaned, looking down at his shoulder, and covered it with his right hand. It felt like the skin was being pinched with a pair of pliers. But there was nothing there!

"YOU FAILED!" screamed the black man. Jif was no longer interested in his questioners. Instead, he focused on his shoulder, which was becoming too painful for him. He clenched the shoulder with his hand to test feeling, but it did nothing, and the pain got worse. Jif looked up at the three men, staring back at him coldly. He placed both his hands on the desk and thrust all his weight onto his arms to heave himself up. But as he stood up out of his plastic chair, his knees went numb. He ground his teeth and gripped the dirty thick edge of the desk to try to hold himself but couldn't hold his balance.

"You should have killed them all when you had the chance!" yelled the black man, thrusting his head forward an inch, tiny globules of spit emanating from his mouth, disappearing into the air.

Jif's legs gave way. He collapsed in a wet, blubbering heap in a corner of the stone floor. Throwing his arms out to break his fall, his palms slammed into the smooth floor, picking up tiny pinpricks of dirt into his soft flesh. The coldness of the floor sank into his clothes. The pain in his shoulder was getting worse, and all he could do was moan and cry.

"I'm in pain," he groaned throatily, unable to stop his tears flowing now. The black man stepped around the desk and walked up to where Jif was lying. With a crack of his knees, he crouched over Jif, expressionless. He thrust his hand into Jif's face until all Jif could see were the black man's eyeballs and the skin around them.

"YOU FAILED!" screamed the black man, the corners of his eyes wrinkling slightly with the movement of his jaw. Jif's vision deteriorated with the tears in his eyes, and everything went blurred.

"Nooo!" wailed Jif. He'd never felt so embarrassed before because he'd never cried for so long. Pain was travelling from his shoulder to his stomach, and his whole body felt terribly heavy, as though he was drunk. All he could do was moan and sulk. He knew what was happening, but he just couldn't react to it.

"YOU FAILED!" screamed the man again, and Jif felt his face crush up into despair. Falling backwards, all he could do was wail.

"AAAARRRGGGGGHHHHH!" Jif screamed as the room blurred out of his vision. The light began to dim. He howled again, and everything went black.

THREE

"Jif! JIF!"

He opened his eyes and found himself lying down in a dark room. There was a pair of eyes staring straight back at him, with a mop of beautiful blonde hair that told him who it was and where he was.

"Yuzuyu," he whispered. His throat felt sore. He looked around and recognised his bedroom: blue ceiling, pink walls, oak brown furniture. The girl slumped off him with a rustle of her diaper to his right side. He found his arms and pushed them behind, thrusting his back off the mattress as he sat up in the bed. "How did I get here?"

"You passed out in the coroner," replied Yuzuyu as Jif's head turned to face her. "So I got a taxi back."

"I don't remember a thing!" he exclaimed. He drew a breath. "Did we see Charlie?"

"I did!" she replied. "They put him in the morgue. He's safe!" She shuffled up closer to her husband and wrapped her two warm palms around his right forearm. "No one can hurt him now."

Jif turned his head and stared back down on the blankets on top of him. White with Bratz pictures and words dotted over it, the sort any girl would love. He knew she was right, but Charlie had already been hurt, and it was killing Jif inside. And what did his dream mean?

"I had a dream," he began, still not looking at Yuzuyu, "more like a nightmare." He drew a breath and looked up at the ceiling before puffing it out. "A bunch of men wanted to know about you!" Yuzuyu threaded a hand through Jif's right arm.

"In your dream?" she exclaimed.

"Yes!" replied Jif.

"What did you say?"

"They said they knew about Frontiera Island, so I told them about how your dad was the mayor!"

"But, Jif," she exclaimed, "we're not even sure ourselves!"

"I know!" he replied. "You know, the British government made me swear not to say anything about Frontiera!" His hands began to shake at this point.

"Nobody knows about it, and if I break down in my dreams, what if someone does it in this time?"

Yuzuyu closed her mouth and pulled on Jif's arm until he lay back down on the bed. His head flopped into the soft pillow beneath. Yuzuyu held his hand softly as her head rested on the pillow next to him.

"Try not to think about it," she whispered, falling asleep. Jif soon followed her.

He wanted to think about the shooting. He wanted to replay the events and see what happened. What he could have done to stop it. How he could have made it less serious. He shouldn't have hired Charlie in the first place, called a voice in his head. Knowing it would make him upset again, he turned his head in his sleep and began to remember the first day. The first time he and Charlie met.

March 11, 2004

It was the second day of his residence in Lime.Inc. He was amazed at how ridiculous it looked; it was half of an apartment block.

The building was all white, a three-story 1960s apartment block with renovated windows. It had its own back garden, with a sandpit for kids, and an outside "hot spring bath." The owner was Japanese.

It was once a hotel, but when it went out of business, the Japanese women bought it and turned it into an all-girls dormitory, rented out to female college students or high school girls wanting to get some independence away from their parents. It was called Babylon Zoo.

But with fewer tenants by the year and rising costs, the apartment manager decided to sell half of the building, and the British government bought it as it was on a busy road in the financial sector of Boston, and it was the closest and cheapest they could get to Washington. In fact, they could have just used the consulate in Harvard. But Jif knew that the operation here had to be careful, and who would suspect weapons would be made and stored along a busy street? That was the whole point of the operation; do something least suspected.

When it was turned into Lime.Inc, all they did was stick some union jacks on the walls outside to compete with the Americans, erect some black metal fencing around the outside perimeter, and install some secondhand furniture. It was strange because it was one whole building divided down the middle with the fence and some partitioned walls.

Jif was selected for this job because nobody else wanted it; half of England was scared they would be attacked by terrorists if they collaborated with the arrogant Americans. And relations with America were at an all-time low after the war in Iraq. Also, it was dodgy; there was little information in what went on in the company. The cover story was that it sold fruit produce, namely, limes.

He had to be careful of his next-door neighbours too. Babylon Zoo, as it was now called, could have blown the cover and all the deals that went on inside. It was up to Jif to keep the cover going.

At the time, Jif was sitting in his office, behind his old rosewood desk. He had an entire box of papers to sort through. He was disturbed when he could hear shouting in the building next to him; his office was right next to the partitioning wall. In addition, there was a red fire exit in his office, which led into the next building which had a flight of stairs. Lime.Inc did not have stairs, only lifts. Even more amazing was this was an internal opening door; in a fire, it would be logical for the door to open outwards, not inwards. He was staring at this door that morning because the yelling was now coming in that direction, along with heavy footsteps.

Jif hastily leapt out of his seat and peered through the pane of glass in the top half of the door. It had wire mesh squares to stop the glass from shattering. Jif's eyes were greeted by a young white man wearing only white boxer shorts. And he was soaking wet.

Jif knew this area should be secure and not allow others into the building without security checks, but something made him feel safe with this boy. He pulled down the grey push bar and pulled the door inwards as the fire alarm started a defining ring.

"Thank you," yelped the boy, his wet dark brown hair slapping against his forehead. Jif's eyes followed him as he stomped through the door and took two more jogs before collapsing on the green-carpeted floor. "Help me!" he mumbled.

Jif looked back and saw at least three girls running down a wooden floor in the other building. He slammed the door shut, clicking it in place, and the fire alarm stopped. He reached over to a bookcase full of folders and binders on the right side of the doorway and heaved it in front of the heavy wooden door. As he did, the door shuddered back and forth. The girls pounded on the glass, yelling and swearing heavily. Jif stepped back, startled, only to be startled again by the office door to be crashed open.

"What happened, Jif? What happened?" yelled Iffy, running into the office and stopping suddenly to avoid the boy. The perils on his yellow jacket lurched forward like snakes. Jif ignored and looked down at the boy with sorry eyes. He pointed his right thumb over his shoulder towards the fire exit.

"Next door is girl-only building!" he said briskly over the noise from the other side of the wall.

"All girl?" replied the boy, gazing back at the door. His accent was a little higher pitched than the usual Bostonian. He was still dripping.

Jif took off his suit jacket and opened it up to the boy.

"Come on," he said fatherly.

The boy complied, right arm first, sliding into the satin lining.

"I forgot my glasses," he said sheepishly. Jif looked at Iffy and jerked his head towards the fire exit. Iffy compiled. Jif cradled the boy in his arms, hand over shoulder, the wetness soaking through the jacket already. The door was opened again, and the fire alarm sounded. Jif looked as Iffy gripped the sides of the doorway and heaved against the angry crowd.

"He's a pervert, he's a pervert!" screamed a female Southern accent.

"Stop shouting and stand up or I will have you shot!" boomed Jif. Quietness set in. He shivered as he drew in another breath. Several eyes peered at him before scraping their feet on the floor and standing out of sight in the other building.

"Come in," coaxed Jif. Iffy stood aside and folded his arms to attention, and the girls walked in single file into the office. The first one was six feet tall and brunette and had a star of David necklace drabbed over her pink robe. Her massively long hair seemed wet. The girl behind her had short brown hair, had a bra but no top, and had grey pants. She was squinting, her eyes narrow, almost closed. Was she blind? The last girl was a short Indian; she had a red spot on her forehead. And dressed in a weird uniform. He didn't know at the time, but it was a Boston Japanese School uniform. All of them were barefooted.

"Stop," he said quietly. "Face me." They complied. It was a government building after all.

Jif looked down at the boy. He looked so helpless. But appearances can hold hateful things.

"What's ya name, mate?" asked Jif as clearly as he could make it. The boy's eyes wandered a little, before looking up and making contact with Jif's eyes.

"Charlie," replied the boy.

"Surname?" asked Jif.

"Ronshoe."

"Why did you go in a girl's dormitory?"

"I didn't know it was all girls."

"Bullshit" came a girl's voice. Americanised, but not from here. A little heavy on the *e*'s. Foreign. Maybe from the Middle East?

"Shut up," replied Jif, facing the enter line of girls. He returned to Charlie Ronshoe. "Why are you here?"

"I came to see my grandmother. She said she had something for me." As he finished, a distant feminine voice called.

"Where is everybody?" came the voice. It was a thick New Yorker accent.

"Ms. Miriam," said the long-haired girl. It was the same voice who'd just swore. The group started pacing out the door and called, "We found a Peeping Tom in our bath."

"And a panty thief."

A short-haired brunette in her fifties poked her head through the doorway. "Allo!" she called in a mocking tone. She started looking around. "What's all this?" The women's narrow eyes finally made contact in Jif's direction. "Charlie?"

"Aunty," replied Charlie in a flat voice. He shook his head pondering what to say. "Hi."

The last sentence repeated itself as Jif's vision began to fade into black. He could feel himself waking up again, but he didn't want to. He didn't open his eyes. He could feel himself on the hot bed again. Smell of baby powder from his wife. Hair on his face. He shuffled himself deep down to keep the warmth on his shoulders. Grinding his eyes shut, he started dreaming again.

Memories of his past flashed by. Hull, where he was raised. The flat town had once a warm feeling around it. Everyone seemed to know each other. But now it was getting conservative, and a whiff of the chocolate factory went up his nose again because chocolate processing smells of week-dead skunk. More images flashed past: stealing fivepence from his mother's purse as a baby, getting lost in the supermarket, breaking his father's car window. Charlie's shooting!

He didn't want to think of the shooting; he knew it would make him upset. He struggled to think of something else. And it came to him.

September 13, 2003, 1410

Jif's dream took him back to Frontiera Island, the place no one wanted to talk about. The place that was really called Gunkanjima.

The Kensuki man escorted Jif in the Mitsubishi Shogun. The driver in front did not speak or look in his mirror. Antisocial or just obeying orders. The car smelt heavily of house plants.

"What's with the smell?" Jif asked in English, facing Kensuki.

"Our boss likes all our car to smell like this!" replied the man with a grin.

The car stopped at the incomplete airport terminal. The driver stayed as Jif was escorted again with Kensuki into the terminal, followed a few glass corridors with overhead yellow signs in English and Japanese, and came to the queue for immigration. The line was short because there were only few passengers on that plane. The immigration kiosk was an all-glass booth with tiny holes at head height to speak through and a slot to put the passports through. The immigration officer sat behind the glass in a dark blue suit and purple shirt, like a bank clerk. One person went through the desk every twenty seconds.

Jif's turn came after one minute, the fastest he'd ever checked through. Kensuki did most of the talking. The officer took a quick look at Jif's British passport, flipped it shut, and handed it back.

Kensuki led him further inside, where construction work was still ongoing. Workmen in white boiler suits and blue hard hat wandered around, some of them on six-foot ladders fixing ceiling panels. Finally they came to the baggage claim: a ten-meter-long rubber belt over a shiny metal bottom to slide the suitcases along. He didn't wait long; he was practically the only one there.

"All right, mate," Jif said as they exited the airport building. "Where's this mystery building?"

"You think I just tell you?" replied Kensuki, in sheer surprise.

"We got to get there anyway!" replied Jif. He stood on the edge of the pavement and scanned the horizon, looking for other vehicles, namely, taxis.

"You think taxi!" Kensuki smiled. "No taxi, we take train!"

"Train! I thought the business was discreet!" Jif sighed, confused. The trip, the job, was confidential, secret. Surely going by train was the worst option; it would attract too much attention. Did they even have a train? Jif was too lost to care.

"How far is the station?" questioned Jif. Kensuki's smile didn't fade.

In fact, the metro station was just outside. The yellow paving looked fresh and bright, as did the wall tiles, with multicolour of red, blue, and green. No graffiti. No bad smell. Jif wondered how long it would last before vandals turned up!

The trains were secondhand from Japan, but impressive nonetheless. One had already pulled up and had its doors open, waiting for its passengers. Plush, shiny carriages with clean, fresh paint. As Jif and Kensuki boarded, a speaker out of nowhere ding-donged three times before the doors slid shut with a creak of metal and plastic.

The carriage's interior was just as good as its exterior. Double the width of the London tube, the carriage featured blue armchairs separated from each other, instead of connected benches. Smell of roses in the air. Magnolia paint on the walls. It looked and felt more like a living room than a public transport area.

"I reckon the British are gonna love it here," said Jif.

"We took inspiration from a man you call Jeremy Clarkson."

Jif couldn't help but laugh.

The train trundled off, slowly at first, gradually picking up speed. The tunnel around him was flashing past, occasionally flashing a metal box or a red light outside.

The train began to shake, much more than before.

"Pardon me, I had some beans last night," joked Jif with a smile.

"It's an earthquake!" exclaimed the man. He stood up and grabbed the yellow pole in the middle of the train near to the doors. "We haven't had one before on this island."

Jif felt his smile fade. He was heaving himself out of his seat when the carriage rocked at an acute angle. As gravity began to pull on his feet, he threw himself back into the seat and clenched the armrests.

Out of nowhere, tiny bits of paper and plastic drink bottles slid across the floor and slammed against the walls. The train was rocking like a crazy horse. The lights began to flicker on and off, sending the train into an occasional pitch-black darkness. There was a horrible sound of metal grinding against a hard surface, which sent a chill into both men as they realised that the train was about to derail.

The Kensuka man clutched the yellow pole tightly, wrapping his arms around it and himself. His face shrank from smiling to bewilderment and disbelief. His mouth was wide open. He kept glancing around, waiting for it to be over.

Jif couldn't bear to watch. He didn't want to see himself die. He screwed his eyes shut and clenched his teeth, gripping the seat. He heard the windows breaking and metal tearing. The rocking was jumbling his intestines about. He lost his grip and fell near vertically onto the train wall. His head smacked whatever there was in front of him. He couldn't breathe under his own weight. He passed out.

FOUR

The telephone trill stabbed Jif's brain like a church bell. Blood rushed to his eyes, and his lungs filled with air as he leapt off the bed.

"UH!" he yelled without thinking. He'd leapt up to the end of the bed, pulling the sheets down in doing so. He knew he'd have to pull them back up again!

"Hello?" came Yuzuyu's voice. Jif shot to the right. Yuzuyu was standing next to the doorframe in her diaper. She looked so cute; her breasts were just starting to grow, even though she was fifteen. Small droopy flat mounds. The nipples were almost black, in stark contrast to her pale skin. She was holding the receiver of the telephone up to her right cheek. Jif was already off the bed and pacing round to her by the time her eyes rolled in his direction. She offered the handset out to him.

"It's Transit," said the girl, sounding deflated. Jif knew she didn't like getting messed up with his work. But even more so with a fatality, Charlie's fatality.

"Yes, Angus!" said Jif into the mouthpiece.

"Uh . . . hello there," he began. His flat accent was Boston born and bred. "Took the words right out of my mouth." His name was Angus Van, but he was called Transit, for no particular reason. Jif guessed it was Vin's idea as it was Vin's builder father who drove a transit van back in Watford. Whilst this was going on, Yuzuyu paced away up to the wardrobe to get her school uniform.

"Am I in the shit?" asked Jif abruptly.

"Uh, yea," replied Transit. "It was supposed to be a party to celebrate two years of Lime.Inc and get some new investors in. But it turned into an awful mess! And it's largely on your watch!"

Jif felt his eyes water. He rubbed his right eye with his free hand until it almost felt good.

"I was told I could hire anyone else I wanted!" Jif remarked.

"But it had to go through Vin first. You sent the paperwork on the day! He wasn't a trained bodyguard, was he?"

"No, but neither's Iffy!"

"Iffy is covered by our insurance, this boy isn't!"

40

"HIS NAME IS CHARLIE!" shouted Jif. He realised his outburst and glanced over to Yuzuyu to see if she was scared. She wasn't. In fact, she was smiling as she laid her school uniform on the bed. It looked more like a sailor suit for ladies. Yuzuyu went to the Boston school for Japanese. It was a prep school for the gifted, on a Japanese theme. The uniforms were bog-standard Japanese: sailor-style white blouse, red cravat, short dark blue skirt. And they asked the pupils to wear long socks too, although this rule was rarely enforced. It was also what Rajah wore day in, day out, Rajah being the Indian girl at Babylon Zoo next door.

"Jif," went on Transit, "nobody cares. Vin wants a sit rep completed by lunchtime."

"Faxed?"

"No, he wants it delivered in person."

Situation report was a military term for an up-to-the-second radio commentary. But Vin adapted the phrase to be used at Lime.Inc for daily reports to be made at the end of each day and faxed to the embassy in Washington.

"To Washington?" exclaimed Jif. He then noticed the wardrobe was still open and Yuzuyu had put a bra on. White. He loved that colour on a brassiere.

"Yep, he's sending a limo to you."

"It'll take hours!"

"It's this or nothing, Jif," Transit went on. In the background, he could hear a young man mumble. There was a clatter of something, a sigh of resignation from someone. "Jif, Dill wants a word."

"Put him on," mumbled Jif. He was then given a blast of heavy breathing through the earpiece. Dill Lexmark was the youngest member of Lime.Inc, and probably the most streetwise, but like everyone else, never took on Vin for fear of getting the sack.

"Hey, Jif!" began Dill's soft, placid voice. He took a long breath and continued. "Vin is going to cut off your head and feed you to the dogs!" The choice of words didn't fit the accent.

"What's the point of telling me this if I can't get out of it?" replied Jif on autopilot.

"It's not about the sit rep, it's about setting an example for the rest of us not to fuck about!"

"What the fuck does Vin know? Everyone is fuckin' about in this company!"

"Seriously, run whilst you can! If you come to Washington, he's gonna sit you in front of us; and by the end of the day, you'll just be a hole with no ass around it!"

Jif knew what he meant. It was a dismissal, but even more than that. It was one of Vin's little mind games to show he was in charge. But looking at Yuzuyu putting on her school blouse just made himself drift.

"I don't GIVE a shit!"

"JIF!"

"A good friend of mine is dead because of that . . . that . . . racist!"

"Racist!"

"Yes, a racist! He thinks he's superior because he's black and all that bullshit about history!" Jif was picking words quickly to handle his anger. He wasn't even sure he knew what he was talking about. Calling a black man a racist? Dill didn't reply, other than sigh through the earpiece.

"He wants to fuck me. Let him! I've told the truth. I got nothin' to be scared of!"

Jif swiftly put the phone down but didn't slam it.

"Jif, is it bad?" asked Yuzuyu. She'd finished buttoning her blouse.

"Yea," said Jif, pacing up to her. "But I don't care. All I want is you." He placed a hand on her clothed shoulder, and she smiled. He drew his hand down her back and started brushing her diaper, making a rustling noise. "Do you need to change?" he asked her as he'd always done.

"No," she replied emphatically, "not yet." She drew her right arm to pick up her dark blue skirt. "But you can help me with my skirt." She said to him with moderate enthusiasm. Jif smiled back.

He took the skirt from her and held it by the waistband. Crouching onto his knees, he held it open. Yuzuyu took a step back and then stepped into the skirt. Jif slid the clothing up her legs and over her diaper until it covered the perils of her blouse. Jif fumbled with the shirt fastening, and it held in place. Yuzuyu's dainty hand covered Jif's own. She tugged at his hand, telling him to get up. He stood up again, and Yuzuyu leaned forward, placing her palms flat on Jif's shoulders. He knew what to do. Half bent, he too leaned in and kissed her lips. She kissed him back and withdrew.

"I like being your baby, Jif," she said childishly.

"Me too," he replied. "But I don't control you, do I?"

"Of course you don't, Jif. You don't ask for sex from me. And you don't order me about either. So don't worry about me! Worry about the job." He knew she was right. "Are you going to walk me to school today?"

He gazed out the window. He'd done it so many times, but not today. He wanted to dream more of Charlie. And think of a way out of this hole.

"No, honey. I can't today."

"It's OK. I can do it."

She put on her shoes and paced out the door. Jif went back to bed, head on the pillow, and heard the ping of the elevator down the corridor. He closed his eyes and thought about what was going on.

How could Vincent be like this? How could he live with himself? Because he could! To run a business, he had to be ruthless.

But Jif still felt as though he was being stabbed in the back. One of life's lessons. He shouldn't have counted Vincent as a friend.

Friends were hard to come by. Girlfriends even more. In nursery, when a beautiful girl he liked refused to hold his hands in the playground, he fell into despair. He despised girls from then on and wanted nothing to do with them. When his friend got girlfriends, he buried himself into food. He ate and ate and got fat. And the results were sitting in his stomach right now.

He knew friends came naturally. A connection of similarities. Charlie and Jif had similarities, that's why he talked to him so much. Yuzuyu and Jif had similarities, that's why she stayed with him all the time.

But sometimes you have to force people to be friends. Or it happens because there's no other option.

Charlie was a wonderful pal, a ray of light in the darkness. Vin was the guy with connections, the one to turn to when no one else would listen. But Jif owed his life to a man few would call a friend.

Ruthless. Greedy. Christ, insults weren't worth getting into.

If he hadn't been where he was . . . would he be alive today?

September 13, 2003, 1901 JST

It was a whirlwind of actions. Jif was on his knees, cradling the dead man's body, when he heard the crunch of a footstep next to him. He thought the gunmen had come back to finish him off. He waited for the men to do their work. They didn't. These men were different. He could sense their honor.

He didn't have time to speak or fight. He was hoisted up by his armpits by four very strong hands. They smelt of fish and salt. He only looked at the short guy, shorter than Jif, with wispy moustache and horn-rimmed glasses and yellow skin.

He felt Fido's body slip away, his head falling against Jif's crotch, slipping to his knee, as he was pulled away. The men raised him until his feet were above the ground, putting all his weight on his arm sockets. He tried to get his feet back down to take the weight off his shoulders, but they started to move and wouldn't let him stand.

He felt he was going to die and didn't want to see anything. He screwed his eyes shut as he was dragged along the messy road, the end of his shoes scraping along the floor.

He felt his left foot hit something hard and metallic. Then his knee settled in a soft fabric. Air-conditioning was on, and music was playing. He was being bundled in a car.

The car doors slammed, and he felt the two men sit up next to him. He could feel their body heat. The car pulled off, quickly. There was a splash as it sloshed through a puddle.

"Open your eyes," boomed an Asian voice. It had heavy *h*'s. Jif didn't comply.

"OPEN YOUR EYES!" repeated the voice. Jif inhaled a shaky breath before doing as he was told. The car was a right-hand drive, as all Japanese cars. This was a Mercedes, however. He saw the three-pointed star from the steering wheel.

The front passenger had turned around, hugging the headrest of his seat, facing Jif in the eye. He was nearly bald, with a goatee and moustache. About midforties. Brown eyes. Serious face. He was all in black: black pants, shirt, jacket.

"Yami yori mo kowai no wa kodoku," he said to Jif in a powerful voice that demanded respect. He was saying, "Solitude is more frightening than darkness."

Jif didn't move his head. And he didn't dare look at the men next to him. But he focused his eyes on the windows. He could see the buildings were becoming older and rougher. Then, he recognized the old hospital. They were taking him back to where he'd started.

The car made a sharp turn and bounced through a few potholes before entering an opening in a wall. The car was engulfed in darkness as the outside faded from view. The Merc ground to a stop, and a light came on inside the room, and the space was dazzled in a pale brightness.

As the driver got out, Jif could see through the windshield a long workbench with power tools. Was he going to get tortured?

Another Jap in a dark suit paced around the front of the car and looked in through the windshield. He pulled a smile and paced off again. The Jap passenger still looked at Jif. Jif didn't react. There was nothing he could do. Everything about today had told him it was best to do nothing.

The passenger's door was opened by the driver. The passenger finally got out, and the rest of the doors opened. Jif was pulled out by the short guy again but, once out of the car, released him. Jif stood tall and felt the other guy stand next to him. Robotic. They were here to watch over him. Jif looked at the other guy. A little taller than the other guy. Thin. Thick, flat black hair. It was only then that Jif noticed that the tips of his fingers were missing.

The room stank of engine oil and dust and had bits of car and cola cans strewn about the floor. It was a garage. And it seemed to be rather dusty. It hadn't been used for years, like most of the other buildings in this sector.

"Come!" called the main man. He was waving them over to a doorway on the wall on the right. The pair grabbed Jif by the forearms and pushed him forward. They were slow enough to allow him to walk this time, but it was still aggressive.

He was pushed through the doorway and into a cigarette-smelling dark den. A plastic picnic table and two dining chairs sat in the middle of the room. In each corner was either a mattress or a sleeping bag. In the far left corner, where a door was wide open, he made out a toilet and a washbasin. It was probably a temporary shelter. But where else could they go?

He was thrust down into one of the chairs before being released. The armrests felt welcoming to him. The bald Jap stood at the other end of the table and pulled his chair, scraping it along the floor, before trotting in front of it and sitting down with a whoosh of his clothes. Then, he closed his eyes and bowed to Jif.

"My name is Atlas," he began. Weird name. His *h*'s were heavy; almost every sentence began with an *h* with this guy. "And I am yakuza!"

Jif shivered. Under the table, he clasped his hands, playing with his thumbs.

"What do you want?" asked Jif. Atlas played it cool and calm. He closed his eyes, pulled his lips to smile, and opened them again.

"I am a patriot. I love my country," he said softly. Jif started to shake his head.

"I don't want to interfere with your country," he whined, about to cry. He thought he was going to be classed as an invader.

"Be quiet!" snapped the Jap. He blinked and carried on talking. "I know you went into the building that burnt down today."

Jif squirmed in his seat. He hated this sort of interview. Interrogations, he felt they were. This certainly was an interrogation. Ever since his first job interview, he felt uncomfortable like this, sitting face-to-face with the interviewer.

"I know Kensuki Kenjiku had involvement there. And I know Rock shot the professor." Jif barely knew Kensuki Kenjiku. From what Vincent had said, he knew he was an investor, and he was involved in freezing dead people. He knew Rock was a dangerous psychopath! But that was it.

"What I want to know is why?"

Jif sighed. He didn't know why the building was torched! Maybe the doc had pissed the boy off. Jif leaned back in his chair and gazed down at the desk, avoiding eye contact.

"We had a lot of equipment in that building. It was going to make us very rich. I AM NOT HAPPY. My bosses are not happy!" He paused to calm himself down. "You see the man next to you?" Jif looked up.

"Finger?" said Jif, throwing his head to the tall man next to him.

"Yes," replied Atlas.

"It was a punishment, wasn't it?" he asked.

"He failed to show his honor in his work," said the yakuza.

Jif turned to face the man, looking up at him. The man didn't make eye contact, looking straight ahead.

"I'm sorry," Jif softly said. Atlas rapped a knuckle on the table, and Jif snapped to attention again.

"Kensuki is a traitor to my country . . . ," began Atlas.

"And you're better, aren't you?" Jif said angrily.

"I am the last chance you have, Kitchen!"

"Look!" Jif started going into begging mode. He couldn't think of anything else because he had nothing to offer them. He didn't know anything of the company, he didn't have money, he didn't know where Yuzuyu or Keitaro had been taken. If they knew he was worthless, they might have got rid of him, maybe deadly. But at least, he knew, the nightmare would be over. "I'm just a white bloke from Hull brought up in a world about"—he held out his hands to make a football—"this big. You've got to know that I don't know what you're about. I don't know what this island is about."

"Yakuza, Kitchen!" stated Atlas, as if Jif was dumb. "Japanese Mafia!"

"I know that. It's just, I'm not involved in what goes on," he explained. He began directing his arms, pointing to nowhere, showing his palms to say he meant no trouble. "I was just sent to look after the building. I don't know what goes on in it. That's my boss's job. Vincent Bird. Take it up with him." Atlas took a tired breath.

"Someone tried to kill you. You don't want to get back at him?"

Jif knew who he was on about.

"His name is Rock, right?"

"Yes. It is Japanese for six."

"Well," Jif began. He pondered what to say, if anything. There was nothing to say. Nothing this guy would have already known. "I don't even know where to begin."

"You went into the building! So you know what there was!" Jif shrugged. Of course he didn't know what was in the building!

"It was just some lab," he stated, shaking his head and sticking his hands on the table again. He racked his brain for what there was in the burning room. Copper pipes. Aluminum cylinders. White smoke from the ice. Liquid nitrogen. The giant copper cocoon. How could he explain that! "I don't know a test tube from a Bunsen!"

"What was the professor working on?"

"I don't know."

"What was in that building?"

"I don't know! It was all on fire!"

"DON'T LIE TO ME!" screamed Atlas. Jif's eyes began to water. His lips pulled back in grimace. His stress levels were roaring, and he began to shake.

"THERE ARE THINGS I CANNOT KNOW!" he screamed back as a tear left his eye.

"If you have any honor for what is left of your homeland—"

As the Jap spoke, Jif's fear grin shrank suddenly. He rummaged through the internal pocket of his jacket and pulled out the brown book. It still smelt of bleach.

"The man gave me this! The professor!"

He gave it to Atlas. The yakuza spun the book round and opened the front cover, spine on his right, the Japanese way.

"I don't understand the writing, but I read pictures. I know it's about that girl."

Atlas turned the pages.

"He also said that the island is going to sink. I saw it myself. The reservoir is seeping into the island's foundations."

"We know that," said the fingers man. He sounded more African than Asian. "Kensuki has ordered a helicopter from Honshu. It is going arrive here at one o'clock Japanese standard time. He'd only do that if he cannot save his empire on this island!"

Shit, thought Jif. That was why Rock had said he was going to die anyway. Maybe another massive earthquake! A major earthquake! But Jif was too scared to ask. Atlas was busy with the book. Jif realized there was something he had missed out.

"Her name is Yuzuyu!" he stated, to which Atlas looked up, stunned, and the rest of the yakuza behind Jif shuffled together, whispering faint sounds to each other.

"Yuzuyu! You sure?"

"Yes. She said so. Why would she lie? We found her in the fire. The other . . . ," he paused and tried to sum it up without getting complicated. "I thought she was a runaway! But she had amnesia! We were going to take her back to the mainland." To which Atlas brought his elbows onto the table, propped up his arms, and slumped his head into his hands. Jif knew he'd said something significant, but there was something bad too.

"You understand?" Atlas said, bringing his head up again.

"No," replied Jif.

"The girl is Kensuki's daughter. She died of meningitis." Jif was confused. He shook his head in disbelief. If she was dead, who was the girl he'd been walking with all this time?

"But if—"

Jif quickly understood. Cryogenics! The father was involved in cryogenics. That was what all the material was in the lab. That was what the ice and liquid nitrogen was for! That was why she was so cold!

"She was reanimated!" Jif gasped.

"The diagrams show her body has been deliberately altered."

"How?"

"There are steel pivots built into her joints. It says they are made to maximize her strength. There are also circuit boards in this girl's head."

"Circuit boards?" exclaimed Jif. "What for?"

"To take away pain."

"Oh shit!" he swore. He'd read enough philosophy and psychology to know how this worked. "If you take pain, you take emotion."

"This isn't a girl, it's a cyborg."

"No, she ain't like that!" cried Jif. He didn't want her to die, even if she was the product of something evil.

"She will be if Kensuki keeps going. He does this not for love! He wants a ruler for this island when he dies!"

"What about that Rock boy? He said he was Kensuki's son."

"Kensuki never had a son. Rock is a boy who follows him like a dog. He'll do anything for his master. But Kensuki won't let him rule this land. He's a loose cannon."

"He's going to kill her, isn't he?"

"Yes. He will."

Atlas smiled.

"You love her!"

"She's given me a purpose. It took me so long to see it!"

Atlas smiled.

"Yami yori mo kowai no wa kodoku," he said again. "Solitude is more frightening than darkness." Atlas leaned back in his chair and put his hands behind his head. Cocky. "Then do it. Make her your purpose."

"How?" Jif asked. He didn't even know where to start looking for her. "I don't know where she is!"

"I do!" replied Atlas.

"You . . . you'll get her?"

"No . . . that's your job." Jif suddenly realized what they wanted. They didn't want info, they wanted manpower.

"You want me to help you?"

"There's no one else here that will help you, English." He was right.

"Of course," he replied. "What do you want?"

"To take out Kensuki and anyone who'll take his place."

"I don't think I can."

"You won't kill anyone, we will. You just clear the way for us and get that girl out."

"Why do you do this?"

"Because there are some things we shouldn't know, and some we should. My country is falling apart from people like Kensuki. This girl will crush them all. I want you to be the deliverer." Jif looked down and rattled like a snake. His stomach was twisting again. He could die trying, but this girl was his chance to prove himself. As a human being. As a father. He wanted to love her, and he wanted her to love him. He had to try!

"I feel sick, but I gotta do this," he said throatily.

"Good," replied Atlas. "Rock is going to kill that girl because he thinks she's an outsider. He never was Japanese!"

"He fears technology," added Jif.

"Hai," replied Atlas. He meant, of course, "yes!"

"Then . . . let's get her out of there."

FIVE

May 10, 2006, 0921 EST

Jif did not remember waking up. He only remembered standing up in his bedroom and pulling on his suit jacket. It was an aging grey thing that smelt of curry vinegar since his student days. He could have worn a cleaner suit; he had four of them. But he didn't feel like it. If he was going to be screwed, it may as well be in a dirty suit rather than a clean one; save the best for better days.

The morning was as dull as could be, a grey metallic sky hiding the sun. The minimal lightness did its best to shine through the windows of the room, but Jif wasn't interested.

He had a white shirt underneath and, strangely, a Homer Simpson tie. He didn't remember buying one or choosing it. His memory must have been playing up.

He turned and looked into Yuzuyu's vanity: an oval-shaped mirror with a white rosary border, hinged to an aluminum platform. He swept back black hair from his temples, pushing his ponytail away from his collar and further down his jacket. He started growing his hair long soon after Yuzuyu came into his life. It was a statement to show that he was different. Not like any of the other men around. There were times people couldn't work out if he was a man or a woman, especially when carrying Yuzuyu around. He liked that because he felt he was like her mommy as well.

In the distance, a telephone ring echoed from his office and chimed its way into the room. It was the public phone number, on a different line, separate from his bedroom phone. So it was more likely to be customers or curious time wasters. He broke off from his thought and paced up to the bedroom door, pulling it open and walking out. He proceeded down the white-painted corridor so narrow his wide stomach made his knuckles brush against both sides of the walls. The corridor itself was pointed J. His office was practically next door to the bedroom, but he was made to go the long way round, all the time.

He reached the door that separated office space from his private space, big and thick, probably fire resistant in line with severe city codes. It was faced in pale oak and had a tiny wired glass window for him to see who would be knocking. He pushed down the silver door handle, and a thousand clunks emanated from inside the wood.

He walked another turn, passing the silver doors of the elevator, and Iffy. Iffy was always up against the wall next to the elevator. That was his order, every morning. Jif turned left to face his office.

The door was the same as the other one, big and thick with a small window. It was handy to have; even though there wasn't much he could do if an uninvited guest turned, he could at least show insults and see their reaction knowing they couldn't get in through this secure barricade.

He glanced in; his office never changed, and nothing had been moved. He pushed the door open as it was unlocked, shut it, and paced quickly to the white 1960s telephone on a corner of his rosewood desk, as it was the fourth ring.

"Lime.Inc?" answered Jif, holding the receiver to his ear. His top lip touched the cold, moist plastic mouthpiece.

"DO NOT COME TO MY SON'S FUNERAL!" screamed a male voice. The voice had a deepness and Irish lilt that Jif had experienced with a New York taxi driver. Even though he never met the guy before, he knew who it was.

"Hello, Mr. Ronshoe," said Jif calmly, pulling up his dining room chair.

"Don't talk to me," growled the man on the phone. Jif knew reasoning with him was futile, but he had to be sure he knew whom he was talking to.

"I need to be sure who this is," said Jif.

"YOU KNOW WHO IT IS!" answered the man. "YOU KILLED MY SON!" Jif had no doubts anymore.

"Thank you for calling. I will not bother you anymore," replied Jif, his voice trailing off in a nervous shake.

"There's nothing you can do . . . ," said the man, trailing off as Jif sailed the receiver from his ear and softly placed it on the cradle. He held on to the handset for two minutes, staring down at his desk and the Lime.Inc letter-headed papers strewn across it.

One of them was an authorization slip to approve Charlie Ronshoe for working in diplomatic protection. It was the size of a paperback book and had weasel words about the person applying for the job and what dangers there were and how that person accepted the risks. It had Jif's signature scrawled on a blank line in the bottom left corner. And in the top right corner was a date of authorization. It was the day before Charlie got shot.

Jif pulled the receiver of its cradle and dropped it with a clop on the rosewood desk. The dial tone hummed its way out of the earpiece in an eerie silence. He sat down on the dining room chair. It had a padded seat and groaned its air out as Jif slumped onto it. He dragged his hand to the papers and turned over the slip because it was making him angry.

He reached for an orange plastic tray that contained blank sit-rep forms. A yellow paper with a Lime.Inc letterhead in green and dozens of black lines and tick boxes. He filled one out every day, even if nothing happened or there were no sales. He only managed to scrawl the date on the top left corner before the biro fell out of his hand. He propped his elbows onto the desk and drew his arms upwards before slumping his head into his palms. And he started bawling like a baby.

He didn't want to think about Charlie again. He forced his mind to think about something else. He wanted to replay the train crash again. How had he survived?

September 13, 2003, 1521 JST

He thought back to that time after he passed out.

He awoke and found his eyes were of no use to him. Everything was pitch-black. He took a breath and started coughing as smoky air tickled his lungs. He could smell the dirt of the floor and oil from outside and wood burning. He began to breathe more slowly.

The only thing he could hear was a low siren, far and distant, as if it was a personal alarm. It sounded like the beacon he had heard from firefighters on 9/11 that signaled they were trapped or in danger after the towers fell. So he wondered if the emergency services were nearby.

He was facedown on something cold and hard. It was the train wall. He found where his arms were and managed to place his palms flat down on the metallic surface, raising his heavy mass off the wall. He knelt up and banged his head into something soft. It was the base of a train seat, facing sideways since the carriage had turned onto its left side.

He was able to stand up and stuck his arms out in all directions to feel anything in his way. He'd taken three steps forward, when the low siren was drowned out by a roaring noise. At first he thought it was another train. It took several seconds for the carriage to start shaking again.

He crouched down, palms flat on the new floor of the carriage. He could hear heavy objects slamming into the sides of the steel carriage, causing dull ringing noises. Somewhere nearby he heard something large and metallic crash out of nowhere, echoing down the tunnel.

After five seconds, the trembling stopped. He stood up again and paced two more steps when his left foot connected with something soft. He could hear the sound of his shoe sliding against a fabric. He looked down to where he thought the object was and bent over with his arm extended. His first finger prodded a cold, sweaty bit of flesh, and he knew it was the diplomat.

He stood up again, recomposed himself, and walked as briskly as he could to the end of the carriage. He ran his open palms up and down the smooth, cold surface of the wall, trying to find the door. He felt something horizontal sticking out from the surface in the black light, about two inches long and five millimeters thick as he ran his finger over it. Curved. Several recesses in it for joints. He figured it was the hinge.

He found the tiny line of space between the door and the wall. He ran his finger along it, sticking his thumb out to try to find the handle. Halfway across, his thumb bumped into a hard object yet again. He used both hands to feel what it was. Box shaped, it felt dirty and sticky. It was two inches big and hollow. He ran his hands down and found the end was open. He felt the ridge at its end, about five millimeters thick and pointed. He dived his hand into the pit of nowhere and felt something cold, long, and plastic. It was the pick handle. He pulled it with his fingers, encountering some resistance, and felt a lock clunk open.

The door jabbed forward a couple of millimeters. A tiny ray of light flooded horizontally from where the door would normally swing open. He stepped back a foot and let the door drop.

It slammed into the steel wall with a dull thud and swung back and forth a little until it lost its kinetic energy. Light flooded the interior of the carriage. And he could see his hands had a splatter of dry blood. He looked back and saw that the Jap had been impaled on a train support. It passed through his stomach like an alien with beads of blood running down its yellow paint. The white shirt was now completely red, or as far as Jif could see, with the jacket wide open. His face was one of sheer panic, with the lips pulled back in a silent scream. His eyes were closed. The hair was a dusty mess.

Jif steadied himself on the edge of the doorway then bent down a little and pushed his head through the opening. The cold air was like heaven. A breeze blew into his face, and he was forced to squint. He looked down at the floor and saw the rough concrete surface obscured by the shiny metal rails on top. Bricks and dried concrete were scattered along the track. Maybe a wall had collapsed. He peered forward and realized that the carriage was no longer connected to the rest of the train.

He threw his hands down, careful not to touch the rails and the electricity within them, and slid the rest of his body out of the doorway. His stomach scraped metal ridges of the doorway, and he heard his shirt tear beneath, leaving a cold breeze on his groin. After his belt chimed past the metal obstruction, his body weight did the rest.

In a messy heap, he landed on top of the rails. Realizing he was not dead or electrocuted, it occurred to him that the rails were not electrified. He stood up again and brushed himself down and saw the devastation.

The light he had seen in the carriage was daylight; the tunnel had collapsed on top of the carriage about three meters farther down. It looked like a mile of concrete had crumpled and fallen down.

He could see the rest of the train, still upright, but pancaked to a thickness of just half-a-meter, huge chunks of broken grey concrete. Dust billowed everywhere.

"What am I doing here?" he said to himself. No one had mentioned before the dangers of earthquakes on this job.

He carefully paced onwards, looking round for signs of life or way out. He didn't know how long he'd been walking for, but he spotted a ladder fixed to the wall on his left. He charged at it, swaying through mountains of drinks cans, bricks, and concrete. He grappled the sides of the ladder and heaved his feet up the rungs. He looked up, and an arch of concrete tunnel still stood above him. He could see a steel trapdoor with several holes drilled into it, allowing long cylinders of light and air billowing down on him. Stepping up, he gazed around. He was nowhere near the opening on the roof of the tunnel, and there didn't seem to be much there anyway. This was probably the best he was going to get.

His weight made Jif nervous. Every step he took made the ladder give a metallic groan, squeaking under his shoes. He held on each time for dear life until he was face-to-face with the door. He raised his right hand, keeping his left fixed to the ladder. He crushed his right hand into a fist and prodded his knuckles into the cold metal door. Amazingly, it was unlocked and opened with a heavy whine.

The door slammed into the tarmac outside with a crunch, and more daylight hit Jif's face. He raced through the opening and pulled himself out of the hole and breathed deeply.

The space around him looked like a building site and a bomb site combined. To his left were sets of partly demolished or unfinished buildings, no taller than two stories, white or sandy-coloured brick, masked by tonnes of scaffolding set up in squares around each building.

To his right were dozens of shop fronts with flashy colour and Japanese words. Some shops had the shutters down, some were open, the glass windows smashed or blown out. One shop front with a bowl-and-chopstick cartoon above the door had a green saloon parked half in half out the store. Broken glass snowed the hood of the car making a white crystal appearance and reflected the metallic sky above, piercing Jif's eyes.

The air smelt heavily of old dog, and bits of masonry littered the road. The road itself was old and grey. It seemed the builders had started erecting the new buildings but had neglected to demolish all the old ones. He knew there were buildings here from the 1930s, but they could have hurried up and restored and got rid of them. Why build right next to old buildings? And where was everybody? It was supposed to be teeming with builders and workers.

Jif grappled whatever was on the pavement in front of him and heaved himself out of the manhole. He lost his right footing and scrabbled in panic, banging his knee against the opening before slipping face-first into the dust.

He ground words of pain as he tried to stand up again. His forehead had collected a tiny piece of broken brick, hanging half a centre meter in his flesh.

The dust had burnt his eyes, and he could barely see his own hand as he tried to find the foreign object. He pulled it out, and the blood started to pour. He ground his eyes shut to wash away the dust as he stood up, driving his palm into his head to stop the bleeding.

He stumbled forward, the lack of sound indicating that no one else was nearby. It dawned on him that this was a ghost town now, and he'd survived an earthquake and a train crash, and now, if he didn't keep the pressure, he was going to bleed to death.

He peered around, surveying his surroundings, and saw the barricade. The shiny silver fencing had been erected across the road. There was a giant high-rise, falling to bits beyond the fence. And he realized that was the old city, the old buildings from 1940s when the Japanese lived here.

Jif pressed on, holding his head until he got to the barricade. Each section of fence was eight feet tall and two meters wide. Each bit fixed to the ground with a bolt. It stretched from end to end. A mini dump truck was parked alongside it. Jif paced about, trying to find an entrance. Eventually he found it; one of the supports had been forced, bent back upwards from the ground.

Jif crawled his way under the opening, dusting his hands and his legs in the dirt on the road. The broken fence dug sharply into his back but didn't tear the jacket. The coldness of the air seeped into his head wound, and he quickly brushed his hand to cover the cut again.

He stood up and wandered forward. Construction equipment was everywhere. JBC's cement trucks, a mobile crane. All covered in red dust. What the hell where they building? Shouldn't they be demolishing first?

"HELLO!" he screamed at the top of his lungs. No reply.

Perhaps the high-rise was being renovated, turned into an office block. Would take a long time! It had been ransacked, windowless holes, paper strewn everywhere, a child's bicycle lay on its side as if its owner was coming back. He pulled out his Nokia. It was on, but the reception bar was blank. He pocketed it again.

He gazed away from the buildings and saw a giant sandy mound. Its door wide open. It sat still, and Jif sucked all the breath he could hold as he paced up to it.

He realized it was a police cruiser, like he'd seen at the airport. It was parked at an angle in the road, and all its doors were opened. Its roof and bonnet were snowed with a thin layer of red and sandy-coloured masonry dust. He came up to the front of the car and looked into the windshield. He could what looked like the shoulder of a man's jacket, poking behind the passenger's dashboard. He walked around the left door, opened. Lying across both seats was a Japanese man in retro uniform. Dark blue pants, black boots, light blue shirt. No tie. He had an inch-thick belt around his waist; on his left hip was a leather gun holster. No gun. Must have knocked it out. In the footwell of the driver's seat was his hat, a black peaked cap with a yellow emblem in the centre.

The man's face was pale. Jif heard a winged insect buzz behind him, and his heart jumped. He leaned in further and rested his left hand on the driver's seat under the man's knee. His right hand crept up and touched the Jap's throat. Cold. No pulse. No reaction. He was dead, definitely. But there was no blood. He must have fainted.

Jif fiddled under the steering wheel, to see if the car was drivable, but the keys were missing. Had someone taken them already? Were there other survivors? He glanced at the man's face again and realized there was a bruise under the jawbone. Shit! He'd been punched. He'd been murdered!

Jif heaved his body out of the car, nervous. He felt being near death made him more likely to die. Panting, he looked around, for nothing in particular. Then something caught his attention.

A signpost. Or a temporary one. It was made out of cardboard and fixed to a broomstick, propped up in an oil drum. Walking up to it, he saw it was written in both Japanese and English.

Katec is what is said. That was the name of the building he was supposed to be in charge of. It had an arrow pointing in the direction of the high-rise.

"Oh . . . for fuck's sake!" There was no way that could have been the Katec building. So he gazed around to see if there was an exit. There was.

A small alleyway sandwiched between the crumbling high-rise and a row of mobile huts. He wandered his way down, crunching on the bits of trash that littered the floor, when the ground started shaking.

At first he was knocked to his knees, steadying himself with the flat of his hands. The aftershock was shallow compared to the major earthquake he'd been in, but it was still terrifying and confusing for him. When he heard something smash, he knew it was time to go. He picked himself up and ran on the shaky ground. His stomach was going into orbit by this time.

He saw a lump of sandy masonry fly in front of him. He skidded and jumped about like a scaredy-cat before racing to the end of the alley. He flew out, to the sound of sloshing water.

He managed to stop before falling into the flood. The water itself was quivering from the earthquake. Then, it suddenly stopped. Jif gazed up.

This must have been one of the island's extensions. A long flat stretch of land. Although he couldn't see much land, or how good it was, because it was underwater. There were six industrial-sized box buildings, sticking out from the brown soup that had engulfed this little plot. Each one white, with a Japanese hieroglyph stuck up in its front. Second from Jif's left was one that had the name Katec in bold blue across the top.

The building still stood, but water was still filling in. He could hear the crashing of the waves nearby; it must have been very close to the shore. Had the defenses been knocked out from the earthquake?

He'd come this far; he was not going to stop just from a little flood. Plunging in, the water reached his ankle, slurping into the soles of his new leather shoes. It was icy cold, and he felt dirty because it was. He sloshed his way through the brownie sludge to an open door. A red carpet greeted him, along with an overhead banner that read, Welcome to Katec Industries. The walls were white and in disrepair; it must have been one of the old buildings that were being renovated.

"Hello?" he called, no reply. He found a flight of stairs. Looking up, he heard a thud of a footstep. As his heart jumped, he raced upstairs. "Hello!" he called again. This time he got a reply.

"AHH!" screamed a man's voice. Jif could smell burning. Toxic smoke. Plastic being melted. A thin sooty smoke spiraled on the tall ceiling; a door was open ahead. Orange flamed in the gap. A human hand appeared. "NANI?" came the voice again. Jif pulled open the door and was greeted on the floor by an old man in a white medical jacket. He yanked the Jap by the collar and kicked the door shut.

"Speak English?" he yelled at the man.

"Yes."

The man had a thick white beard and moustache. He was mostly bald except for a thin line of black hair around the base of his skull. His breathing was croaky, and he kept on coughing. He looked up, using his eyes to plead with him. Jif knelt down and saw how red and irritated the eyes were. He could hear crying in the distance. A child's voice.

"I don't know what to do," Jif said, being honest. The old man reached under his pants and pulled out a tiny brown book.

"Keep," he whispered in English, shoving the book into his hand. "This island is falling apart," he began. "Reservoir!" he paused. "Break . . ." He closed his eyes and stopped breathing. Jif put a hand in the hands and throat. Nothing. He rested the man down, slowly and carefully. His first day and he'd gotten three dead men on his conscience.

"Hey!" screamed a young voice. There were more people. Jif looked to his left.

That sound was overtaken by a creak like a pumpkin splitting open. *Bang!* Something collapsed! Jif turned around to look at the wall behind him. It had caved in, and black smoke was billowing out.

"Hey" came the voice again. It was a young man's voice, Asian, and coming from the stairs. Jif couldn't see anymore as the smoke began to engulf. He held his breath.

"Senpie," said the boy, muffled. His face came into view, an inch from Jif. The boy had spiky black hair and had his grey nylon clad right arm over his mouth.

"Casualty," Jif coughed, pointing down at the man. Another figure appeared through the smoke, and the boy stood up and disappeared. Jif grabbed his jacket and thrust his collar over his mouth. He felt his own sweat from his cheeks. His heart was pumping into overdrive. He squinted his eyes and stepped forward, trying to see where the crying was coming from.

Through the hole in the wall, he felt the floor creak beneath him. He waved his left hand through the smoke to clear a way and signal to whoever was out there. As soon as he could see the orange flames thrusting up from the floor in front of him, his nose started to itch. He could smell melting rubber and almonds. There was cyanide in the air. He had to get out soon.

The illumination of the fire showed up the interior of the room. There were gas cylinders all around. Oil drums. Plastic boxes holding bits of everything were burning thick black smoke and melting.

There was something bronze in front of him, copper. Like a coffin. A pod. It had a sliding section on top and was partially open. It was on fire on the outside, but it had white smoke wafting out its interior. Was it dry ice?

The smoke was burning his eyes and his lungs. He wanted to get out of there! He couldn't breathe. The heat was intense, yet the fire was two meters away. The crying was still audible and gut-wrenching. He wanted desperately to help, to prove to himself he was heroic, but he could not decide if he should save himself. Then she appeared.

The girl was Asian, but pale, almost ghostly. She grunted a sigh of despair; her mouth wide open, lips stretched back in fear. Her face was wet with tears, and a few strands of her short hair had got stuck to her cheeks. She didn't appear to be wearing clothes. She seemed to be walking with a cloud of mist around her, on tiptoes, shaky, her hands at head height trying to avoid the flames. Jif could not believe it; he was in the presence of a naked female. Her hair was honey blonde, very alluring. He fought against the erection that was coming on.

Jif approached cautiously so as not to scare her. He reached out his hand. He expected warmth. There wasn't any.

She was cold. So cold, the ends of his fingers burned.

"AAHH!" screamed Jif, thrusting his hand into his left armpit. It reminded him of being stung by a bee. It caused him to gasp through his jacket, and he started choking. Bent double like a hag, he knew he was in trouble. The smoke was stealing all his strength.

"Sir, get out" came the voice again. He felt himself being pulled by his trouser waistband. Virtually blind, he threw out his hands to feel if he bumped into anything and focused on his feet to feel the floor condition. He felt a recess in the floor, and a gust of clean, cold air hit his face. He realized he was at the foot of the stairs. He looked back to see where the other guys were.

"HEY!" he screamed back, spluttering a cough. He felt his ribs contract and ran down the stairs. The smoke trailed him as he got to the doorway.

He threw himself into the water. Cold, glorious water. If dirty and smelly. He sank his head down, cooling away the heat, blowing through his nose to get the smell of the smoke out of his system. And realized he could taste shit.

He stood up out of the liquid, feeling his eyes burn again, this time from the sewage. He sloshed back towards the door, saw more smoke gush its way out, and heard the rapping of feet on the stairs.

An old man with a black moustache and goatee appeared. He must have been the other guy. He leapt into the filthy water as it went up to the knees of his blue jeans. The man's grey porkpie hat doffed about as looked back to the doorway, showing the dirty black line on his beige jacket. And the boy, ashen faced, leapt out.

The boy was holding the blonde girl. She was naked, her soft round ass drawing Jif's attention. She was gazing around in curiosity. Jif waded up to the group when the old man snapped.

"Rego da sododat de nani o!" screamed the old man. "What the fuck was that!"

SIX

May 10, 2006, 1034

Jif woke up again on the rosewood desk and couldn't go back to sleep. He raised himself off the desk, heaving himself with his palms, when there was a knock on his door. Mitzvah was peering through the glass, her face obscured by her head scarf and veil. Most men he knew of were scared of the veil, but not Jif, mainly because Mitzvah wore Western clothes under her veil and not the all-black dress that other Muslim women wore around Boston. As he sniffed, he realized his face was wet again. He wiped his eyes and waved Mitzvah in. She turned the handle and pushed open the door. Iffy followed her in.

"Is your phone off the hook?" she asked in her thick Bradford accent, her veil twitching as she spoke.

"I didn't wanna be disturbed," replied Jif.

"Then why d'ya let me in?" she said back, her arms outstretched, palms open, showing that it was nothing personal. Jif could almost see the smile under her veil. She drew a breath as Iffy stood to attention behind her, hands behind his back. "Ambassador Vincent Bird wants a word with you."

Jif's heart sank. Vin was his best mate, the guy who got him this job; and now if he wanted a word, it meant bad news. The phone call should have warned him of that, but it didn't. He drew a breath.

"When?" asked Jif.

"Today, at the embassy," replied Mitzvah. Jif looked around, pondering what to do. Did he have any appointments? And how was he going to get to Washington at this short notice?

"He has sent a limousine to pick you up," Mitzvah went on to say. "Should be here in ten minutes."

"That was quick," Jif said, in complete surprise.

"You know Vin. He thinks before telling anyone."

Mitzvah turned around and paced out of the office. Iffy stood perfectly still as the elevator outside chimed. Jif was still pulling himself together, staring at the phone, and decided to cheer himself up. He looked at Iffy and asked a question.

60

"How come Thatcher fall from power?" he said through clenched teeth as he always did when setting Iffy off.

"All did turn against her when she introduced a gobbling tax!" replied Iffy in a gravelly voice. He drew a breath and finished off the sentence. "THE TROLL TAX."

Iffy had a form of torts syndrome. He would respond to certain sentences by being another character. In most cases, Gandalf from *Lord of the Rings*.

Jif gave himself a smile and stood up from his chair. He made his way around the desk and walked past Iffy through the doorway. Iffy turned on his heel, following close behind Jif, and pulled the door shut. Jif stood at the elevator. His hand hovered over a shiny steel plate on the wall as his index finger lightly pressed the single button in the middle of the plate. The tiny red LED light inside the button came to life.

The elevator pinged, and the doors opened. Jif stepped into the car and stood at the back as Iffy shuffled behind. The door closed as Jif turned around. Iffy did the same and reached over the control panel for level 1.

There were four buttons to press. R for the rooftop, 3 for the third floor, 1 for the first floor (or ground floor in his native England), and CP for the basement car park. There was no button for the second floor; in its place was a keyhole. A special key was needed to enter that level because it was where all the equipment was made. Up to ten scientists worked there on a deniable operation of research and creative weapons. Jif never saw them. He'd only been on that level once. It would have been too dangerous for him to have talked about it anyway.

Jif felt the car moved down with a whine of motors above their heads. The car was dark, with just one fluorescent tube light in the ceiling. The interior was metallic grey, all metal, not shiny. Jif's mind was still racing with thoughts: Was he going to get fired, or could he argue his way out? What would he do next for a job? Lime.Inc wasn't very good with references. And would he be given "executive action"? It was the polite military word for execution.

He felt the car slow down to a stop. The car pinged again, and the door slid open. Lime.Inc reception area. Jif stepped out; his leather shoe clopped on the tiled floor. Mitzvah wasn't behind the desk, but Shiffs was. His name was Robert Shiffs, but everyone called him by his surname. Six feet tall, slim build, and charcoal grey hair, he was quite good-looking but failed to win any girl. If he wasn't manning the reception, he'd be wanking to Internet porn in the back room, so he'd gotten a bad reputation as the village pervert. He'd even been looking up girls' skirts on flights of stairs.

Shiffs had his head down, pretending not to notice Jif, scribbling away at some papers behind the white desk of the reception. Jif placed his hands on the desk, leaning over to drift his shadow over Shiffs, and the boy eventually looked up.

"Did Yuzuyu walk to school today?" questioned Jif.

"Yea," replied Shiffs in a southern English accent. "She had her bags, set off, and Panget let her out." Jif drew a breath.

"When she gets home tonight, let me know. I wanna cook her dinner tonight."

"Will do," replied Shiffs, snatching a business card from a tray and scribbling away. Jif turned around, ready to leave.

"What time will you be back?" called Shiffs, looking down. Jif turned around again.

"Well, I'm going to Washington. I'd say, three hours, minimum. Even on High 93, its miles and miles away—"

"Seven hundred fifty-one kilometres, actually," cut in Shiffs, poking his head up again. Jif hated it when he was too specific. Why couldn't he just be general about things?

"Mate, why do ya have to be so exact?"

"What's ya problems, man?" replied Shiffs, leaning back in his chair, defensive. Jif sighed and threw his hands up in the air.

"I don't know why we can't just take the plane," he whined. "Or better yet, just hold it at that British consulate in Cambridge." One Memorial Drive was a ten-story structure of glass and steel that held the British consulate for Massachusetts; Jif had been there once to chat with Vincent before doing the Lime.Inc job. Ironically, it was within spitting distance of MIT, the place he'd fought so hard to get Charlie into. He paused in position for ten seconds, expecting a reply. There wasn't one. He turned on his heel and walked out.

Jif paced out into a glorious sunshine, with Iffy in tow. He was still kept from the road by the eight-foot-high black metal fencing just two meters from the footpath. Next to the gate sat a brand-new wooden garden shed; it was the home for the resident police officer. Panget stepped out in his British police uniform: black pants, white shirt with black epaulettes. His black turban, beard, and glasses actually made him look more peaceful; and that hid his grumpy mood that morning, until he spoke.

"Haven't you ever heard of a telephone?" grumbled Panget in a soft Glasgow accent. Jif could see a burn mark on Panget's brown-skinned knuckle. He reached his left hand back in the shed, and the first gate opened outwards, slowly.

Jif was going to greet Panget a good morning, but the grumbling made him change his mind. Avoiding eye contact, he kept on walking into the first section, up to the second gate, to allow the swinging gate to close without bashing into him. He didn't bother to check as the gate behind him swung within an arm's length of his elbow. It closed with a dull ringing noise, and then the second gate slid sideways open.

Jif stepped out as the sliding gate clanged behind him. He dipped his hands in his pockets as the process was repeated for Iffy. The smell of car fumes was intoxicating. There was so much traffic noise he didn't even hear or feel when Iffy stood next to him. In front of Jif stood a five-story building, grey with glass and steel; he never knew what the company was. He peered left, and he could just make out One Federal Street, an enormous skyscraper housing many financial institutions. It was quite busy, even at nine in the morning. A low rumble of an engine mixed with hissing of air-conditioning became audible from his left. The white stretch limo pulled up on the sidewalk two minutes later. The driver honked his horn and wound down the window.

"Pickup for a Jif Kitchen?" he called in a soft American voice.

"Yes," replied Jif, not making eye contact. The driver opened his door. He was in a smart-looking chauffeur's uniform, grey peaked hat, cashmere raincoat, and knee-high black leather boots. He paced to the back and opened the rear passenger door. Jif followed suit and entered the car, with a thanks. The driver pulled a pleasant smile.

The car smelled heavily of roses and beer. A party must have been held in here shortly before it arrived. Jif clambered over the leather seat and held on to the minibar next to the door, before plumping down into the side-facing row of leather on the right of the car. The red leather groaned beneath his weight, a sound repeated by Iffy as he sat in the opposing seat behind the minibar. He'd managed to climb over the bar as Jif had his back turned.

"Martini?" asked Iffy, raising his eyebrows.

"No, thank you," said Jif, shaking his thick finger toward the black man. "Have one for yourself."

Iffy's hands disappeared behind the bar as he looked down, making dozens of clattering noises. Jif tilted his head back against the wall of the limo and felt the car pull forward slowly. The surroundings of the interior were not plastic, but a synthetic material, so Jif could not feel the car's vibrations. Feeling more relaxed, his brain tried to make sense of what happened all those years ago and how it affected him today. He felt sleepy and was about to close his eyes when Iffy went off.

"Mmmrrrhhhhhuu!" spluttered Iffy like a horse. Jif looked at him to take notice. Iffy went quiet again.

"What, mate?" questioned Jif, eyes narrowed to show he was annoyed about being woken. Iffy jostled his arm up, waving his finger at the window.

"You always wanted to see the park!" Iffy said quickly. Jif shook his head.

"Ya talking out of your ass!" he snapped. Jif knew it would be impossible to see Boston Common from Federal Street, unless you were onto of a building. Jif felt the limo steer right and then left. Jif peered out the door window next to Iffy and realized they were on Congress Street, streets lined with boney trees and giant black skyscrapers.

The limo started to pick up speed. Jif was curious; it was normally packed at this time of day. Jif gazed around the large space and fiddled with the seat when they overtook a white roaring bus.

"Iffy," called Jif, "how do you wind down the partition?" Jif pointed at the glass wall divide at the other end of the limo. "I want to speak to the driver!" Without a flicker of emotion, Iffy raised a black brick with a wire at the end. It had red and white squares on top. A sort of remote control. Iffy sank his thumb, and something clicked. With an awful electric whine, the glass partition wound down.

"Sir," called Jif, "what's up with the traffic?"

"Virtually no traffic!" called the chauffeur without turning his head. "Amazing for Boston!" He said nothing more, and Jif couldn't argue and ask anymore. Jif turned to Iffy and waved his first finger in a circle. Iffy wound the partition back up again.

"I would have chatted with him . . . ," said Jif, his head bowed down. "Why is everybody so antisocial today?" he questioned as he looked into Iffy's face. Iffy was serious faced again, staring straight through into nothing.

"I hate these things. It's gonna be a dismissal, and I can't get out of it." Jif was getting angry. He threw a fist into the seat next to his thigh. "Why do they always have to drag their employees for"—he searched for something to say—"a word! All the time!" He put on a London accent. "Mate, can I have a word?" He returned to his normal voice. "Why can't they just get on with it and say, 'Hey, you're fired!' Why can't they just be honest? They're all so uptight and dishonest! Every employer! Everyone I've ever been with, they stab me in the back!"

Iffy still didn't respond. Jif sighed. He felt the car fly along the road, bouncing, gliding through curves. He worked out they were on Lomasney Way, heading towards the spaghetti junction. Jif felt his eyes water up. He rubbed his face with the back of his right hand. He felt if he lost his job, he would be able to support his wife. She was the only thing good in his life, other than Charlie. If he lost her as well, he'd have nothing. He'd be nothing.

Jif turned around and peered through the window behind. They were doing about 60. He saw Ford Crown Vics fly past the limo as they entered one of the freeways. Overpasses fencing flew above him as they sped along. He felt the car dip in a bend. He saw a freeway rise out of the ground and become level, coming side on closer and closer, until the limo joined this lane. Highway 93.

"Well, this is it. Nothing to stop now," whined Jif as he swiped up his left sleeve to see his watch: 1042. It would be an awfully long drive.

He peered back through the window. Trying to stare down the window, down the road. They were coming up to the Thomas P. "Tip" O'Neill Jr. Tunnel. An ugly square hole dug into grey concrete. The mouth swallowed them up, plunging the limo into a mild darkness that was pierced every second by a flash of yellow from the overhead lights in the tunnel.

The darkness made Jif even sleepier, if uncomfortable. Closing his eyes and bowing his head, he tried to think of Charlie but couldn't. Instead, the thought from earlier came back. The darkness reminded him of it.

September 14, 2003, 0016

In his memory, he found himself running down a dark corridor, lit by only a tiny ray of light from the door up ahead. He was in the Kenjiku Plaza, and he could hear his heart racing madly, his breathing emphasized by the motorcycle crash helmet he was wearing. At the end of the corridor was a metallic door. It was unlocked and ajar. He could hear yelling inside, grown man arguing in a Japanese dialect that he couldn't understand.

He crashed through the door, bearing in mind the element of surprise, and trying not to drop what was in his hand. Straight ahead, Kensuki Kenjiku, suited in beige, matted, unkempt black hair, looked, turned right to face his intruder. He was standing in front of a Kenjiku uniformed guard, who also turned to see what was happening. The room was small, illuminated by yellow light beaming in from a streetlight outside through a window, and only had a single desk behind them, about a metre long and reached end to end of the room. Jif immediately got clear of the door and spun right to drive his left shoulder into the men. Soft, warm flesh engulfed his arm, banging his wrist into his stomach. Two windy grunts hummed their way into Jif's helmet along with a scraping sound of furniture. He felt his right gloved hand start to burn as the liquid in the glass sloshed over, dripping down its stem. A black peaked cap cluttered over his visor and fell to the floor. The weight on his arms subsided with double yelps.

Facing right on, he heaved away from the men and charged for an open doorway which led into the huge room filled with the smell of urine. On the smooth tiled marble floor, Keitaro was lying facedown, an arm stretched out and curved above his head. Jif leapt over him and looked up again. His eyes were met with dozens of black electrical devices stacked against the walls, some monitors, some plastic things with no obvious use. The boy that had only been known as "Rock" had his back turned. His short black hair was spiked up in all directions, and the black combat pants and red fleece did nothing but anger Jif; it reminded him of the shootings earlier in the day.

In front of the boy was Yuzuyu, arms raised in surrender, standing in a puddle of liquid. The brown skin beneath her blonde hair was so wet it reflected the little light that was in the room. She was still wearing the dirty blue coveralls and the oversized men's shirt. The sleeves had dropped right up to her elbows. Rock slowly turned around, his eyes looking like black holes. Jif threw what was in his hand directly at Rock's face. The beer glass tilted in the air, ejecting a small globule of liquid from its inside. The fluid looked alive, with little rainbows of colour.

The whole glass impacted Rock's head from the corner of his left eye socket. The glass broke in three pieces, and the liquid flowed all over his face. Jif didn't wait for Rock to scream as he ran past and charged at Yuzuyu. He threw his arms out and scooped her up. She slammed into Jif's chest with an "uh" from the back of her lungs as he heard Rock screaming in agony. The smell of sulphuric acid was now obnoxious. Her weight was a sudden pull on his legs; but leaning forward, and shaking his head through the wave of her blonde hair, he ran for the nearest exit.

The door next to them was unlocked. Another dark corridor; Yuzuyu did not react. As shouts of pain from Rock blended in with yells from other men behind him, he ran and could hear footsteps slamming on the floor behind. He could feel the dampness of Yuzuyu's wet trousers seeping into his smock. He could see a junction ahead and a large window. Jif didn't slow down as he approached.

Throwing himself forward, the glass slammed his crash helmet down onto his skull with an awful *smak*. Glass shattered around him, and Yuzuyu howled in fear.

"JIF!" she screamed. Wind began to whisk past both of them as they plummeted from the thirty-second floor of the plaza. Jif gripped Yuzuyu's dress as hard as he could as his right hand reached the pull string in the strap of his backpack. A quick rustle shocked his body before there was a gradual, not quick, slowdown of their descent. Even with the parachute, they were still falling quicker than he would have liked.

May 10, 2006, 1158

Jif stirred in his seat. Not wanting to wake up, but wanting to know if he was there yet, he squinted his right eye, took a peek, and raised his right hands to view his wristwatch: 1159. Lunchtime and he still wasn't hungry. He'd been dieting for two months, but about this time, he'd normally have a porkpie or a slice of Cracker Barrel on Jacobs. He couldn't stand the British tea that was imported here; Tetley tastes weird. He'd settle for a Nescafe or trot over to Starbucks.

He gazed at Iffy. He had his eyes closed, but his head was still up, as if he was sleep sitting. Silently, Jif shuffled around.

He leaned over to his window, putting his forehead on the cold pane of glass. They were on a freeway, doing about 70. A colossal speed for such a big vehicle. But the sooner they got there, the better. He looked for a landmark. Where were they?

The landscape was whizzing past, along with roaring tankers, buses, and vans. He could see mass car parks and ugly tall white-walled industrial warehouses. Somewhere near Massachusetts? It was New Haven.

His vision was temporarily obscured by a pillar. The opposite freeway lane split away in a curve. Roads flew above him. They were going through another intersection.

Jif coughed. He started feeling sick. He wished this car would stop and he could just run with Yuzuyu from this awful country. It once had so much hope, but it stabbed him in the back, just like everyone else in his life.

"What's the use of family?" Jif asked himself out loud, not caring if Iffy woke up. His breathing had caused condensation on the window. "They tie you up, drag you down, and die and break your bloody heart!"

As the mess of overpasses flew past, the sunshine suddenly broke through. He squinted, and then crushed his eyes shut. The blinding light caused his brain to ache, and Jif could feel his blood easing into his eyelids. The brightness continued, and his vision became engulfed. All white.

Jif knew this wasn't in his memory. It was too long. He was now seeing his imagination. Everything was white. He could feel himself looking around. A mass landscape of white. Nothing else.

He felt himself move his hands. In front of his face. He saw them. But that was it. A hallucination? An out-of-body experience?

"Hello?" he called. He heard his echo bounce back.

A spot of black appeared on the horizon. At least it wasn't white.

Seemed to get bigger. And bigger. It was coming forward, at a colossal speed. Jif felt his knees shake. He wanted to run. But he wanted to confront what he was seeing. The object started to take a recognisable form. Human shaped. A young man. Asian. Dark green jacket over a white shirt. Blue jeans. White sneakers.

It was Keitaro.

He stopped about a meter in front of Jif. He was wearing the same clothes as when he died. He was smiling.

"Are you alive?" Jif sheepishly asked.

"No, Jif," said the boy. He spoke in English, heavily accented in Japanese. "This is just your brain coping with whatever shit has happened to you." Jif nodded his head. And he realised, he was dreaming.

"I know. It's so stressful, all this!" Jif whined, throwing his arms at his sides. "A good friend of mine died—my fault—and now I'm going to lose my job! It's so insensitive!" Jif panted, thinking up more things to say. "I know you're just a hallucination, but if you were 'ere, would you come for Yuzuyu?"

"No, Jif! We both know I'd never have made a good husband. You needed her more than me!"

He knew he was just saying that.

"Jif," Keitaro suddenly said in a sinister tone, "everything is going to change."

"Nani?" replied Jif. He felt himself unable to use English. He'd been learning Japanese since Yuzuyu arrived in his life, but now it was all he could think of. "Nani do sisfa?" Jif asked.

Keitaro faded away into the light as Jif felt his lungs exhale.

And the dream fogged its way through his brain as he thought of something else. And the paleness of the light put him on track to think of his wife. The paleness of the sky and the thought of how Yuzuyu's skin was so pale came to mind.

She was born in Japan, yet she was white. How could that be? It was the same question he asked himself when he and Yuzuyu arrived back in England. At his terraced house in Hull, Jif had made her feel at home, when the question kept fuming through his head.

It took a week before he worked out what it was. Vitiligo. Or leukoderma. "A chronic skin disease that causes loss of pigment, resulting in irregular pale patches of skin" as the encyclopedia told him.

A trip to the doctors suggested that Yuzuyu's case was caused by a combination of autoimmune, genetic, and environmental factors, something Jif did not have time to understand. What was important was that it was not life threatening. So Jif decided to act as if this was normal.

It worked! The vitiligo affected her whole body, not patches! So to anyone in the street, and especially to Yuzuyu, she looked like a normal Westerner. A pale one at that.

But that was not the most serious problem.

May 10, 2006, 1206

Jif felt his eyes open again. It was dark. Yellow fluorescent lights flying past above him again. Were they in the Boston Tunnel again? No.

Out of the tunnel, the limo emerged among four-story red-and-white-bricked buildings. Jif could see they were in the Bronx, near New York. He twisted around in his seat, peering through any of the windows, trying to see the Statue of Liberty.

Grand Theft Auto IV was coming out next year. He hadn't played video games since he arrived in the US because of the job and Yuzuyu. But he was still highly interested. GTA IV would be set in Liberty City, a mock-up of New York. It would have many New York monuments incorporated in the game. He wanted to see how different the Liberty Statue would be to the Statue of Happiness that would be in the game.

He saw the road suddenly shrink from a two-lane highway to just one. They were going over the George Washington Bridge. The road felt bumpy, and the limo vibrated as though it was having an orgasm. The low-level bridge barrier whisking past, he could see a beautiful little forest beneath him. He wondered what it would be like to live in the woods, like Robin Hood. Like Tom Good out of *The Good Life*. Away from civilization. Away from the need to pay taxes.

If he had lived down there with Yuzuyu, feeding off deer and building wooden shacks, it would be likely people would come to criticise him. And he could have sex with Yuzuyu without anyone bothering him. But Yuzuyu was content with technology. She loved her computer. He could take that away from her, not now. What if he'd taken her to the woods before all this?

"No! Don't think of sex!" cursed Jif to himself through clenched teeth. "That's what paedophiles do!"

The bridge ended, and they were in New Jersey. Behind his head, on the left of the car, was a multi-storey purple building made of glass that looked rather similar to the hospital on the TV series *House*.

Jif sighed and sat back down, resting his head uncomfortably on the edge of the backrest, since there was no headrest. He wanted to think of Charlie. "Really?" exclaimed Foxy. "You're an MIT student?"

Twenty minutes after the scuffle in his office, Jif had escorted the boy back into Babylon Zoo for a chat. Having dressed and dried off, the Charlie boy put on some glasses. It turned out he'd actually been called over by his grandmother, to run the place.

"What's an MIT?" asked Rajah. By now Jif had gotten to learn everyone. The long-haired girl was Naomi, an Israeli, also trying to get into MIT to do the maths degree. The Southern girl was called Foxy because her eyes made her look like a fox. He wasn't certain of her real name. And the Indian was called Rajah. There was also a Japanese resident, but she wasn't in today.

"So you should be a sophomore by now?" said the New York aunty. She wasn't involved very much with the dorm. She only ran the small café outside, which shared the now-tiny car park in front of Babylon Zoo.

"Well, actually, Aunty Miriam . . . ," began Charlie. He was sitting on a couch in the living room; the aunty was kneeling her elbows on the backrest behind him. He was cut off when Miriam covered his mouth.

"So that's the story! He's been studying his brains out all these years! I'd say he'd be an impressive manager." Then she pulled her hand away.

"Manager?" exclaimed the boy. He still wasn't in MIT! Perhaps she was trying to do him a favour to give him this job.

"Of what?" asked Jif. "The apartment?"

"No, wait!" exclaimed the Israeli. She paced up to the coffee table in front of Charlie and started shaking her finger. "We can't have a man be the manager of an all-girl dorm! That's totally unacceptable!" She was throwing a tantrum when Foxy interrupted.

"So, Mr. Manager . . . what exactly are you an expert in?" asked the Southern belle.

"Well," started Charlie nervously, "my goal was to do the computer course and—" She cut him off.

"Oh yea! Check it out! Hear that! A computer geek! He'll be the next Bill Gates!"

"Will you stop playing up!" shouted Naomi.

"What's the big deal? Hell, he even looks like Gates, man!"

"Look, this guy just peeped us in the pool. What do you think he'll do when he's workin' here?"

"Well," softened the aunty, "I think it's best he stays here for the night, and we take this up in the morning."

"Ya sure?" asked Jif.

"I got to get back to the café, unless someone else wants to take my place?"

The living room swiftly emptied. Miriam showed Charlie to the manager room, and Jif accompanied him. The boy was glad; he felt uneasy.

"Look, you're not an MIT student, are you?" questioned Jif while he slid the door shut.

"No, I'm a ronin!" answered Charlie. "I've failed to get in twice." Jif felt him strike a cord in his heart. This guy didn't just look like Keitaro; he had his spirit too.

"Look, I admire you!" Jif stated.

"What?" exclaimed the boy.

"I'm not a cop. I'm not gay. I just want to know that I can help other people somehow."

"Uh, can you get me into MIT?" asked the boy. And the rest of their lives began.

September 13, 2003, 1557 JST

After wading through the water and watching the building burn down, Jif and his newfound friends wandered between the crumbling ruins of two buildings, before holding up at a 1970s monstrosity in yellow brick.

Jif was still dripping, his clothes sticking to his skin like cling film, weighing him down like a sack of bricks on his shoulders. With the boy and girl behind him, the old Jap thrust the shoulder straps of his backpack off his shoulders and swung the bag onto his right arm before plumping it against the yellow brick. He turned around and smiled, throwing out his arms. Jif paced up to him.

"You . . . you American?" pointed the Jap.

"No . . . English!" replied Jif.

"Ah! England! We never had England in Tokyo." Jif knew what he meant. He knew of very few English people connected with Japan. Except for Lucy Blackman, British tourist murdered by a Japanese businessman. Jif decided to test what little Japanese he'd learnt.

"Vatashina noni hongoto taragatoviNaomi," he told the fat man. He was basically saying, "My Japanese is shit." After a two-second pause, the old man burst into a laughter that caused him to bend over, holding his stomach.

"Hahaha!" laughed the man. He stood up straight again. "Fido," said the man, tapping his chest with the tips of his fingers. "Fido," he repeated again. He was telling Jif his name. Jif didn't believe that was his real name; perhaps his real name would be unpronounceable. He leaned over and placed a palm on Jif's shoulder. He felt warm. "You?"

"Jif," replied the Yorkshire man.

"Jeff," said the fat man. "Coma . . . Jeffrey?"

"No, just Jif," he replied with a corky smile. "Weird name." There was a crunch of broken glass from the left. Jif looked over at the boy as he stepped over the broken fragments. His dark brown hair appeared shiny, even in the dull light.

"My nephew," said Fido, "Keitaro."

Keitaro pulled a smile, and Jif nodded, as if saying, "You don't need to thank me." He was still holding the small girl in his arms, right hand under the girl's bottom, left hand across her back, her legs around his waist. They looked like brother and sister.

"Eeh," called Jif to the boy, in English. "Was she cold when ya got her?" He'd burnt his hand reaching out to her in the fire. He was certain it was because she had been exposed to something freezing, enough to burn! But Keitaro didn't understand. The boy pulled a confused face then sat her down in the corner, before removing his jacket. He held it open and waved her forward, but she didn't respond. So he draped jacket the over her right arm, gently placed his hands on her shoulders, and arched her forward a little before draping the jacket over her back and dropped it over her shoulders and arms. She rested back, still looking curious, eyes full of wonder. Jif loved the way she looked; he could see himself in her. She reminded Jif of himself.

"Arigato," the girl said, for the first time. High-pitched, squeaky voice. Jif was already pacing towards her. He knelt before her with a nervous smile; he'd never been good with girls.

"She no talk," lied Keitaro, waving his arms out. Jif nodded without looking at him and trying to think up something in Japanese but couldn't.

"Uh . . . you have a mum and dad?" he asked. Dumb question. She didn't respond. Keitaro leaned and sat next to her.

"Aru de aruka?" questioned Keitaro in the girl's direction. He was asking, "Who are you?"

"Vatashima bere beradaru?" replied the girl. Squeaky and innocent. It was a question. She was asking, "I am who?" Keitaro's smile shrank away.

"Ya," replied Keitaro. Jif knew what that meant. "You camedita de searu . . ." He was saying, "You're supposed to say . . ." Jif was already losing track, so they proceeded to walk away and leave them with their Japanese lesson.

She had thin, not boney, legs, in the 1940s style. He'd been taught through pictures in textbooks at school. *By heck, she's beautiful*, thought Jif as he radiated protective feelings and feeling of another sort which bothered him. His botheration forced him to stand up. He walked back to Fido, who had opened his bag and was sucking a bottle of mineral water through a straw.

"Drink?" offered Fido, doffing the blue bottle upwards.

"Yea, all right," resigned Jif. He was thirsty anyway, and anything would taste better than the shitty odor in his mouth. He gently wrapped his thick fingers around the plastic as Fido took his fingers away. Jif could smell him; he smelt of cooked noodles. He downed a gulp of the refreshing mild water when Fido started talking again.

"Did the professor give anything to you?" asked Fido. Jif felt suspicious. How did he know he was a professor and not just a doctor? He lowered the bottle and hissed through his teeth.

"No," he replied, placing a hand on his left pocket, where the brown book was. He didn't yet trust him enough to share that book or share the words uttered to him in the building. Reservoir. What did he mean? Surely they would have finished demolishing the old structures and building the new buildings before doing anything so massive, like a reservoir. He decided to test their honesty. "How did you know he was a professor?"

"I was after him," replied Fido. This was interesting.

"Why?"

"There is a bounty on his head. One million yen. He did illegal medical operation in Tokyo."

"Dead or alive?" asked Jif. "The bounty."

"Alive," replied Fido. "So now we no get money."

"Well," began Jif, "how did you get here? 'Coz I came by plane, from . . ." He trailed off. Fido took over.

"We had a boat. Ferry. But our driver took off and left us when the earthquake hit."

"So how do you plan to get back to shore? 'Coz I'm not familiar with . . . this part of the world."

"We have flare. We set them off at night. Choppers will come at night. We seen them."

"Have you?" questioned Jif. He felt more uneasy with these people, when another aftershock hit. Fido steadied himself against the wall. "Oh, bloody hell!" cried Jif as his knees buckled. He fell on his knuckles, dropping the water bottle into the rippling pool on the pavement.

"COME, COME!" yelled Fido, pulling at Jif's collar. He was running up to Keitaro, who was picking up the girl already. He followed them, and they were going around the yellow brick building. It seemed to have a block to it and a recess. They were heading to the front. There was a doorway, or what was left of one. The doors were long gone.

The interior was white, plaster walled, dirty with dust and cobwebs. The floor was wooden, its shine long gone, covered in broken glass, unused light bulbs, clipboards, and dead rats. It looked medical almost; it smelt of antiseptic but mixed in with the scent of dirt and decay.

There was a reception, the single desk set up against the wall with a shattered blackboard behind it. Wooden chairs were strewn around, overturned, and connected with cobwebs. Jif gazed around wondering what to do as his body shook to the point of collapse with the earthquake.

"Stairs!" cried Keitaro. They started to disappear in narrow corridor. Jif followed and found a flight of concrete stairs. They'd been tiled once upon a time, but many of the ceramics had been ripped out, leaving a rough surface and a sharp edge to each step. He flung himself up as he felt bits of nothing become dragged over his hair. He heard something collapse in the reception. A masonry sound. Maybe a wall had fallen down. He was making for the third floor when he heard them call him from below. They were on the second floor. By the time he got to them, the aftershock had stopped.

May 10, 2006, 1301

Jif felt his eyes open again. He was staring up at the roof of the limo. It had a poster of the Sistine Chapel; he hadn't noticed it before. His neck was aching, and he looked forward again, spotting Iffy. He'd fallen asleep as well.

A thought-provoking hum filled the cabin, and Jif glanced around to see where it was coming from. It was the glass partition from the driver being wound down. The two front seats and the flat head of the driver appeared in silhouette against the bright light through the windscreen.

"We are on Massachusetts Avenue, Mr. Kitchen, approaching the embassy!" the driver called out without turning his head.

Jif was surprised. There already? Jif brought his left wrist in front of his face and raised his sleeve to expose the Ariel wristwatch: 1310. He raised his eyebrows in surprise. He'd been sleeping for four hours. But how? He decided not to bother with questions and just get on with it.

"Cheers," replied Jif, easing himself from the hot seat to get ready. As he stood, he felt a rush of cold air flood the back of his thighs. He shuffled, bent double like an old man to stop his head from hitting the roof, to the passenger door. He peered through the window as the car continued its journey, gradually slowing down and easing towards the sidewalk. A white-walled building passed by, followed by a couple of enormous trees before the glass walls of the embassy came into view. Jif's heart suddenly sank, not just from what lay ahead of him but because he felt chilling reminders coming into his head yet again. He felt his eyes close as his mind filled with the thoughts of Frontiera Island.

September 14, 2003, 0000 JST

Jif was sitting in the rear seat of the brand-new Mercedes sedan, behind the front passenger. Jif checked his watch: midnight exactly! The man next to him was supping him with all information needed.

"The head office is tenth floor," the short Jap sitting next to him mumbled in broken English. He was handing Jif lots of things. The combat jacket. The red motorcycle helmet. The parachute.

"I hate heights," grumbled Jif as he zipped up the Kevlar-lined camouflage jacket and fastened the three buckles of the parachute across his chest. "But tonight there is no other way. Even I know that."

"Most or all of us will die tonight," said the front passenger, facing the windscreen before turning around to face Jif. "But if you survive, tell everyone, tell everyone what you saw. They have to know about this!"

"I will, Atlas," replied Jif. In a last act of preparation, Jif pulled the motorcycle helmet over his head, slamming the rim down into his shoulder. He struggled to find the buckles before connecting them. He still had his suit underneath, and he was getting very hot.

The car made a turn and rumbled over an uneven surface. A huge white-walled building came into view, and the car pulled up alongside it. A thick black metal sign stuck up out of a small nursery of flowers. It had writing in white, first line in Japanese hieroglyphs, second line in the English translation: Kensiku Industries.

All car doors opened, Jiff was almost on autopilot. The other men were putting dark blue bulletproof vests with TV written in yellow on the chests. Jif could feel his heart racing, his breathing amplified in the helmet.

"We go now!" said the baldy, standing next to him. As he said that, a silver figure appeared in front the glass doors. It was a Honda android, walking upright at a regular pace with a mysterious black head on top for its radar.

"Keep still," said Atlas. "It will pass by." It did. The android simply walked around the patch of flowers and passed the group of men and headed towards the rest of the unfinished or demolished buildings.

They paced forward as one, until Jif's foot connected with something. He looked down. A car battery. Black plastic face. Red Japanese writing all over it. It had its red carry handle sticking out. Jif quickly squatted down and picked up the battery before returning to the group. The cobbled floor was still intact, as was the glass door. The reception area was immaculate, if unmanned. White-tiled floor, beautiful light fixtures, ceiling fans, black leather furniture in the corners, and white desk on the left.

As the door swung open, someone shouted out of nowhere. "OI!"

May 10 2006, 1302 EST

Jif woke up again. The car door was open. The chauffeur stood in front of him, holding open the door, his smile never vanishing.

"Need a minute, sir?" questioned the chauffeur. Jif stared at the man for ten more seconds before easing back on his seat. He closed his eyes again and drew a breath before pulling his legs upwards and placing his left foot on the sidewalk. He could feel a coldness rush through his foot. His heart thumping deep into his stomach, pumping more blood in his head, swelling his cheeks, increasing his sweat, and making him more nervous about what was going to happen next. Cowering out of the doorway of the limousine, he kept his head down, slowly looking up to see the building that would decide his fate.

On the edge of the sidewalk and in front of the embassy, two low redbrick walls with grey edging on top housed some short yellow flowers that Jif didn't know the name of. Beneath each pot of flowers was a bench built into the wall, made of grey slabs about a meter long, big enough to sit three people. The gap between each wall was about two meters long, to give ample room for anyone who wanted to walk along the paved gangway up to the stairs or for kids to play on the grass outside the high walls.

Jif was focused on the black plaque, which read British Embassy in letters of gold. The wall it was on had seen better days, covered in green from the trees and rain. The plaque was just next the set of steps that led to the big black gate and the industrial fencing that surrounded the embassy. He could see a British bobby standing behind the gate, swaying to and fro on the balls of his feet.

After the gangway came the embassy itself, two stories high. The glass-walled building was in the shape of a giant circle, with a one-store rectangle next to it to house the reception. The windows were massive, the glass reflecting the sunlight and obscuring whoever was in the building, and thin strips of white concrete in between each window, making it look like a construction toy. It was only a few meters away, but surrounded by the black industrial fencing and the low brick walls in front, it felt like a mile.

Realizing he was still standing in front of the car, Jif moved forward two steps, allowing the chauffeur to close the door behind him.

"Iffy!" called Jif. He was still in the car.

"The ambassador told me your bodyguard could not enter the building. I'll go in with you," explained the chauffeur. His explanation was plausible. Iffy was unpredictable, and Vin was cautious about the embassy image.

"I'll take your word for it." Jif nodded as the chauffeur turned on his heel with a squeak from his boots. Jif paced forward as slow as he could; he wanted to drag this out as much as he could to soften the blow he would feel. He heard the chauffeur creep inline behind him; he didn't care if the man was lying or not; he was outside an embassy with dozens of policemen, the worst place to attack anyone. He shuffled through the gangway between the short walls and felt a paving slab wobble beneath him. Swaying up a flight of concrete steps, he made his way to the gates. They started to open inwards with a low hum even before he hit the last step. He stepped over a white line from where the gate had just been. Just like at Lime.Inc, the British bobby stopped behind the line since this was considered British soil. This PC was a pale forty-year-old white guy with short stubble on his chin, white shirt, black epaulettes, black tie, comfortable shoes for walking, a proper helmet. Jif tried to keep his eyes as straight as he could but couldn't look away from the cop. The man's eyes were deep set, like black holes.

He approached a set of glass sliding door which had been left open. Ahead of him was the plush lobby that housed the reception. He hesitated a second then stepped in.

The air-conditioning was at full blast and sent goose bumps all over Jif's body, making his shirt prickly. The lobby was white walled and tiled floored, smelling heavily of bleach and disinfectant, like a hospital. Only furniture and people gave colour. The reception desk was curved pine and, as he got up to it, smelt of forest. Two men and two women sat behind, answering phones and looking down. An elderly woman in her sixties looked up into Jif's eyes. White haired, brown eyes, her mouth held dozens of creases around it. Jif felt his jaw open, but no words came out; the woman cut him off.

"Mr. Kitchen," she said in a London accent. She looked down again, and her arm disappeared beneath the desk for a moment and reappeared with a plastic tag. "Wear this please!" Jif took it from her, obedient. "Take a seat. The guard will be with you soon."

He made his way to the leather chairs and sat with a groan from the fabric beneath. He examined the tag. One inch wide by four inches long. Translucent plastic. The blue card inside read Visitor 09 in black, font 18 letters. Beneath that, in tiny letters were weasel words of how it was property of the British embassy. There was a small plastic loop and a shiny metal clip to attach to clothing. Jif sighed and pinned it to the peril of his jacket. He placed his hands on his lap and realised his stomach was burning, from hunger and from nervousness. He looked around, trying to amuse himself in the surroundings, but the walls were plain, and there was no one else around. Yet he could hear the traffic outside;

it was so loud. He found himself staring at the doors, waiting for something to happen, someone to come in and tell him everything would be all right. Instead the chauffeur stepped. Still smiling, he kept eye contact with Jif as he approached the chairs and sat down, giving the same groan as Jif, but less audible.

"I'll wait for you," said the chauffeur.

"Hello," said a young male American voice. Jif turned his head and made eyes with a young man. No more than eighteen and with blond hair creeping up his hat, the boy was dressed in a white shirt, black "plasticy" waistcoat with a shine to it, black pants, and a dark blue baseball cap with Security marked in white on the front.

"Come with me please, Mr. Kitchen!" said the boy. The guard spun on his heel and paced towards the reception again but was led to the left side of it, to a frosted glass wall, about two metres wide and six feet tall. Jif followed behind, feeling his heart racing. The boy glanced over his shoulder to spot Jif then pulled a smile and got back to work. On the far left was a keypad. The boy waved his fingers over it, and a series of dull hums murmured away above their heads. The glass wall became a door, giving a *pchuf* as it slid to the left, slowly disappearing into the wall. Once the door came to a stop, the guard waved forward. Jif complied.

"What's gonna happen?" asked Jif. The guard did not reply.

"Don't get too shocked. Everyone goes through this," said the boy.

Jif saw the boy crush his left hand into a fist, and it disappeared out of view. He slammed the red button on the left wall he'd seen earlier, and the door behind slid shut with a *shuff*. Jif looked to the right and saw an LCD display, whirling away at maximum speed. Maybe it was just for show. Sealed in the chamber, Jif felt bewildered and began daydreaming again, even though his eyes were open. Everything around him reminded him of that fateful night.

September 14, 2003, 0013 JST

Deafening gunshots exploded out of nowhere. Jif couldn't see any flashes, and even with the helmet encased around his head, the blasts still echoed into the ears.

His accomplices ducked and pulled out black pistols from their pants. Jif followed and dived for the reception. Atlas fired two warning shots into the ceiling, causing a sprinkle of white dust to snow around the group.

"KENJUKI MASISETSA ITERRU FOSHTE NATUNAOMI!" screamed Atlas. Jif couldn't understand since he was speaking so fast and tried to hear for pauses in the speech break the sound down into logical, possible English alternatives. It took three months for Jif to find out he was saying, "Kenjuki is going down and taking you with him!"

Jif was leaning against the reception desk, cold. He was unarmed, except for the car battery in his hand, when an Asian man appeared from the corner, just before a set of silver elevators. Jif only concentrated on the top half.

"AH!" yelled the man. He had a wafer-thin moustache below his nose. His black peaked cap held an emblem he didn't recognise, but the black epaulettes on the shoulders of his white shirt bore the English translation "Kenjiku."

A close gun blast vibrated Jif's helmet. Jif felt his right ear clench up as the guard collapsed with a gasp. Jif spun his head and saw Atlas was behind him, with the smoking pistol.

"YA SHOT HIM!" yelled Jif, muffled by his helmet. Atlas didn't respond. He turned back and peered further out to see the man. He was on the floor and had his back against the elevator doors. He was pushing both his hands into the black trouser leg of his left thigh.

"I can't believe you shot him," mumbled Jif under his breath as he soon saw blood trickling in a steady stream away from the man. He was about to ask why he'd been shot, when he noticed the silver pistol on the floor. It wasn't there before, and everyone else had black guns.

Jif fought to look at the blood and stood up. On the desk, he found an empty beer glass. It was stringy with beer froth and a tiny trickle of flat yellow liquid in the base. Jif quickly snatched it and scooped up the car battery.

"Jif, what did you do?" asked Atlas as Jif made his way around the desk. He didn't reply. At the opening, Jif was greeted by a hidden recess behind the main desk, which held an immaculate-looking telephone unit, an idle computer, and a notepad with Japanese symbols scribbled in blue biro. The only other thing was that everything was coated in a sprinkle of white ceiling dust.

Jif placed the battery on the recess next to the phone and pulled open the white wooden drawer beneath. Among the pencils and pens, he found some long paper scissors with a yellow handle. He opened it to its maximum length—handle to blade—and held it. He drove the other end of the blade into the clip of the battery and started digging.

"Jif, idegimas!" Atlas was saying that he was leaving, when he was really waiting for Jif. The lid of the battery case clipped open after Jif tampered with all corners. He disguarded the lid and looked down into the pool of acid. It gleamed a shiny colour. Sparkling with all different colours.

He took a breath and raised the battery up to the ridge of the glass. He tipped it forward, and the liquid sloshed its way into the glass, fizzing eerily on its way. He shook the last few drops out and dropped the battery. Clenching the glass tightly, he made his way round the desk again.

The group was already in the lift, except for Atlas. Jif felt his foot tap on the hollow metal floor of the giant tin box. As the doors closed and the car rode up, Jif couldn't help but feel the interior was wonderful. Mirrors everywhere, shiny keypads . . .

But he had to focus, and his stomach was burning with sickness. He was about to commit a crime, but it was one he knew would be beneficial for the greater good.

The elevator pinged, and the doors opened. The floor was just like the reception. Plush shiny white walls with corporate decoration. As one, everyone stepped out of the car and turned left. They paced a dozen steps as they approached a wooden door that was the same colour as the walls around it, except for a brass doorknob with a keyhole.

"The junction box is here," said one of them. Jif couldn't make out who. The one with the missing finger pulled the fob in his bracelet. He squeezed it slightly, and a slice of metal popped out. It was a key. He slid it into the door lock and turned it slowly. Pulling back the master key, he turned the knob and opened the door.

A thunk of something soft hitting the marble halted the procedure. Jif spun his head round, making sure no one was getting ready to charge at them with a rifle. Out of the corner of his eye, he saw Atlas's head shake.

"Fileto inasai," snapped Atlas. Jif could work out he meant "get on with it."

The man at the door pulled it open. The interior was dark, but it quickly became clear it was a cupboard. One foot in was a black plastic box with a shiny silver handle. The Jap pushed the handle down with an *eeek* and opened the junction box. His hand went into his suit pocket, and he pulled it out again with a yellow-handled Phillips screwdriver. At this point, Atlas turned to face Jif. Jif locked eyes in turn to show he was paying attention.

"Get ready!" Atlas spoke in English. Jif nodded and took a step back, sticking his hands out to get ready for his blindness.

The man's hand disappeared into the box. He heard metal connect with metal with the fiddle of the screwdriver. There was a short buzz, and everything went black. Except for a string of yellow hallway lights along the edges of the walkway.

"GO!" yelled Atlas. "GO!"

And Jif spun round and ran as fast as he dared. He knew what would be behind the door.

May 10, 2006, 1308

There was a *ding* out of nowhere, and the frosted glass door in front of him opened. The muffled sound of office work flooded into the chamber. Yet there was no one in sight, except for some movement at the far end of the corridor. It was a corridor, tiled wall, tiled floor, tiled ceiling. The tiles must have been a light colour, like beige. Even so, it did little to reassure Jif.

Two men appeared from both walls. They were guards again, but more formal, peaked caps and blue tunics. The one on the left was stocky and old and had horizontal lines all over his face. The right one was slim and younger and, strangely for Jif, looked rather similar to Charlie.

"Hold it," said the stocky one in a Hackney accent, pointing a dirty finger. Jif complied. With no one else around, he didn't have much of a choice. He felt he was going to die here anyway.

The old guard put his left hand behind the right sidewall, where some dial tones echoed their way into the chamber. They both peered back in Jif's direction, to his right. Jif looked up at the LCD bar. It displayed in red "101KG." They were measuring his weight. A security precaution to make sure none of the people inside take anything with them, like a computer, or leave anything behind, like a bomb.

"OK," said the young guard, waving his right hand forward. Jif complied as the old guard stood to the side. The young guard spun round and started walking, his leather shoes echoing his footsteps, like a teacher emphasizing his authority in the classroom. Jif followed, swallowing his now-dry throat, weary that his fat stomach was pressuring his belt with a squeaking sound, and heard the old guard fall in behind. Professional escort.

As he was frog-marched through the embassy, he felt the same sensation when he was in the Kenjiku Plaza. He felt he was going down the same dark corridor where he rescued Yuzuyu. But this time there was no hope. And it was not dark, it was light.

The plaster corridor ended, and he was in an open office. Ten meters wide by ten meters long. Telephones ringing. Suits sitting in front of PCs. Women running across holding bundles of paper. Jif was escorted through the chaos to the other side of the room. Yet another narrow corridor, this time, very short. At the end was an oak brown door. The security guard pulled out an ID card and swiped through a silver card reader on the left side of the door. A green LED light appeared in the box's corner, and the door lock clunked. The guard pushed the door open and stepped aside.

"Mr. Kitchen, Ambassador!" said the guard, looking straight ahead and not making eye contact.

"Thank you, Mr. Ralph. Wait outside!" said the voice of Vincent Bird. The guard stepped out of the way and stood up against the walls of the corridor, arms folded. Jif nervously stepped forward. Peering into the room, lit by the grey sky through the large windows at the back, he could see a single white plastic garden chair sitting in the middle of the room. He gazed left. Main members of the company were sitting behind a five-metre-long table, draped with a white tablecloth. They sat in order of seniority: Vin Bird, CEO at left end and next to Transit Van, CO and mayor of Boston; Roberta Heseltine, advertising manager; Charles Howe, finance manager; and lastly Dill Lexmark, spokesperson and youngest of the lot. All clean-cut in sharp suits, even Heseltine, although she looked like the spokesperson for a biker clan; she was a Goth, always wearing spiked-up hair, black lipstick, and huge hooped gold earrings.

"Sit down, Jif," Vin said coldly, his half-bald head reflecting the dull light in the room.

Jif had no option. He paced to the garden chair and sat down on it with a creak of weak plastic. He drew a deep breath, and he could almost taste the hostility in the air.

"You signed an official denial," began Transit Van, his thick moustache twitching lightly with his lip movement. "So far you kept your promise, but with this situation, we have to wonder if you're a loose cannon to this company!"

"I accept whatever choice you have!" replied Jif, looking down at the floor. The board shuffled in their seats, bewildered.

"What is this, Jif?" whined Dill. "Stand up for yourself!"

"I want this all to be over with!" he replied in a flat voice

"The problem is not you, Jif," began Vin, "it is your wife!"

"Leave her out of this!" he snapped back in a slightly louder voice, finally looking up.

"The fact is, you took her from hostile land and made this company a target!"

"He wasn't after you. He was after me!"

"When there's an attack in one branch, the rest look weak. There's going to be a ton of attempted attacks on Lime.Inc. We're hated enough as it is with the Israeli contract!"

"What am I supposed to say?" asked Jif, pointing his palm at himself. "Sorry there was a shooting? A good friend of mine is dead!"

"And you have our sympathy! But this company is at stake! All these jobs, all this money could stop from all this!"

"This is why I accept whatever your agreement is! I already know I'm no longer trustworthy, and you'll never look at me the same again! I could argue all I want, but it won't change ya minds, so I'll just take the easy way out." Even as Jif spoke, his hand started to shake.

"Then why didn't you just give in your resignation?" yelled Vincent, annoyed. Jif paused and looked down again.

"I thought there might be some hope!"

At this point, Heseltine spoke, "Is all this necessary? No one can be sure of an attack. Especially from a guy from three years ago." Her voice didn't go with her face. Squeaky, innocent, enthusiastic, not like her aggressive appearance or anyone else sitting next to her; they were all tired and bound to the company.

"No, I changed my mind!" snapped the ambassador suddenly, looking up with a pissed-off face. "It is you, Jif! YOU WERE THE ONE WHO HIRED THAT BOY AND GOT HIM KILLED!"

"You told me I could hire anyone I wanted for the extra security for—"

"Yes! Proper security!" interrupted Vin. "Not the boy next door!"

"—the party!" continued Jif, unchanged. "A party with guests I barely knew. In a building with incompetent staff! A SHABBY FACADE SO THAT YOU COULD SELL WEAPONS ON THE CHEAP AND DO DEALS WITH PARLIAMENT ON FOREIGN SOIL!"

He thrust his right arm in a downward motion twice towards the board. His throat burnt like he had inhaled fresh cigarette smoke. Jif had never screamed so much. Not since that time on the island. Even now he was picturing it.

September 13, 2003, 1610 JST

"There were supposed to be a hundred men working on this island, building it up! So where are they?"

"You tell me!" replied Fido, rummaging through his backpack again. Everyone was sitting in the trash of the giant room; it felt like a classroom. Bits of wood, broken plaster from the walls, and a child's multicolored tricycle littered the floor. Everything of monetary value had been stripped out long ago; Jif could see holes in the walls where electric sockets used to be. It stank of urine.

"This used to be a hospital!" stated Fido in English. "This was the children's ward. I was here for two days because I broke my toe."

"So you been here before?" asked Jif. Keitaro started to get up and flipped over a plank of wood as he did, sending a cloud of dust in the air. Yuzuyu flinched back, defensive, pulling the perils of her jacket closer together across her chest.

"I was here for five years," stated Fido, "before the company closed down and all the jobs disappeared. Now no one is welcome here!" He threw a black cylinder into the piles of trash next to him. Jif couldn't figure out what it was for. Keitaro had disappeared but reemerged from the doorway, carrying a bundle of washing.

The boy muttered something incomprehensible, and Yuzuyu seemed joyful, giving a pleasing "Wah!" As Keitaro waved the clothes in his hands, Jif caught on. He was going to dress the girl. Even though he'd seen her naked, he knew when to give privacy.

He stood up and leaned up to an open window. Actually, it was just a hole; the glass and even the frame and windowsill had been ripped out. Jif rested his elbows on the rough edges of the bare brick and cracked cement as he pulled out the mystery book, breathing through his nose, trying to get some fresh air to drive away the awful smell.

As he pulled open the worn brown leather cover with no title, he saw this was no ordinary diary. The first page held a blue biro drawing of a human figure, with the joint of the arms and legs circled untidily. Hieroglyphs were all over the page, but Jif couldn't read Japanese, only speak it.

He turned the page. Two pages of just words. Meaningless. Page 3 had a paperclip attached to it, but nothing to hold. He turned the page to see if the other side had anything. Jif's heart stopped.

Attached by the paperclip was a four-by-seven-inch photograph. It showed a Japanese man in a green sweater overlooking a pretty little Asian girl in a floral dress playing with a set of Barbies. He had no doubt; the girl in the picture was the girl in this building. The girl he'd rescued, well, not quite. He turned his head around. Keitaro was dressing her. Men's clothes. Green pants with a hole in the knee and a dust-coated white shirt. Too big for her, but anything would be good to keep her warm. A lot of giggling as Keitaro used a rope for a belt on her.

He flipped the page. More Japanese writing and drawings of what looked like a car disk brake. Two disks connected together. Arrows at either side of the drawing pointed in opposite directions. Maybe it had something to do with her joints. Pivots maybe? To add strength?

He flipped again. Measurements now. And he recognized something straightaway. "Twenty pints of blood." It was in English in the same pen ink. But the rest went back to Japanese again. Some sort of operation was being done. But should Jif be getting involved?

He turned again. Diagrams of a large rectangle encasing tiny cylinders, squares, and dozens of lines in all directions making interconnections. A circuit board. What did this have to do with her? He turned the page, and everything else was blank. He sighed as he pocketed the book.

"What you got there?" called out Fido. Jif felt his testicles contract; the guy was suddenly talking again, breaking this peaceful silence.

"Nothin'," replied Jif, a little angry. He spoke through the window, not turning around.

"Oh, you don't want to talk?" went Fido sarcastically. Jif sighed. The guy had changed his tune. Jif shuffled around and thrust his hands in his pockets.

"What, mate?" said Jif, trying to be as reasonable as he could.

"This island is only 400 by 140 meters," started Fido, pointing a poky finger downwards. He still had the bag in his crotch. "And they managed to cram five thousand human lives onto it. Now, you people gonna do that again?" Jif knew where this was going.

"Look," started Jif defensibly. He was trying to defend himself and assert himself. "I just want to work! I want a job! I want to get paid! That's it!"

The argument was interrupted by the sound of scraping. The girl was kneeling on the floor with her new clothes, arching over what looked like a newspaper. She was holding a chunk of black rock. Charcoal. Where the hell did charcoal end up in this place? Keitaro reappeared again, with a bemused look as he too saw what was going on.

As Jif placed his hand over his pocket that held the book, his stomach tied itself into a knot. He gazed over to Yuzuyu, realizing the hole he'd just entered.

He approached the girl slowly so as not to disturb her. His heart was racing.

Jif peered over her shoulder to see what she was doing. The piece of newspaper lay under her hand as she scrawled English letters in black ink. He could make out some scribbled letters. *K, I, T, A.* She was trying to write Keitaro's name. Keitaro joined him, peering over the girl, and that's when she reacted. Her head spun round as she gasped, and her eyes connected first with Jif's then with the boy's.

"Vatashima machia sterio stika?" she asked, gazing back at the newspaper. "Did I do it wrong?"

"Ya," exclaimed Keitaro, smiling and waving his hands up to his neck to show there was no trouble. "Da choro emoniomokoto anetano kari ke sore da." He was saying, "I was just wondering how your hair was grown." Yuzuyu turned her head back to Keitaro again and dropped the "pencil" to reach her head and threaded her hands through her hair.

"Keitaro," she began, "ika niki kono vu vatashino ke?" She was till holding her hair. Jif roughly figured out she said, "How would you like my hair?"

"Ah . . . ," sighed Keitaro with a grin. "Ana kono ke uma kuaru, fedira oni." Jif sighed as he worked out his reply. "Your hair is fine as it is." Probably the best thing to say. He knew the girl liked him. He drew a breath and pulled a smile as she turned to make eye contact with him. He didn't feel comfortable speaking Japanese, and he felt this girl knew English too, so he chose his native tongue.

"I was wondering . . . ," began Jif, in English, when he was interrupted.

"Yuzuyu!" called out the girl.

"What?" exclaimed Jif. There was a *ching* as something connected with the floor from behind. Fido must have dropped his water, again.

"Yuzuyu is my name." She spoke in English! She could understand him. Jif wanted to pick her up and cheer, but his insecurity held him down. It was Keitaro who did the celebrating for him.

"Ah, miru!" cheered Keitaro, leaning into the girl and patting her back. Jif started standing up, feeling unwanted. "Vanitina kiorgu!" he said to her. "You're remembering!" He started saying how she would start remembering her mother and father. "Sununi kyoku mama doshdi papa . . ."

Suddenly, Jif heard a distant mumble of voices. Outside, more than one person. Certainly not from here.

"Did you hear that?" he interrupted the conversation.

He made it to the hole for a window and peered out. Two stories below, two men in strict-looking black uniforms and very big peaked caps were directing their arms at each other.

"There's more people," cried Jif, with a six-inch smile across his face. He genuinely thought he'd found salvation. He rushed past Fido and through the doorway, leaping over a bemused-looking Keitaro, and clip-clopped down the concrete stairs, his footsteps echoing around him. Out in the open again, he kicked a plank of wood out his way and cornered the building, skidding suddenly. A black sedan was parked in front of the gateway; it wasn't there before! He panted and placed his hands down, leaning over the hood of the car, the bonnet still warm. He could smell exhaust fumes in the air.

"MAYDAY!" yelled Jif. He could see an inch of black uniform from behind a leaning steel structure about three meters away. It twitched, and he saw a face appear. His mouth was wide open. Then he disappeared.

Jif heard a Japanese yell.

"Jif, get back in! They're going to shoot you!"

"What?" exclaimed Jif. He stopped and turned his head. "Why?" He turned back again and spoke to himself, arguing the point. "We haven't done anything wrong! They're coppers. They're supposed to help us."

Then, a guy appeared. Like the dead police officer he'd seen earlier.

"There are five of us, one little girl. We . . ."

The boy in the red top and black combat pants stomped up. His expression didn't change. His automatic glinted in his right hand. Jif felt his intestines collapse inside. The boy raised his gun.

Jif was throwing himself off the car when he heard the blast. He'd spun round. He didn't feel anything! He was racing for the stairs, his heart pumping into overdrive, his skin suddenly gone cold and wet. As he got to the last step of floor 2, he felt the blood. In his left shoulder. He dragged over the wound to see the blood loss. A streak of red lined diagonally across his palm. He wandered dazed into the empty ward.

"Fucking hell, man! I told you!" screamed Fido on the other side of the room.

"How was I supposed to know?" yelled back Jif, holding his shoulder, and shaking like a vibrator. He was getting cold and felt lighter, as if he was getting high. Through now-chattering teeth, he spoke, "Anyway, what should we do now?"

Keitaro had already picked up Yuzuyu in a brotherly cradle when Fido rushed the doorway where Jif was. He grabbed a handful of Jif's shirt and yanked him back into he room.

"This isn't the time to play fights!" yelled Jif. He figured he was going to get punched. Instead, Fido threw himself through the wooden partition, which splintered to the sound of a Jacob's biscuit cracking. They were in another ransacked room. A doorway was in the corner.

"Run you!" went Fido as he charged for the opening. Jif turned his head and waved Keitaro forward. Women and girls first, he believed.

"What are you doing?" yelled Keitaro as he rushed past, crashing through the trash on the floor. Jif made up to the arch and chased after them.

Fido led the group along a massive dark corridor, up to a shut door. As they grouped together, Fido was pushing his hand down on something. There was a clunk, and the door swung open. Darkness. He went out and made left. Jif was about to see why.

It was a set of stairs. There were a few windows, but little light came through. He went through the fire exit and kept up with Keitaro; the girl, looking back, looked so bewildered. The stairwell was dark and claustrophobic. Jif let his hand slide along a cold steel banister, using that as a guide through the moderate darkness as the stairs turned before him. They passed another door, one floor to go. *Smack smack smack,* with their shoes on the steps. Out of sight, there was a squeal of metal against metal. Jif rounded the next corner. Daylight. Fido had found the last door. Ahead of him appeared to be a stack of trash: bed frames, tables, anything made of wood. Jif went through the door and made straight where they were heading. There was a tight gap ahead between two box houses; they'd already gone through. Jif squeezed his way through, scraping his soggy chest against the brick. He stubbed his toe and ground his teeth, and he fought to keep up with them, when he heard a car engine behind him. A spout of energy filled his legs, and he milked every bit of it.

They ran along the road, sandwiched between the giant grey brown buildings. Concrete all around. Bits of wood, general trash, and kids' toys littered the way. Jif leapt over a smashed TV set; plastic casing and circuit boards shattered on the floor. As he kept up with the men in front, he could see that Yuzuyu was uncomfortable. Keitaro was holding her like a baby, but her head kept on slamming into his shoulders with every step he leapt. She was practically crying. Jif reckoned she was begging him to stop running.

The gap started to widen up ahead. Jif followed in a line, and they emerged in an open space. It was like an alien planet. He was now running on new pavement! It was black. Looked as fresh as today. And yet in this patch of new, there were crumbling buildings all around. This was a shambolic building exercise being done here!

"Key!" cried Keitaro, with his head turned over his shoulder to face Jif. "Go there!" He took an arm off Yuzuyu and pointed straight in front.

There was an opening up ahead. A hood made of brick. Red. Recently made. White signs with black hieroglyphs on the overhang. A stairway to a subway. A train station.

"GO! GO! GO!" screamed one of the men. Jif didn't know who; they both sounded the same at this point. Those in front started to sink below ground level as they made for the stairs of the subway. Jif followed, leaping two steps at a time. He was swallowed by the tunnel opening and found himself on a station platform.

It was clear this structure wasn't finished. There were plain redbrick walls all around, giant red cabling and flimsy fluorescent lights hung from above, the ceiling was incomplete. There were no ticket kiosks, barriers, benches, or the other normal things associated with a train station. Bricks, wall tiles, wooden planks, and strips of metal were lined up against the rough wall. Power drills,

saw blades, and hammers were strewn along the floor, some of the spiraling long red electric cable. He saw Fido trip over one of these cords, falling flat on his stomach before getting up again.

They ran into the platform as another earthquake started up. How many more times did this have to happen? Jif felt his feet become numb. An overhead sign with hieroglyphs vibrated. Ceiling panels creaked above him and started to fall down. One white aluminum panel smacked his head before clambering around his feet. He tried to focus on the group ahead of him while negotiating around DIY tools and trash in his way. He heard Fido up ahead yell something in Japanese while running along the platform. Keitaro turned his head to translate it for Jif behind him.

"We're going onto the track!" he yelled. As he went to the edge, he began to disappear. Jif could barely see because there were no lights on in the station. Not wanting to go blind, Jif reached into the side pocket of the jacket and pulled out a cigarette lighter. He never smoked, but people often asked him for a smoke. It was a good icebreaker in his opinion.

They leapt from the platform onto the track. Jif felt his knees almost compress to the sudden stop of the jump. He gasped deeply and leapt after the Japs into the darkness. Flicking the lighter three times, it finally ignited, and he could see an arm's length ahead. The rails were bronze in colour, on top of dark grey concrete slabs.

"Is it electrified?" cried Jif, talking about the rails. He got no reply. The only sounds he could hear were the footsteps, echoed by the tunnel. And his own panicky breathing. Then, a gun blast from maybe a shotgun echoed down the tunnel.

"Fuck!" screamed Jif. There was no flash, and he couldn't be certain in which direction the sound had come from. They ran along the track, Jif trying to stay in the middle to avoid touching the rails. Keitaro was turning round, running backwards while holding Yuzuyu, waving Jif to come closer. *Bang!* Another blast. Then sporadic gunfire, an automatic weapon. Jif raced the last amount of strength he had and caught up with the boy. His skin looked yellow in the orange light of the flame.

"Give me the light!" demanded Keitaro over the gunfire. Jif handed it to him; he might put it to a better use. Keitaro swiftly passed it to Fido, who'd slowed down. In the light, his hat cast a shadow over his face, giving Jif a chill down his spine. It reminded him of the boogeyman. Fido muttered something Jif didn't hear and disappeared again. The gunfire was still going! Then the light appeared again; he was holding it above his head.

"He's got a lead!" spluttered Keitaro, who was running out of breath. Yuzuyu was grasping the boy's collar. A shiny line of a tear was on her check. She was scared down here.

The shooting had stopped. In the darkness of the tunnel, they were trailing into nowhere. They had all become a train, holding on to each other's shoulder to avoid getting lost in the darkness. He knew Fido was leading. Jif held on tight to Keitaro, in front of him, but secretly wishing he could hold on to Yuzuyu.

Then the light went out. Black! Darkness!

"FUCK!" Jif was screaming at the top of his lungs.

May 10, 2006, 1323

He was back in the embassy again. He could feel the eyes burning their gaze into him.

"Why d'you come here, Jif?" yapped Vin. "You bring in a twelve-year-old girl in a nappy to attract everyone's attention. YOU GET MARIED TO A MINOR! I'M THE ONE WHO HAS TO EXPLAIN EVERYTHING TO OUR INVESTORS!" Vincent had never been like this before. In Hull, Jif and Vin stuck together through the roller coaster of school. They were both minorities: Jif was fat, Vin was black—the only black in school. They had taken raps for each other and promised to help each other out. It was Vin who had recommended Jif for the Frontiera Island job and the Lime.Inc job because he knew Jif could be trusted, and he knew Jif would do as he was told! Even Jif knew that! But all that trust, all the honour, had evaporated! Now it was all one man for himself. And Jif could feel it, the coldness, the loneliness.

"All I can say is I'm glad I'm not dead or in prison," croaked Jif.

"You always helped people out," Vin started saying, almost complimenting. "You're too kind, that's your problem, Jif. You let these people take advantage of you!" It felt like a father-son talk. Vin may as well have been his dad; he was older and had taken care of him. But the coldness in his eyes, sitting across from the table, left Jif with a sense of hostility.

"If I hadn't taken the job, I wouldn't have met the boy. I wouldn't be cryin' over 'im. I wouldn't be so weak, like, now."

"Our mind is made up." Vin sighed. "We all have a job to do, and you've done yours."

"I signed your bloody paper!" Jif started yelling. "I signed the official denial! I have not broken it! I ain't done nothin' wrong! I thought there would be some respect in this job after all the shit I've held for you guys!"

"Jif, you're out!" said Transit, elbows on the table. Vin leaned back in his chair, arrogant. Dill pulled a sorry smile and showed his palms to say there was nothing he could do.

"Right," Jif replied automatically. Even though he showed no emotion, the redness in his cheeks filled up to a rosy colour. He wasn't surprised, he was relieved.

"You have one week to pack your bags and leave Boston!" the mayor went on to say. He bent his head to read a sheet of paper in front of him "You will receive a pension of fifty pound sterling a week when you turn fifty, and you will receive a reference form, stating that you worked in our despatch department. You know how to drive a van, don't you?"

"Sure."

"Time to leave," snapped Vin, with a click of his finger, pointing to the door.

"Is the army involved?" asked Jif all of a sudden. His face was impassive; and for the first time, the board showed nervousness, leaning back in their chairs and looking at each other. Vin mouthed "what the fuck" to Transit, and Transit shook his head in denial. The ambassador's mouth was still open when he made his reply.

"No comment." His voice was a little shaky. Jif was unsurprised that they were holding stuff back, but since the official denial was brought up, he'd been thinking that he hadn't dreamed the interrogation after all.

"Three men wanted to talk about Frontiera!" Jif exclaimed. The board was suddenly interested.

"When?" asked Howe in his deep voice.

"Less than an hour after Charles Ronshoe was shot!"

"Why didn't you say before?" questioned Transit, emphasising his authority in his voice.

"Because they drugged me, and when I woke up I was in my bed," replied Jif. At which point, Vin sniggered, his shoulders shuffling up and down with each laugh. Everyone turned to look at him.

"Get out and shut up!" barked Vin with a smile, cocking his head to the door. His arms were folded, defensive. Jif had got to him, and he was glad of that, but any sense of friendship, any sense of hope, was gone. He was looking at a stranger. And Vin was going to have the last word. He didn't care.

Jif heaved himself off the garden chair, the plastic groaning behind him. He blurred his vision to avoid looking at the people's faces as he turned and walked as casually as he could to the door. His right hand reached the doorknob.

"Jif," called Vin quietly. Jif stopped. He didn't turn around to face him. Vincent talked to the fat man's back. "I know you tried, I know you failed. It happens all the time. We just accept it and move on. Lesson number 3."

Jif twisted his wrist to turn the knob and pulled open the door. The guards stepped forward, one on each side. Jif fell in between them and marched out the corridor, feeling sick.

He was relieved it was all over, and he was no longer responsible now for anything. He knew what Vin meant by lesson number 3. But up until now he was able to live a life of ease; all he was to do was overlook the building, and he got paid for it just because it was top secret. Now, everyone would think he was just a van driver. He was going to have to graft all over again, and he didn't even know how!

But more important to him, the boy he had worked so hard on was gone. His major work had nothing to show for. He blamed himself, he blamed Rock, there had been times today he blamed Yuzuyu for her vague association with the gunman. But there was one person he hated most of all: Naomi! If it had not been for Naomi, Charlie would not have been so desperate to take that job; he would not have been so insecure, he would have been confident in himself and be able to find another job. And he would not have needed to scrape money for the girls to pay bills and party or to buy all the shitty things for Naomi.

Jif was in front of the sliding glass doors again. The two guards stood behind him, out of the chamber. The door behind slid shut with a *shuff.* Enclosed in the glass chamber, he felt his eyes burning again as tears welled up in his eyes. He took a couple of sighs as he brought his grey suit sleeve to wipe away his tears as the motors started whirling above his head. The frosted glass pulled to the right, and the sound of traffic and quiet chatter flooded in. He could still feel the wetness on his eye sockets as the brightness hit him.

He stepped out into the plush lobby. Cold! The chauffeur's peaked cap was visible from behind one of the leather armchairs. Even though he was close to others again, the loneliness was still there. He paced a meter forward when the chauffeur suddenly leapt up. He turned and faced Jif, eye to eye, hands behind his back, formal.

"I'm ordered to take you back now, sir," he said informatively. Jif rotated his head, wondered how to reply.

"Yea," he finally said, sniffing through his blocked nose; it had started to run.

The chauffeur spun round and marched towards the rotating doors. Jif followed quickly, not wanting to be left behind. He staggered out of the embassy again and up to the limo, a broken man. The chauffeur opened the passenger door and stood to attention, waiting.

He climbed into the limo again. Iffy was still sitting behind the bar, upright, rigid, and staring into nothing. That was how he always was, connected and isolated at the same time. Only when Jif sat down on the seat did Iffy turn his head.

"Drink?" he questioned. Jif was feeling sick again, but anything to drown his sorrows would be good. He hadn't really drunk since his wedding.

"Is there any absinthe?" asked Jif. Iffy looked down and ducked behind the minibar before reemerging with a pear-shaped bottle of translucent green liquid. It had a paper card attached with string on the bottle's neck and the label on the front clearly stated "absinthe original" in Victoria letters. Jif leaned forward, stretching out his arms to take the bottle. Iffy leaned over the bar. The bodyguard's black fingers made contact with Jif's as he cupped the bottle with both hands. He felt a bite of ice-cold through Iffy's fingers. Leaning back, Jif ogled the bottle and noticed a stick on the base that read in red letters, "Imported by Lime.Inc for consumption of the British embassy only!"

Jif sighed. Of course. He was foolish to expect absinthe in America. It was banned! But the limo driver had already thought of it. It wasn't even Jif's favourite drink. He grasped the neck in his left hand and squeezed the bottle top with his right, turning it until the seal broke with several snaps. He spun it with his fingers and held it loosely, raising it off the mouth of the bottle before putting it to his own.

Air rushed through a tiny gap between his top lip and the glass as the green liquid bubbled its way into him. He swallowed. It tasted liquorish. The burning sensation in his mouth left a welcoming feeling. The mark of his scream in his throat was no longer there. He felt his heart rise again, and a small smile came to his lips. Bringing the bottle down to his seat, between his open legs, he suddenly recalled how at home he was in the car.

"You should try this seat, Iffy," jeered Jif. "It's so comfortable!" He grasped the bottle top and spun it counterclockwise in the mouth of the bottle until the liquid stopped spinning. His eyes felt heavy. He wanted to remember his wife.

September 15, 2003

When Yuzuyu first arrived in England, she greeted everything with excitement. Especially her new clothes. Clothes that Jif had bought; he got them on the cheap from eBay. Two days after arriving, and buying ten items of teenage girl's clothes, including knickers, Jif set about feeding her. Amazing, she had not asked for food or complained about being hungry since her arrival.

Jif gave her a tall glass of Coca-Cola, which she swallowed within a minute. Jif remembered that moment, when she handed back the glass back to him, and smiled. She liked the cola. It must have been her first drink, outside of a cryogenic freezer.

He was at the stove, making steak pie and boiled potatoes for him and her. She was wearing electric blue jeans and a pink T-shirt with a heart picture on the front, the cutest thing on the planet with her blonde hair. Jif kept on glancing at her as she sat at the kitchen table, drawing with pencils and paper.

"I'm drawing you, Jif," she called to him as he opened the oven.

"That's a nice idea, Yuzuyu," replied Jif, trying to sound encouraging. After checking on the pie, there was a piddle paddle sound coming in Yuzuyu's direction.

When Jif turned around, Yuzuyu was stepping up from the chair. She turned to face Jif but looked down at herself, mouth in open in surprise, her drawing still in her right hand.

"I'm wet!" she exclaimed. The inside legs of her jeans were of a darker shade of blue than they had been before, all the way down to her ankles. Urine was in a small puddle on the chair behind her and under it as well.

"Didn't you feel that?" asked Jif, a little lost for words. Yuzuyu looked up at him.

"No!" she replied truthfully.

Jif spent the next ten minutes undressing Yuzuyu, cleaning her up and redressing her. She didn't complain or cry. She was more shocked than anything.

Jif decided to do a test. He gave her a drink yet again and timed with his watch how long before she needed the toilet. She never asked. She wet herself again in thirty minutes.

Jif decided that Yuzuyu was incontinent and began buying Pampers for her. And upon buying the first pack, lust got the better of him, and he decided this could be the best way to indulge in his voyeuristic fantasies.

He wanted to be her father figure, and he got his wish. He persuaded her to let him change her all the time. And she did so with trust. Jif loved to change Yuzuyu's diaper; he made her feel safe and warm, and he got to see her genitals and backside.

But he never touched her in a sexual way. He attempted at least twice, but every time, his heart raced, and he became sick.

He gave up his sexual exploits and became just a father figure to her. By now, she had become accustomed to wearing nappies or diapers and enjoyed Jif changing her.

"I'm too lazy to get out of diapers," she once said to him.

To be both motherly and fatherly, Jif turned to television for the answer. His role model soon became Lois Griffin from the animated TV show *Family Guy*. A doting wife and mother of three children, she showed utter care and consideration to her family and placed her feeling aside to the anchor of the husband and kids. She always showed a smile, never shouted, and helped out when she could. And Jif lapped this up perfectly, making a perfect little family of his own.

SEVEN

May 10, 2006, 1749 EST

Jif drifted in and out of sleep. He could feel himself laughing, even though he didn't know what he was laughing at. He took another swig of absinthe; the burning sensation came back, as did his smile. Iffy was asleep again and hadn't moved. And the sunlight beamed its way into the car, illuminating his face. He still didn't flinch; deep sleep.

"Iffy," called Jif, waving the bottle, "treat yourself!" He clutched the bottle to his chest and tried to hold himself, not sure where his left hand was in the seat. "You never had, like, a proper beer." Iffy still wasn't reacting. Jif was wondering whether Iffy was dead or if he was dreaming. "Iffy," he called. Still no response.

Jif felt a frown on his face as the car slowed down. He peered through the glass and saw he was pulling up outside Lime.Inc. He was home again, but he wasn't happy. He felt the loneliness return in his body. Even with the sunshine, he still felt cold and unhappy.

Jif felt a slight dip in the car and a slam of a car door. The chauffeur came back into view and reached for the door. The door lock clunked. A swoosh of cold air flew into the car along with the sound of regular traffic. A squeak from Jif's left told him that Iffy was moving and awake.

The chauffeur didn't say anything; he just kept smiling. The limo was Lime. Inc's property, but it probably had another job to do somewhere else, just as Jif had to pack up and leave. He took a deep sigh and swooped his foot out of the footwell, onto the sidewalk outside. They stood up outside and paced towards the black gate, with the sound of Iffy scuttling behind him. The car door slammed shut behind him, and the clip-clop of the chauffeur's shoes echoed in Jif's mind.

"Panget," called Jif, his throat feeling like sandpaper. He stuck out his right hand and chimed the bottle against the irons bars several times to make a dull ringing noise. The gate swung open, and Jif stepped forward into the chamber. He was going over the same laborious process that left him feeling terribly lonely. The gate slammed shut behind him, and the gate in front swiftly opened. He took two steps forward out of the cage and spun round to the gate, which slammed shut again. The same process was repeated for Iffy, and he waited for him to come through. Side by side both men walked into the building; Jif didn't want to walk on his own.

"Hello, boys," mumbled Mitzvah from behind the desk without looking up. Jif took another swig from the bottle as he paced to the elevator. It was open and ready for use. Iffy snuck into the corner and pressed the button. The doors slid shut, and the car moved up. After ten seconds, it pinged on the third floor, opening the doors. As one, the men stepped out, but Iffy suddenly stepped sideways and stood up against the wall. Jif hesitated but said nothing, clutching both arms to his chest, defensive.

He walked by himself along the beige corridor to his bedroom, and the loneness filled every inch of him. Closing the door of the bedroom, he downed the last of the absinthe and spun the empty bottle towards a paper bin under one of the windows. It missed and chimed in the carpeted floor. He eased himself down on the Bratz duvet, rested his head on the pillow, and closed his eyes. He could feel his brain rotate, not sideways, but backwards. It had been a while since he was drunk.

He started thinking about Yuzuyu. She now went to school by herself; the year before, she always clung to Jif like a baby to its father. He felt like a father too. She went to school at the Boston Japanese School. It was a two-story building in Chinatown. Strange, as it was Japanese and everyone around it was Chinese. But pupils all over went there. There were white Americans, blacks, Latinos, even Iraqis. It wasn't just a school for the Japanese; it was a place to learn about the Japs. It certainly helped Jif learn his wife's language—a little better.

He loved that uniform. Sailor-style white blouse, red cravat, short dark blue skirt. Such a short skirt. So feminine!

Then he thought about himself. Hull, the Orchard Park Estate.

He'd lived in Humberside all his life. And he hated the place. Nobody knew anything about politics; when he made a joke about the prime minister, none of his friends knew who the PM was!

He'd tried getting into politics, but no one was interested or supportive. In desperation, he went on a suicide mission, standing in the middle of town with a loud-hailer, preaching about human rights and the corruptness of parliament. He tried to make himself as the alternative PM, even though he was nineteen, and fat.

He was either ignored or spat on. His old foe, Roshan Peking, threw a bottle at him. Children would tell him to shut up because he was boring.

He promised new jobs, better public services, lower taxes, and "make everythin', like, wonderful!" But he wasn't against immigration.

That was his downfall because the residents, and his own parents, believed that immigrants were taking all the jobs in Hull. But Jif saw immigrants in a different light. The girls and women in his area were rough and unfeminine. The migrants were a lot softer. He had a spot for them. And that cost him. At any rate, in his area, politics was a dead end.

The local supermarket in his town was a branch of Tesco's. At first, it was the only employer that showed any interest in him. When his attempts of being a member of parliament or running for council failed, Tesco always took him back in. He started out as a trolley boy and didn't move up. But someone there liked him because a new store was opening in Watford, Hertfordshire. His manager asked if he wanted to work fifty miles from home, for extra pay. He accepted.

Tesco's Watford was huge! Four acres of car park space! Wearing solid shoes and a yellow fluorescent jacket, he had to scour this whole area.

His job was simple: pick up the stray trolleys in the car park and stack them into a line in the pedestrian walkway. Another guy operating a three-wheeled remote cart would connect the trolleys to the machine and drive the trolley train up to the shop front.

Few people talked. And he was regularly yelled at by yobs and general customers. It regularly rained, and he would sweat heavily under his work jacket. But one day he saw couple in the car park, struggling with a baby basket. He knew straightaway that they wanted the cage trolley.

"Would you like the specialist trolley?" he asked the black man.

"Uh, yes, please, if you have any," replied the father.

Jif ran off to a trolley park and pulled out the cage trolley he'd seen earlier that day. The couple gave Jif a terrific smile as they took it from him. The man slipped Jif a business card. His name was Vincent Bird.

Jif drifted, from his sleep, to just lying with his eyes closed. He didn't just hate himself; he had no one to turn to. He had his wife, and he loved her, and she loved him, but the fact that she was a minor, and incontinent, left him feeling nervous. He wanted to have sex with her but knew full well it was wrong with a girl her age. So he felt restricted.

Charlie wasn't just a friend; he was his project. A man has to keep himself busy. Once he had taught Yuzuyu English, he found himself someone else to help. He could see himself in Charlie, and the fact that he was always picked on by Naomi further emphasised that. But it also gave him someone to hate! If Naomi hit Charlie, he would further hate her. And make sure Charlie had the fighting chance he deserved.

But Charlie wasn't the dorm manager for fun; he was on a mission, as Jif found out soon after his first meeting.

March 18, 2004, 1906 EST

"When I was five, I made a promise," began Charlie. He was sitting in the office on a tiny office chair. Clutching his hands in his lap, Jif knew he was embarrassed talking about his love life, his childhood memories. "I promised a girl . . . we would get married!"

"So why didn't you?" asked Jif. He was lying back in his chair but found himself staring out of the window. The darkness was setting into the room, and the light had been blown out, leaving only the traffic outside as an illumination.

"We promised we would meet up again at MIT!" Charlie said, not making eye contact. His glasses were reflecting the contents of Jif's desk. As Jif leaned forward, he glimpsed himself in the reflection and, for a moment, thought he saw himself in Charlie's face.

"You didn't make it in, did you?" said Jif. Charlie's hair was spiked up with hair gel. His green T-shirt and khaki shorts gave the ordinary feel around. Jif felt aware his stomach was bulging.

"I flunked twice!"

"You know her name?"

"All I remember is that she had strawberry panties, every day!" Jif spluttered out a laugh.

"Mate, come on! You gotta have more info than that!"

"We used to play, in the hotel playground, before it got sold." Jif sighed. He was aware there used to be a sandpit and a swing set in place of the car park; he'd come across the old plans of the buildings.

"Charlie, I gotta tell you! You and me, we ain't so different. I like you, I see myself in you! And I want you to find this girl! But you ain't gonna, like, survive with that Naomi kickin' you around all the time!"

"I know," whined Charlie, "but she's the best payer of the lot. This business depends on the girl's rent."

"Mate, tell you what! You do some odd jobs for me, and I'll use my contacts to find this girl and get you into MIT!"

"You'd do that?" exclaimed Charlie, making eye contact for the first time since sitting down. Jif waved his arms out.

"We're friends, aren't we?"

Jif opened his eyes. They'd been closed for . . . he didn't know how long. Yet they still burned. He didn't know whether it was from tiredness or from stress. He spun his head round to the left, propping his left arm down onto the bed to steady himself, and stared into Yuzuyu's vanity mirror. He loved watching her dress herself in front of it, doing her hair and stuff, though she didn't use much makeup.

Jif was looking at himself, pondering all the weeks' events and wondering what to do next. The hatred inside him was burning up again. He wanted to end it all, but he didn't know how. He finally stood up off the bed and paced around to the vanity, never breaking from his own reflection. His heart was racing again. What to do?

He bent down on the dressing table and reached for a pair of yellow-handled hair scissors. The smooth plastic handle was cool against his finger and thumb as he hoisted them into the air. He diverted his eyes from the mirror as he thrust the scissors behind his head. The horrible sound of the blade scraping each other rang into his ears. He felt his head become lighter and he heard the hissing sound as the scissors cut through the hair. Again and again, he opened and closed the blades. Something hit the carpet. His ponytail was gone.

He continued his attack with the scissors, cutting where he could. Inches of hair flew down in front of his eyes, some fibers catching on his nose. The prickling in his skin was unbearable, yet he kept on going. Tiny fibers like dust landed everywhere, falling into his collar and digging into his neck. His face felt as if it was on fire.

The scraping sound of scissors and hissing of hair became almost constant. His eyes screwed shut, and he could see what he was down. Time passed agonizingly slow until he lost track and finally opened his eyes again. He didn't dare look in the mirror. Instead, he dropped the scissors and dashed for the door. Briskly he marched down the corridor, radiating anger, authority, and control. Iffy didn't budge as Jif stamped past him, opening the office door. He didn't even close the door behind him as he passed the desk and reached above for the Exit sign. He ripped out an electricity wire and pushed down the bar of the fire exit door. The alarm didn't go off. He paced out, his footsteps emphasized on the wooden floor of the girls' dormitory that he was now entering. Walls were plaster, yellow, and fun. Shallow shelves held pictures of past and present tenants against sunny backgrounds. To his left were a flight of stairs, the emergency stairs. Jif continued his march on his reckless mission.

In the kitchen area, all the girls were hunched over the oak dining table, waiting for lunch. The Japanese tenant was dressed in kendo trash and leaning head down in the table with a towel obscuring her head. Rajah and Chelsea were at a 1990s stove, boiling chicken curry and rice on silver saucepans that had lost their shine ages ago. The cupboards around them were a horrible white and cheesy yellow and coated with grease. Two separate side windows let in the light, which gleamed off the white plates stacked up in a plate rack on the left side of the room.

"I'm so bored I think I'm gonna scream!" whined Foxy, holding her head in her hands above the table.

"You will be in five minutes!" replied Jif, pacing around the corner and into the kitchen.

"Oh," exclaimed Rajah. She had a heavy Indian accent and the red Hindu dot on her forehead. She was dressed in her school uniform, like Yuzuyu's: blue skirt, sailor-style white blouse, red bow tie. "Hi, Jif. We're having tikka masala. Care for a plate?"

"What happened to your hair?" exclaimed Foxy. She was genuinely surprised.

"I want you out," he began. "ALL OF YOU!" he screamed.

"What!" exclaimed Naomi in sheer surprise.

"You heard!" Jif shouted back, unrepentant.

"What's your problem?"

"You are my problem, Naomi!"

"It's been just a day, Jif! Come on!" She brought her hands up and down in defense.

"He died for you!"

"Shut up!"

"He died trying to make enough money for you guys so that you could get drunk, and sleep and SHIT!"

"I have a job too, you know!" snapped Foxy, slamming her fists into the table.

"I'd like you both to shut up!" Motoko said, raising her head from the bowl of hot water. "You're making all of us nervous!" She tossed the towel off her head, and it flung up against Jif's shoulder. He didn't flinch.

"He took that job to prove to you that he wasn't a perv!" he said, his eyes still burning into Naomi's face.

"You were the one who gave him the job!" she replied.

"You drove him into it! Admit it, cunt! You wanted him dead!"

"You bastard! I loved him!"

"That's ridiculous! You can't love anything! You're a monster!"

"I see his smashed face every fucking day. You got no idea how I felt for him! You . . . you just wanted him to . . ." She struggled for the words, gritting her teeth and shaking her head. The rage was boiling inside of her. "He was your meal ticket to heaven! You just saw him as a project."

"If you loved him, then why did you keep PUNCHING him?"

"Because he kept invading my privacy!"

"You didn't have to hit him! And how can you love someone if you keep smackin' 'im around?"

"You don't fucking get it! It was for his own fucking good! To learn"—she jerked her hand again, trying to find the right words—"not to do stuff! Like Shiffs!"

"Charlie was never a Shiffs," Jif replied quietly, before screaming, "HOW DARE YOU COMPARE HIM TO SHIFFS!" He drew a deep breath through his teeth, his face still deep in rage. "Every time I look at you, all I see is hatred! I can't stand it." He paused and then made for the dining table. "I want you all gone! All of you!" He picked up the stack of white plates in both his hands and threw them all, as one, onto the oven. The black girl gave a high-pitched scream as she dived out of the way of the flying plates.

The crockery crashed against the steel surface of the tiled wall above the hob, shattering into dozens of fragments with an ear-piercing chinking sound. The kitchen swiftly emptied of occupants, except for Jif and Naomi. A warm, soft fist rammed into Jif's neck, just below the brain stem. He fell forward a little, head back, arms out, turning around to see who it was. Fully turned, Naomi slapped him across the face, knocking his left eye. His eye began to water.

"You see!" Jif gritted through his clenched teeth, holding back from crying. "All you do is hurt people! You can't be with anyone!"

"It's you who's the problem," replied Naomi, punching Jif's shoulder blades as he paced out of the kitchen and into the hallway. "You always put people in harm's way!"

"You're waste to humanity!" shouted Jif, his face now wet with tears as his other eye gave way to the hurt inside of him. He made for the stairs.

"Most people get their high from beer," Naomi went on, with a kick up Jif's backside, "or drugs." Jif heard her draw a shaky breath behind him. Maybe she was crying as well. He could see the fire exit door just a few paces from him. "But you, you're addicted to chaos!"

"Stop talking about yourself," Jif said quietly as he reached the door. It had been jammed open with a bottle top on the archway above him. Pushing it fully open, the fire alarm rang into life with deafening effect. Behind him, Naomi drove her fingers into her earholes to drown out the sound. Jif was unfazed, walking casually to the office door.

"Iffy!" shouted Jif at the top of his voice, trying to overcome the ringing. The office door flew open as Iffy stood with his yellow jacket and ever-serious expression on his face. Jif kept on walking while giving orders. "There's an intruder in the office! Get rid of her!" He threw his arm behind him to point out Naomi. Iffy complied immediately. He ran into the office, out of Jif's sight.

"Hey!" yelled Naomi as Jif walked through the doorway. "He broke all our plates!" Jif made it to the elevator and hit the single button on the wall. The LED light inside came to life. "GET OFF ME!" shouted the girl. Jif was wondering why she hadn't punched Iffy through the wall as she had done so many times with Charlie. Maybe Iffy was too heavy for her. The elevator pinged, and the doors opened.

Jif stepped into the car and turned around to watch Iffy run in the elevator just before the doors slid shut. Once he felt the car move down, he let out a long-held cry. He covered his eyes as his sobbing became uncontrollable. He wiped his eyes. He took a stammering breath. He hyperventilated to control the crying, timing when the lift would stop. He felt the car slow down to a stop. The car pinged again, and the door slid open into Lime.Inc reception area.

"Hello again," muttered Shiffs without looking up. Mitzvah wasn't around. Jif stormed out of the elevator, the cold air now breezing through the gaps in his hair. He stomped past the reception desk and made his way, angrily, to the doors.

"Uh . . . Jif?" called Mitzvah out of nowhere. Jif didn't reply. Iffy was jogging to keep up with Jif's strides as he marched down the footpath. Panget appeared again.

"Open the gates please, Panget," Jif requested, quietly, under his breath. His voice was shaky.

"Sure," replied Panget, compliant. This time, both gates swung open at the same time, so there was no need to wait for the other. Panget could read Jif's mind after all. Jif made for the gap, not flinching when his knuckles banged against the metal fencing. He turned left on the sidewalk, against the traffic, with Iffy following behind close by. There were surprisingly few people out today on the sidewalks and on the road. The clouds seemed to vanish on cue, and the sun came out, bathing everything in gold. But Jif still wasn't changing his tune.

He'd been stomping for a minute and was already one hundred meters from the building, passing offices and more hotels. The busy street of Boston's financial district failed to notice him. Cars, trucks, and taxis roared past without a care in the world, spewing their toxic fumes. He felt tiny, dominated by the multistory buildings around him, but seeing grey concrete of the Federal Bank Reserve growing taller just up ahead of him made him feel in comfort; there were people he knew there. They could help him, but he wasn't sure his body would last that long.

He wanted someone to stop their car and ask him what was wrong, but it never happened. Jif tripped on a cracked paving slab and staggered forward to regain his balance. He drew a shaky breath, leaned forward to the edge of the sidewalk, and embraced a parked car. Hands and head over the roof, and the smell of burnt oil and pine filling his lungs, the flaky faded lemon colour of the car reminded him of his childhood; his father had a Cavalier with just such a colour. He stayed there for thirty seconds, panting, before pushing himself away again. He staggered forward a few paces, passed a red fire hydrant and a 1960s streetlight with a shiny rectangular sign stating parking times, before reaching a black Ford Crown Victoria. It was exactly the type of car Jif had bought for Charlie, just two weeks before the shooting. The reminder broke his heart. He slowed down his pace, turning right towards the car, head down, and spluttered a tearful breath. He hissed a gasp between his teeth, spun round towards Iffy, and yelled into the air.

"I DID NOT KILL MY BODYGUARD!"

He fell to his knees before rocking backward and slamming his spine into the car's right front wheel. Bringing his arms over his face, he sobbed like a baby. The bodyguard stood and watched, unflinching, as the whole of Boston flew by without a care.

The sounds of the traffic slowly began to drown out of his ears. His arms felt heavy, his spirit lightened. He knew he had to get over Charlie, but his pride was killing him. The only light left in his life was Yuzuyu. He was so nervous when he realized he was married to her. He thought it would end him. But it turned out to be the best thing that could happen. She made it clear she wanted to stay with him.

Jif struggled to remember his wedding night, but he couldn't. Most of what he knew was from other people telling him and the video.

The only thing he genuinely remembered was walking along the Strip in Las Vegas, and temporarily losing his balance, bent over and staggering forward in a drunken move, all he saw was the dirty maroon tiled floor of the sidewalk. And it was so ridiculous, he had to laugh. And once he started, he couldn't stop. He just kept laughing hysterically like a maniac, knowing he was in trouble. He remembered his head was burning, as were his cheeks, filled up with blood.

"I think he's had it," someone behind him said. He never found out who said that. He remembered seeing several pedestrians pass by, bewildered, or giving dirty looks. He saw a bride and groom pace out of a hedged walkway and turned into that path and saw the wedding chapel before everything went black.

He didn't remember anything else, and he hated himself for that! How can you not remember your own wedding!

The only consolation was that a man he did not know had recorded the wedding for him. Seeing himself on that tape always made him angry.

The whole mess had started soon after arriving in Boston. Jif had been ordered by Vin to secure a contract to a casino boss, who needed military firepower to control his rivals.

The deal was a complete success, but Jif made the mistake of accepting a drink from the customer. He'd also brought Yuzuyu with him and left her in the limo that Vin had lent to him. Drunk, he climbed back into the limo, somewhere in the Strip, and asked to be taken back to Boston.

On the way, however, Yuzuyu noticed a wedding chapel. The banner out front said Any Age Welcome. Yuzuyu asked Jif if they could marry there and then; and Jif, under the influence simply said, "Yea . . ."

On the video, Yuzuyu was beautiful. A gorgeous white wedding dress that covered her feet. The teasing veil. Her wonderful smile. Compared to him, he had been dressed in a black suit, white shirt, and a red bow tie; he didn't remember putting any of those things on. His then security team, two black Southern men with blue jackets and baseball caps with Security written in yellow on the front right breast, were holding him up by his arms because he could no longer stand up. His legs were bent, and he was continuously struggling because he felt restricted.

The tape showed the background as white tiled, with several dark brown pews behind the congregation, empty, and a distant archway that led to the Strip; the viewer could clearly see pedestrians and cars driving by in the night sky.

The priest, a thirty-year-old man in white robes, with straight black hair and a thick beard, read out the vows, "Do you take this woman to be your lawful wedded wife?" Unfortunately, Jif's head was somewhere else as he blurted his reply.

"Have I had too much to drink, or have I really got two jugs?"

The priest sighed and shook his head.

"Do you want to marry this girl?" shouted the priest. His yell echoed across the tiled walls of the chapel.

"Yea, yea," replied Jif in resignation, bowing his head.

Jif refused to see any more of the video after that. The fact that he had been allowed to marry a minor tore him up inside.

Deep down, he loved Yuzuyu. He wanted to love her as a wife and have children with her. But he knew that because she was still a minor, he would just have to wait, or give up his dream entirely.

But as the year passed, he realized it was a gesture of her love. The fact she'd married him meant she'd saved herself only for him. She even told him, he could make love to her when the time was right.

He still had to be careful though.

Ever since his first meeting, he had suppressed all sexual urges for her. But others weren't so convinced. Jif simply took his pleasure from changing Yuzuyu's diaper and wiping her clean. She depended on him, and he was happy for that.

EIGHT

May 10, 2006, 2107 EST

By the time Jif had snapped out of his dream, it was pitch-black. He was still leaning against the car, his back aching at its base, his shoulder blade flattened under his weight like a pancake. He felt damp; he'd been sweating heavily under his suit jacket. His armpits, his forehead, and his underwear felt wet. Even though he'd been sleeping so long, his eyes still felt tired, a deep burning sensation under his eyelids.

He was facing one of the many office buildings along Federal Street: three-story, grey brick, big windows. It was too dark for him to read the company name, and he never paid attention anyway. He moved his hand to his back and felt the cold steel of the car's wheel rim.

The headlights of a passing car woke Jif up a little more, just as its engine hummed past. His hands scraped along the rough surface of the sidewalk as he tried to steady himself. Leaning forward with his knee bent, he slammed his palms down in front of him, and his weight on his shaky arms, pushed his legs up, and stood tall. He looked around. Iffy was gone, and he felt so alone. The fact that nobody had some time for him, stayed with him, left him feeling that nobody did care about him.

His eyes growing wet, he faced the direction of his building and made the lonely walk back to Lime.Inc. He felt his shoes slamming onto the sidewalk paving, crushing little bits of nothing under his feet. There was a slight breeze that night, and some newspaper pages blew onto the sidewalk; Jif simply walked onto them. There was little traffic, so two cars with headlights on blinded him a little. It wasn't until he got to a streetlight that his sensitivity to the light began to diminish.

He looked into the sky, no stars. It was terribly cloudy tonight and dark. Making him feel even more depressed. He tried to think about something else to feel less lonely. He wanted to get into bed and hold Yuzuyu and promise to change her diaper in the morning. He knew she'd be back from school by now and worried about him. But if she was, why she hadn't called him, he thought. He had his mobile with him, and he kept it on at all times!

He could hear yelling further down the sidewalk. Under the glare of a streetlight up ahead, he saw two men in jacket and jeans swaying about in zigzags. Jif didn't want to be next to drunkards, with two of them and one of him. He glanced behind to see the traffic and then back down again and ran across the street. On the other sidewalk, he found a rusty green Pacer. Ducking behind the driver's door, he glanced through the mud-splattered window. A glass bottle flew its way into his view from the opposite sidewalk, smashing into the concrete. The two men soon followed in front of him, staggering about, laughing and swearing at each other; he could make out a word they were saying. One was short and white and had a mop of curly black hair, like the interrogator he saw in his dream. The other was thickset, tall, and black; didn't mean anything to him.

"I hope he wakes up," yelped the white one. What was that one about? They wandered out of Jif's sight. He didn't move until their yelling had died down. Glancing, he gripped the car's wing mirror and pulled himself up. As he did, a white semi-truck thundered past. A hurricane of papers and sweet wrap slammed into his face. He wiped his eyes and dusted down his jacket. Repeating the Green Cross Code, he dashed across the street again.

After losing count of his steps, he made it to the tall black barricade of Lime. Inc. In the darkness, it looked more gothic and frightening. Jif located the gate and knew it was closed. He saw what looked like a piece of paper lodged in the bars but thought it was just trash shoved in by a drunk. He made a light fist with his right hand and chimed his knuckle against a black steel bar until it made a dull ringing noise.

"Panget!" he called, raising his head so it could be heard over the fence. He stopped rapping and waited patiently for the gate to open. It didn't. After a minute, he reached for a silver box on the right, with six horizontal holes, five inches long by half centimeter wide, and a small button down below. He pushed the intercom and expected a buzz, but that didn't happen. He leaned down anyway and spoke into the speaker.

"Panget, it's Jif. I know it's late, but . . . ," he pondered what to say. "I'm havin' a bad day." He panted and peered through the bars to look for any activity. Nothing. He pushed the button again. "Panget, come on!" Jif panted again before heaving off the intercom and sidestepped along the fence to look for Panget's shed. He found it, and his jaw dropped. Its door was open. It creaked eerily. Jif could see into the side of the shed, Panget's bed. It was empty.

Panget never deserted his post, and if he did, the building was insecure, so Vin Bird would send in the heavy security. But there was none of that. And the building itself appeared lifeless.

Jif glanced at his watch: 2120. Even at this time, a light would still be on in one of the rooms, even his bedroom. But not tonight. Then he thought about what Vin said. "You have forty-eight hours to pack your bags!" Jif's heart started to race. Had Vincent thrown Yuzuyu out early on purpose? Or had Jif been asleep for two days? Or was the building evacuated?

Jif sidestepped again and looked for the paper he saw earlier. He found it. It was in a plastic wallet and fixed to the iron bars with white plastic cuff. The letter was large and bold for even the partially blind or dyslexic to understand.

"Lime.Inc has moved to our new address in Washington. Please consult our Web site!"

Jif's eyes began to water again. They'd done something without telling him. He felt the whole world had turned against him, and all his strength had left. He knelt down and blubbered.

"Why?" he kept on saying. "Why?" He didn't care about the job. About money. All he cared about was his girl. But even then he felt ashamed. Yet she was the only thing good in his life, and the only thing he hadn't messed up. She'd stayed with him no matter what. And even when he said she could be free and leave him, she still wanted to be with him.

He wiped his eyes again and suddenly became aware of how cold the top of his head was. He stood up, put his back to the fence, and reached into his jacket pocket. Pulling out his mobile Nokia 3310, he knew the embassy would be closed and that Vin wouldn't want to talk this late at his home address, but Jif still had to try as there was no other way. He scrolled though the menu of contacts and reached "Vin home." He clicked the green button to make the call, and the screen went to calling mode. He put the earpiece to his ear and heard the rings chirp away.

The double beeps rang four times before there was a clunk on the other end of the line. Jif drew a breath; he knew what was coming.

"Hello. This is Vincent Bird. Leave your message at the tone, and I will get to you in the morning." And the message ended with an ear-piercing hum. Jif's eyes continued to burn.

"Vincent, by the time you get this . . . did you move the Lime offices?" He breathed heavily as he tried to think of more things to say. "Where's my wife?" He was no longer authoritative. He was now just whining. He felt dejected, and he knew full well the message wouldn't be listened to anyway.

And he realized there was no point in trying anymore. He had his chance, and he blew it. He thought it would never end, but it did. As Vin had told him, "Except it and move on!" He pulled the phone from his ear and hung up. Brushing his eyes with the sleeve of his jacket again, he took two shaky breaths, on the verge of crying, and looked across to the other side to the fence. Where Lime. Inc's fence ended, Babylon Zoo apartments began. He paced forward and looked into the vacant car park and the blue front door up ahead under the porch.

His mind was ticking. Oh! Why hadn't he thought before? He could go through the apartments and break through the fire exit in his office! The front door was shut and locked all over, but the windows weren't. He could try it. But his pride wouldn't let him. He didn't want to be under the same roof as the person he held responsible for Charlie's death.

His left foot was on its ball, waiting to move. After thirty seconds, he sat down flat again. He blinked several times and closed his mouth. His mind was made up. He had nothing left to lose now. He had a duty to serve. For his friend!

He spun his heel and pulled a serious face. Focused, he marched down Federal Street. He knew where he was heading now. But he was still thinking up the plan in his head. And he pondered on the reasons. And the alternatives. And Charlie!

At the end of Federal Street is a junction, where the road becomes High Street. Repeating the Green Cross Code again, he dashed to the other side of the street. He found himself on a small shopping precinct, full of 7-Elevens, late-night burger bars, and one gun shop.

It was called Hired Guns, its name embedded in red on a green canopy above the one-story shop. Separate from the rest of the shops, it was a yellow-walled building with two massive windows either side and a single blue door in the centre. The glass in windows and doors had internal white strips to keep the glass from shattering and avoid ram raids for the guns. The two windows would display mannequins in combat gear holding rifles, as well as banners claiming a "blow-out sale!" But tonight, that was obscured by the two steel grey shutters which locked to the floor.

Next to the door and under the right hand window lay an aging bench. Metal feet spiraling up to form the armrests on each end, painted green, holding eight or ten long strips of wood, its varnish peeling off like bent nails.

Jif rested his right arm on the green metal armrest and glanced at the door. A cardboard held to the door's window told the opening time: 0900 tomorrow. It was 2130 now. Jif clambered onto the bench, lay on his back, and hoisted his legs over the other armrest. He jammed his left arm under his head to act as a pillow and drew his right arm over his eyes to cover out the lights of passing cars, if they came by. And he was plunged into darkness.

It was uncomfortable, but he didn't care. He had to go through with this! And he started to dream. Oddly enough, about his childhood, and his fear of the dark.

November 1992

"Please, Daddy," sobbed the boy in pajamas, clutching hands together, standing at the foot of his bed. "I can't stay here." Jif's father was having none of it. He slapped Jif twice, across both cheeks.

"Enough of that crying or the boogeyman will get you," mumbled the man, pointing a tar-stained finger at Jif.

His dad was Scottish and worked as a bus driver, along the Orchard Park Estate in Hull where he lived. His mother would work on and of as a till worker for some retail company. She never said which one. And Jif began to believe she never worked at all.

Jif's father had a long line of fathers who were aggressive. So he understood why he got punished; he just didn't believe it was fair.

His real fear of the dark came when one night he'd dropped a bowl of sugar in the kitchen. Jif was frog-marched by his dad into the tool shed and locked in. It was raining, and without light, it felt frightening for such a small boy. The roof began to leak, and he couldn't get out of its way. His hair would get wet; he felt dirty and useless. In the dull light, plastic bags and hammers would glint like a creature's eyes. He'd convinced himself the boogeyman was there with him.

He pounded the door and screamed for his life.

Then, his childhood memory faded away, to give way for another memory.

September 13, 2003, 1714 JST

"Where is it?" he shrieked.

Fido was waving the lighter from side to side, the glow of light bouncing off the rough brick of the tunnel wall. Then it went out.

"AHHH!" screamed Yuzuyu. "Put that back on!"

They were still running, but without light, they were running blind. Jif controlled his breathing, still holding Keitaro's shoulders. He heard Fido hit the flicker three times without success, before slamming the head of the lighter into his palm. Two furious smacks later, the light came back on.

"Is that water?" asked Yuzuyu. Jif listened carefully and could hear gushing water. He wasn't sure if it was good or bad. The light gazed over the walls, and on the right, flaking concrete partially obscured a steel door. Everyone sighed in relief. Keitaro pulled out the crowbar and handed it to Fido.

The tool chimed on the wall as it was smacked. Bits of cement tinkled onto the floor. The door eventually gave way, and they found themselves on an industrial metal walkway. The water was beneath them, gushing at a heart-pounding speed. It was a tunnel, dark and damp and smelly. It was too big for a sewer and certainly not a flooding subway. The group pressed on.

They climbed a flight of stairs and continued in the direction the water was traveling. Jif could see white mist of splashing water. A waterfall?

When they approached a slight bend in the walkway, they could see another flow of water in the opposite direction. They kept going and saw another flow from another tunnel opposite them. Jif looked down, and his heart sank.

"Oh, wow, I can't see the bottom!" exclaimed Yuzuyu.

The hole was about as wide as a sedan car and bottomless. Water from all three sources were falling and splashing together into the hole and disappearing into the blackness. Even so, the splashing caused droplets of water to fly up onto the group, and Jif felt his shirt suddenly go damp.

"See that?" Keitaro was pointing down at the other side of the tunnel. "That's the waterline, where it used to be! Look how low it is now!" He was right. The top half of the tunnel was light in colour; the rest was dark. The darkness being where the water level once was.

"Maybe this is a reservoir," said Jif.

"Is that the adjustment reservoir the man was talking about, when he spoke to you, in the fire?" asked Fido.

"I guess. The water was up there . . . then the earthquake happened, and this hole opened up . . . the water drained. It's . . . it's convincing."

"But where's the water going?" Yuzuyu asked.

"Down there!" replied Keitaro.

"No, where does it drain?"

"Into the foundations!"

And Jif suddenly realized that the city, the island, was turning into a sponge. The buildings would start to subside as it had once done in Tokyo. Or even the island would sink.

"We got to get back to the surface!" Jif said with his teeth chattering.

"This is dangerous, but so is up there," stated Fido. "We get shot!"

"If we get far enough, we can avoid the shooter."

"I have to agree, the only rescuers going to come are for the workers here," stated Keitaro. "Not many helicopters are going to come."

Fido relented. "OK. We see what this way takes us. OK?"

They started to pace along the steel walkway. Each step felt like walking on eggshells as the walkway wobbled and swayed like the deck of ship. They paced on about ten meters when the walkway ran out.

"There is a hole here!"

The tunnel wall had a jagged hole as if something had been driven through it. Bits and bobs started to fall out the hole as Fido tried to step in. It was stationery. Pencils, rulers, envelope. They were under a shop.

"It's a steep climb," stated Fido.

"What do you mean?" called Jif over the roaring water.

"The shop floor has collapsed," explained Keitaro, turning his head. "It's at an angle." That explained why the stock was falling out. Fido was already scuffling in through the hole, pushing bits of debris out onto the walkway. Then Keitaro went in.

Yuzuyu was hoisting herself in when the walkway started to groan. Jif looked down and saw the platform he was standing on was almost off its supports. He gasped and lifted his right leg as the metal twisted beneath him.

Spink!

He felt his weight disappearing as the platform swung out from under him. He fell straight down. No time to scream. He threw his arms out. The platform he once stood on was hanging like a flag under the other platform. His fingers stabbed through the tiny gaps. His mass pulled on them, as if they were being yanked from the knuckle. His body slammed into the grill. It rattled like a drum set.

"ARRRGGHHH!" he shrieked. He gripped to the iron grill with every ounce of strength on his fingers. Yet his mighty grip, and his weight, was causing his fingers to bleed as the thin steel cut into his skin. "Fuck," he squealed. Having to bend his head upwards was tiring on Jif's neck and was putting pressure on his windpipe.

"NO!" screamed the girl. Out of sight, he heard two separate footsteps rattle down the loosening walkway. The girl's pale face appeared first, with Keitaro just above her shoulder.

"Are you OK?"

What a dumb question. But he knew what she meant.

"Leave me!" screamed Jif in a restricted voice. He knew the bridge would collapse with his weight any minute, and even if the group could pull him up, there was every chance he would pull them in too. "Go!"

They didn't. Keitaro was the first to throw his hands out.

"Take my hand!" he yelled.

"Leave it. I'm too heavy for you!"

"Do it!"

"No! I'll pull you over!"

"Look! I've got a hard-enough time getting throughout the day without your death on my conscience! Shut the fuck up and help yourself!"

Jif looked into his eyes and saw something he never had! Honour! He released his right hand and threw it upwards. Keitaro grabbed it and yanked it for all his worth.

"Agh!" Jif felt as though his arm was popping out of its socket. He knew it was futile.

Then Yuzuyu took his other hand. He was still holding on to the grate. She prized her dainty fingers under his palm. Jif tried to give her some leeway. Her soft fingers encased his palm, and he felt weight and pressure become sudden on his elbow and shoulder.

And he looked up in amazement. Yuzuyu was standing up, gradually, with Jif on her hand. Her face was emotionless.

And he knew, the strength in her body was not ordinary. And he realized, the drawings, the designs for the body in the books that he had must have been for her. Which meant the obvious! That she was the intended target! But also, they were all going to get killed, simply because they knew her. And he wasn't going to let her die! Never!

May 11, 2006, 0857 EST

Morning came with a glint of sun in his eye. Jif stirred on the bench, easing his sore muscles. Opening his eyes, he saw the sun was only going to last two minutes; the cloud was all gathered around it like a flock of sheep herding around a farmer. He thrust his left wrist in front of his eyes: 0858. Jif sighed and pushed himself up. He felt sore everywhere, even in his ass, as he sat upright. There was a jingle of keys to his right. A redneck in his fifties held a jail ringer's set of keys in the door lock of the gun shop. *Boy, what a redneck*. Brown cowboy hat, Sundance leather jacket, blue Levi's jeans. The only thing out of place were the man's grey sandals.

"If you are waiting for the fat fighters club, it's in the Boston mall," said the redneck with a smile. He had a Texas accent. Jif blinked his tired eyes and drew a breath, holding back a giggle from the man's joke.

"I'd like a gun," said Jif.

"Well, you came to the right place." The redneck's movement of his mouth added several more creases to his already wrinkled cheeks, yet his forehead was still smooth. Jif was trying to see what hair colour he was, with what little hair was poking out of the hat. It looked dirty brown. "What do you want?" he demanded, peering over his shoulder as he made his way behind the glass counter, laden with silver revolvers.

"Winchester pump!" Jif said without hesitation. He knew it was a tall order, but it was the only weapon he felt comfortable with.

"Wow," exclaimed the redneck, pushing himself away from the counter with the heels of his palms. "We ain't sold those in a month. You buy today, I might close early."

"Uh, what's the waiting time for this type of gun? I ain't ever had a license."

"Well, what's it for?" The redneck held up his hands at shoulder level, open to the sky, to show it was a standard question.

"Protection. I run the Lime.Inc building down there." He pointed out of the window to nowhere in particular, other than Federal Street. He knew he was lying; he no longer worked there, but what did this gun salesman care? He was just here to make money.

"No waitin' time, sonny. We all know you Limes ain't trigger-happy." He turned his back and reached for one of the guns hooked on the wall. He picked a long, shiny silver rifle and raised it off its mountings before turning around again with a smile and started talking in a mocking English accent. "Cor blimey, haha." He drew a breath through his smile and placed the massive lump of steel on the glass counter with a *ching*. "Yea, I seen you before. I reckon you'd be cool." He pointed to the gun. "On me. All you got to do is fill the license, and I'll take care of the rest. You'd be out of here in five minutes."

Jif raised his eyebrows. This was too good to be true.

"Sounds great. Uh, can I have a look please?"

"At what? The gun?" questioned the redneck.

Before the redneck said any more, Jif already had his hands on the gun. Jif held the Winchester across his chest, like a trophy, stroking its barrel; he breathed heavily as his heart raced. He knew the power, he knew the danger. He knew what to do. He dry fired. *Click!*

"How much?" Jif asked as he lowered the gun to the table again.

"Two hundred dollars."

"Done!" he said, pulling out his wallet.

"What, no haggle? Most sonnies push it down to one eighty."

"Not me. I just want a gun now."

"Well, yippy hoo!" said the Texican, doing skip hop on the spot.

"And I'll have a box of ammo as well."

The gun seller squatted down out of sight and made a shuffle of metal. He reemerged with a red box that smelt of fireworks.

"Ten rounds," he began, "that's another twenty dollars."

Jif gazed down at the money again and pulled out another two tens from his wallet and laid the wad of money on the table. The Texas man scooped the cash in his hands and shuffled the bills from his right to his left, gripping his lip as he counted silently. Finally he looked up and smiled.

"Happy to do business." Jif suddenly saw his own reflection in the man's glasses. "Would you like a bag?"

"Yes please," replied Jif. The gunman reached for the piece and the shells with his right hand and kept them at his hip as he sidestepped to the left. Out of sight, he tapped some keys on a cash register, with an audible beep, before the sound of coins being shaken filled the room as the money tray was ejected. A plastic bag was shuffled and paper was torn. The man reappeared with a long white plastic bag with the name Hired Guns splashed across in red.

"Have a nice day," said the Texican, bringing the gun over the counter. Jif took it from him, lacing his fingers into the handle holes before bringing it to his waist and opening it to look inside. The gun and ammo were there along with a tiny receipt. Jif looked up, smiled, and turned in his heel, making for the door.

And Jif was out, with his brand-new gun!

NINE

May 11, 2006, 0907 EST

As he waited for a break in the early morning traffic, his mind began to wonder. He was thinking about Frontiera again. He wanted to remember a particular moment when he was with the group. Ultimately, the reason he was here. He was thinking about the rushing through the tunnels, running away from the uniformed gunmen, when he suddenly snapped out of it.

His attention was suddenly drawn to a break in the traffic. He looked left and saw a white Boston taxi had actually stopped for him. The driver was waving with his right hand to cross the street; Jif thought it was a little too courteous. He gazed back to the right and saw no other cars approaching. He dashed across the street, his gun swaying like a pendulum under his hand, slamming into his ankle as he got to the other sidewalk.

Already he was feeling sick. His conscience was telling him to stop, but his will carried him on. As he proceeded down Federal Street, and the buildings dominated him again, he started to think of Frontiera.

September 13, 2003, 1829

The group decided Jif should go first. It was quite a climb, and the shutter was partially closed, leaving a small gap underneath. If Jif wouldn't fit, then nobody else would try it.

So Jif pulled his way up to the collapsed floor, dragging his body up to the doorway. It smelt of mud and shit. Jif crawled under the metal shutter. He felt tiny pinpricks dig into his chest through his shirt. Pulling himself out, he turned around to see the gap again. It looked smaller than it actually was. A splotch of yellow flashed in the darkness, and Keitaro's head was appearing. Jif pushed himself to his feet and stood, looking down on himself. His shirt and jacket were streaked in brown-grey dust, peppered with bits of tiny black stone stuck to his white shirt. He breathed deeply and, for the first time all day, felt his lungs actually push his ribs out.

112

It was another alien site again. More collapsed or abandoned old buildings and a brand-new road in the middle. How can new things be made when all this trash was around? A pile of rubble was to his right; at least something had been done. Then, something he couldn't believe.

"Fuckin' hell," he said quietly. Over the rooftop of one-story box was a brand-new skyscraper, maybe a few yards away. A bog-standard tower filled with glass and steel, looking grey in the clouded light. A must for any central business sector. And yet there was all this trash around here! This was unbelievable!

"Uh," Keitaro groaned as he crawled out the gap. Jif bent down and offered his hand. Keitaro looked up and threw his arm out. Jif gripped the boy and gradually hoisted him forward. He went for the armpits, sweaty, hot, and pulled his whole body out. He released him and let him be.

"Feel's like being born again," said Keitaro. Jif chuckled.

Yuzuyu was next. She crept though quite easily, so Jif didn't offer his help. He didn't really want to touch her anyway.

"Keitaro's over there," said Jif, pointing him out. He reckoned she wanted to play with him anyway. "I think he might want some help." Yuzuyu understood and trotted off.

"Give me a hand," called the old Jap. Fido stuck his arms through the gap. Jif held the hands and slowly pulled back. Fido got jammed at his waist. It took three jostles to release him. Fido ushered Jif away and crawled to his feet.

"Jif, get over here!" yelled Keitaro. Jif sighed, stood up, and paced over. Keitaro was kneeling on the ground, hunched over something. He seemed shocked! His skin was pale. Something had scared him. All this time, he hadn't showed one bit of fear.

"What, mate?" went Jif, sitting down next to him.

"Jif, I think I'm gonna die," stated the boy, staring right into he ground. He didn't want to make eye contact. Jif felt like giggling.

"What?" he replied.

The boy was staring into a pool of water. Jif didn't know at the time; but in certain cultures, if you see "things" in the reflection of a pool of water, it will come true.

"Jif, I'm not a man. I'm not a father. I don't know how to take care of a girl."

"Mate, why are you saying this? This girl loves you. You have the perfect chance to live a life of solitude with her."

"I won't live that long," replied Keitaro. "Trust me, I know it." Jif thought it was just the nerves talking, but he secretly hoped he was right because he too wanted Yuzuyu.

"Don't you think I got a better chance of dying?" replied Jif, angrily pointing to his stomach. He knew fat men died early. He didn't know what age, but he knew he was on a death train.

"Just, promise me this," demanded Keitaro. He looked up and made eye contact with Jif. "Promise me that if I don't get out, you'll take care of Yuzuyu." Jif sighed. He hated these holes.

"I already wanted her. But I know she'll never be happy unless she's with you," he replied, pushing his palm over the boy's shoulder, trying to offer some comfort. He stopped suddenly and looked behind him, at the rubble. He heard a distant rumble of a car engine. Jif staggered forward and edged the curb. He was sure he could hear a car. Then, they appeared.

"Hey!" he shouted. "I see cars!"

The group paced to where he stood as Jif stuck both his arms in the air and started waving above his head. There were two cars: the first was a sedan, the one following was an SUV. Both black. The sedan splashed through a puddle and avoided a large piece of masonry in the road when a set of red flashers in the grill started pulsing.

"Police?" asked Jif to no one in particular. He could make out it was a Mercedes. Then he noticed a figure in the passenger seat. He recognized him. It was the boy from earlier. The one who shot at them! He stopped waving.

"Geronimo!" he shrieked as he bowed to the right where everyone had stood next to him. He threw his arms around the group and thrust forward. It felt like running through water.

"What are you . . . ," yelled Fido. There was another splash, and squealing! The cars screamed to a halt.

A gun fired. It missed his knee by an inch as a tiny hole blasted its way out of the sidewalk. Jif felt his hands shake again. Fido dived to the left, out of Jif's vision, while Keitaro was herding Yuzuyu back to the shop front. There was the sound of shattering bricks out of nowhere, when Jif tripped on something in the walkway and lost his balance.

"Shit!" screamed Keitaro as Jif landed facedown in the dirt, tiny pinpricks digging into the skin of his forehead. Car doors opened, and there was smacking of footsteps. Pushing his palms into the painful grit of the ground to stand up, Jif cocked his head. A tall Jap aimed a pistol at him. Midthirties, black tunic, white shirt, and no tie. He looked evil, but not as bad as the gun boy behind him. Jif felt his heart beat its way into orbit. He felt helpless, now crawling along the floor like a baby. There was nowhere to hide.

"Ahhh!" screamed Yuzuyu. Jif caught sight of the girl and Keitaro. They had been forced to the floor; two men in suits were scrabbling with them. Jif managed to push himself up as Fido appeared again, screaming at the top of his lungs, running with a long chunk of grey masonry in his right hand.

Bang! Bang! Bang!

A small hole appeared on Fido's jacket. His face contorted as though he'd been kicked in the balls. Jif couldn't bear to watch him die and thrust his arms under his head and dug his face into his biceps, obscuring the light. He heard the huge brick fall from Fido's grasp, with a chink and a sort of rattle. He hissed breaths through his teeth, trying to avoid sucking into dirt and trying to avoid his body rattling. The possibilities were running out; he would die either now or later. Footsteps stomped and squeaked around him. There was a shallow murmur of Japanese gossip, and he heard Keitaro yell something unintelligible in the distance. A car door opened and closed again, then something curved and leathery slammed into the side of his belly.

Jif winced in pain but didn't turn over. Another kick winded him, but he still didn't budge. Then, a foot jabbed into his right shoulder and thrust him sideways. He held his arms to his eyes for as long as he could as he was rolled to his back. He felt a warm fleshy hand grasp his wrist and pulled his left arm downwards. Jif opened his eyes. It was the evil-looking Jap. Crouching down over him. Angry face. His eyes like pits of fire. He just stared at Jif. Then he stood up and walked backwards. Jif lifted his head and wished he hadn't.

The boy from earlier approached Jif. The one who'd shot him in the shoulder. His black automatic pistol was aimed at Jif's head. He had short black hair, spiked up in all directions. Jif could feel the evil piercing him through the boy's aviator sunglasses. He was still wearing them even though it was cloudy and getting dark.

Jif noticed the boy's black combat pants were peppered with specks of dried blood. He'd been killing someone else today. So Jif knew what would happen next.

"Just tell me this . . . ," wheezed Jif, "who are you?"

"I am Rock!" replied the boy, in Americanised English. "Son of Kenjiku!" He cocked the gun. "You tell you god . . ." The boy put the gun to Jif's forehead and drove his head slowly down into the grit of the road. He felt tiny specks of grit pierce into the soft skin of his head. "I will take no one else to run this island."

Jif's head lost all heat as his body realised what would happen next. He felt so useless. So futile. He started to think about the day and the days before that. And he said to himself, "What have I done with my life?"

Just then he felt a rush of blood as a tear filled his left eye and streamed down his temple. The boy drove the gun deep into Jif's skull until it hurt. Jif didn't complain but closed his eyes as he waited for the inevitable. *Click!*

No bang!

He waited ten seconds to be sure then opened his eyes.

The boy was smiling. The gun was in the same place. But had not fired.

"Must be your lucky day. I'm out of shells," mocked the boy. With a crunch of gravel, the boy eased himself to his feet and slid the gun back into the waistband of his pants. "You gonna die anyway!" he yapped as he walked backwards, nodding his head upwards. His cocky body language was saying, "What are you gonna do about it?" and he was right. There was nothing Jif could do.

The screams of Keitaro and Yuzuyu were unbearable, but all Jif could do was push himself up with his palm to spot the hostages in the back of the cars. Yuzuyu was crying and trying to hide her face. Keitaro was shaking back and forth in the seat of the Mitsubishi, yelling his head off and trying to get Jif's attention.

"Don't let them take us!" screamed Keitaro. Jif could only shake his head as shame swept his body. "SAVE YUZUYU!" he screamed. "YOU MUST SAVE YUZUYU!"

One suit each got into the open seat of each car, next to each hostage. As they pulled the doors shut, the child's screams diminished into murmurs. Rock got into the front passenger seat of the Merc, and the convoy drove off slowly.

Jif tried to push himself to his feet, but his legs were useless as he slumped to the floor again. He crawled on his hands and knees along the rubble-covered road to see one last look of the cars. Peering along a broken building, he saw the convoy bounce over dips and bumps in the road and saw a wing mirror fall off one of the cars, before they turned another corner and disappeared.

He felt ashamed. Not angry but ashamed. Because it was his idea to go back onto the road, so he'd led the group into the lethal grip of the bad guys. He turned around, still too weak to stand, and spotted the man.

Fido lay where he was shot. His porkpie hat was upside-down, sitting just above his head on the tarmac of the cracked road. His skin was pale and grey. The whole in his chest was the size of a fist, and the body smelt of fireworks. The blood was splattered in penny-sized spots all over the shirt and on the tarmac around the body. The man's open mouth showed how he'd taken his last breath.

Jif slid his hands under Fido's shoulders and pulled him up, so his head reached Jif's chest. Cradling him, he felt a quiver of emotions fill his body.

And he started to cry.

May 1, 2006, 0910 EST

He swung the bag like a pendulum as he paced down the street, still going over the thoughts in his head, when he leapt out of his pants to the blast of a siren. He leapt round, expecting a cop car ordering him to stop. It turned out to be a fire truck. A brand-new Mini pulled to a stop next to Jif as the truck roared past on the opposite side of the road as cars veered out of its way as it went to the end of Federal Street. The Mini drove off again, and the road returned to normal.

"Not far to go," Jif said to himself. He'd already passed two hotels and an office block. How he wished he could have taken a step inside One Federal Street, the plush-looking skyscraper at the other end of the road.

The iron fencing was starting to come into view. He walked past the café, where Charlie's aunt would work, but today it was closed. Jif was amazed it didn't have any graphite on it.

He eased into his right and entered the car park for Babylon Zoo. Foxy's blue pickup had been reversed into a stop up against the iron fencing, alongside Naomi's brand-new grey VW Beetle. They were here all right.

He marched across the pavement and avoided the front door. He went to the window. White wooden frame. The glass itself was feebly in place. He put his hand against it. Wobbly. He pushed his fingers in and dug in between the pane and the frame. He pulled forward. There was no putty, just adhesive strands.

Jif yanked the pane of glass out of the window frame. Too easy. He propped the whole pane up against the wall by his feet and leaned in through the gap. He hoisted the bag in first and gently placed it on the interior floor. He wriggled through the space and got his stomach clear. As he plumped his way into the floor, a flood of memories came rushing back.

April 11, 2004, 1210

It was several days after the black girl had become a resident. Her parents were restaurateurs, and so she was a great cook. So good, Yuzuyu wanted to go every day.

"Thanks for inviting us," yapped Jif as he waltzed into the kitchen.

"What do you mean invited?" moaned Naomi, who was dishing out the plates onto the table. "You invite yourself! You just turn up whenever you feel like it!"

"Ayyy! I'm paying for the food, aren't I?" retorted Jif with his cheerful grin. He loved being challenged; it gave him an excuse to be naughty and nice at the same time. "A hundred dollars is way too much for a meal anyway," he said as he threw a wad of bills into the middle of the dining table. It was to help with the rent anyway, to make things easier for Charlie.

"Anyway," Yuzuyu would often say, "I love Chelsea's cooking!"

"I'm glad you like it!" Chelsea would often reply with a smile, and she stirred whatever she was making at the stove. It would be the best moment of her day. She was a social recluse and was often reluctant to celebrate or take compliments. Jif could sympathize, but there was nothing in common with him or her.

"So," Foxy would always say in her Southern accent, "what is it like to run your own business?"

And Jif, after sitting down, would give the big lecture that it was not HIS business. Another common topic was "do you sell guns?" Jif always said no and always felt his stomach go empty when he lied.

"Some weird-sounding things come in," he said that day. "We got Gahanna now."

"Is that Mexican?" asked the Japanese girl, Motoko. Her voice was deep, which was unusual for a Japanese woman. That day she wore red blouse; no cleavage exposed. She was very conservative.

"No, it's Brazilian," replied Jif.

"Ready," called Chelsea. And as she picked up the pot, Charlie came in.

"I'm back," he called, holding a wad of cash. And as he paced around Jif, being the klutz that he was, he slipped along the floor. "AHHHH!" The dollar bills went up into the air and fell like confetti whilst Charlie slid forward, narrowly missing Chelsea, who pulled the pot out of the way, and finally fell forward next to Motoko. In his clumsiness, his hand hooked into the sleeve of Motoko's blouse and ripped it open on his way down to the floor. The young woman's white bra was an alluring sight.

Jif could do nothing but grin, and the girl's blouse buttons flew through the air, twinkling like snowflakes. But by the time, Charlie's body connected with the floor, Naomi was standing up, with clenched fists.

"YOU PERVERT!" she screamed as she knelt down out of sight making a dull thud as her fist slammed somewhere into Charlie's body. "YOU'RE A PERV! I NEVER LIKED YOU! I WANT YOU DEAD!"

Jif had lost his smile by the time he stood up. He couldn't take it anymore. As though his body was not his own, he yanked the Israeli to the cabinets, squatted, and scooped up Charlie into his arms. Charlie had wrapped his arms over his head to defend himself, but Jif could clearly see the bruise mark from a fist in the back of his neck. He almost lost balance but was able to carry Charles out of that kitchen, insults flying around.

"Take him and keep him!" yelled out Foxy.

"He owes me a new blouse!" snapped Motoko.

Yuzuyu followed close behind as Jif tried to run to the fire exit door to his office. Jif sidestepped though the doorway to avoid slamming the boy's head against the frame.

"Jif, stop it," whined the boy through his hands as Jif laid him down on his desk. Yuzuyu closed the door, and everyone sighed.

"Why do you do this, man?" asked Jif, shaking his head in disbelief.

"What choice do I have?" replied Charlie. He was almost tearful. As he pulled his hands away, his broken nose became visible. Blood trickled like water from both nostrils. Amazingly, his glasses weren't broken.

"You could fuck that job and live in here!" said Jif, thrusting his head towards the door.

"But that's the easy way out!" retorted Charlie, throwing out his open palms.

"Sometimes you have to take the easy way out!" explained Jif, raising his eyebrows in a sympathetic face. "If you stay there any longer, this job will kill you!" He drew a breath. "You heard what that Israeli said! When someone says they want you dead, they mean it!"

"Jif," whined Yuzuyu in her childlike voice, "you can't be serious all the time!" Jif knew she was right. He placed an arm around her shoulder.

"I know, honey," he said motherly. "But in these times, I cannot assume anything's a joke." Charlie propped himself up with his arms. His hair was disheveled now, and the blood was still trickling.

"Jif," he began, "I know you've done a lot for me, and you're the first friend I had. You believed in me!" Jif knew a put-down was coming. "But I'm not that boy from . . . wherever it was."

"You . . . ," stuttered Yuzuyu. "He does!" she exclaimed, looking up at Jif. "I never noticed!"

"I'm not Japanese! You can't have a second chance. Once it's gone, it's gone!" went on Charlie. It felt as thought the roles were reversed. "Just like with MIT."

"I just . . . want to know that I can help!" explained Jif.

"My only chance is with this girl. And even if she isn't my promised girl, she can still get me into MIT!"

"Even if she punches you every day?"

"I think it's a risk worth taking."

"There's no other thing I can think of," Jif suddenly said, shaking his head and looking at the floor.

"What?" asked Charlie.

"You're a reincarnation of Keitaro," explained Jif. "No offense, but it'll just make me easier to keep going." And Charlie smiled an embarrassed smile.

"I just told you I'm not!" he said as he pulled some tissues from a box on Jif's desk and held them to his nose.

Ten minutes later, a private ambulance pulled up outside Lime.Inc. Jif and Yuzuyu took Charlie, to Massachusetts General. They returned to Federal Street two hours later.

May 11, 2006, 0916 EST

He sat on the floor of the passage. Not really a passage. The front door led to an open space, the lounge. It was decked out with two old couches, a coffee table, and a flat-screen TV. The floor was veneer but had dozens of floor mats and rugs over it.

Smells of girl's skin, roses, and perfume filled his body. He pulled the gun out the bag and laid it across his lap. He took the box of shells and opened it. Cordite filled his nostrils again, and images of Charlie came flooding back.

Charlie lying on his back. Mouth open. Blood oozing. The iron smell of blood gripping him! Gun smoke intoxicating his mouth!

He crushed his eyes shut and shook his head. He had to focus. The shells were red and ice-cold. He found the chamber and slid it open. Holding two shells in his left hand, he slid one in and jabbed it forward. Then he pushed the other one in and sorted that as well. He loaded two more rounds and put the rest into his jacket pocket. He put the bag and the box into the trash can next to him.

He stood up, gun across his chest. He walked on, passing a utility room with a washer and a dryer. It also had a steel sink on board a worktop. Today it was covered in a mess of washing powder boxes, green liquid, and someone's bra draped over the taps.

Jif pressed on. A closet sat wide open, doubled up as a cleaner cupboard. Raincoats of all sorts sat on hangers on a shiny horizontal bar. Beneath the tidy stash, Foxy's army jacket and sun hat untidily lay over an upright vacuum cleaner. Charlie would use that vacuum on the length and breadth of the apartment. Jif had even given him a hand.

He passed Charlie's room. Charlie's glorious room. The door had Apartment Manager embossed on a white plastic plaque. And beneath that, a torn piece of lined paper with scrawled blue ink that read Charlie. The door was a sliding one; with runners. Jif pulled it open sideways with a rattle. It was about nine meters by nine meters and three meters high. His bed was made up, ready for use, but it never would be. Tucked in the left corner, it felt claustrophobic.

He gazed up. There was a rough broken hole through the ceiling. It led to Naomi's room, which was directly above Charlie's.

The hole was covered from the floor above with a plank of wood. Charlie had said, and Jif had seen, that they would communicate between rooms that way; and Charlie would pop his head into Naomi's room for a chat or a question. Charlie would often do it at the worst time, like when Naomi was getting dressed or had a "boy" over. One time he climbed through the hole in his pajamas, and the pants got caught on the splint of the hole and pulled them down, showing his genitals.

Every time, Charlie would get a broken nose and a day of name-calling. *Damn it, Charlie.* It pissed Jif off, but he wanted something else to remember Charlie by. On the right was a secondhand light brown school desk, masked in black-and-blue pen ink graphite. It was littered with books on computer science, programming, system networks, and brochures on MIT.

His closet was shut, but hanging on its door was a dark green bundle of washing. It was an old RUC uniform, from his grandfather. The red emblem of a harp on the peaked hat was glinting in the dull light.

He had used it previously as a TV extra. Jif remembered seeing Charlie wear it one time and hearing him do Irish accents. "Can I git 'ure a rose?" The memory brought a dry smile to his face.

He moved on. Approaching the stairs, he carefully stood on the far corners of each step next to the skirting board, or the wall, so as to make less noise; the centre of the steps would be most in use and would make more noise.

Approaching the second floor, the light suddenly disappeared from the window on the landing.

He stepped slowly, knowing that Naomi's room would be on the first left. He thought about her, her anger, giving Charlie a smack or punch and calling him a Peeping Tom. The very thought drove Jif's brow down in anger.

On the bright yellowy sliding door were two white wooden name boards, held on by brass screws. The top one was in English: NAOMI, in blue capitals. The one below was black, in Hebrew:

$$\text{נעמי}$$

He knew her name, Naomi, came from the Book of Ruth; she was the mother-in-law of Rut, or Ruth. Even then, he could think of nothing nice and no reason to stop now.

He gripped the handle and heaved it to the right. The door rattled on its rollers, loud enough to wake anyone. The light in the room was on. A female figure was bent over a chest of drawers. He could see the head; she was looking down. Her hourglass figure looked pretty above her tight Republic jeans and the blue bra she was wearing. Jif aimed the gun and squeezed the trigger.

Kpow!

There was no flash! Just a deafening bang and a tiny puff of smoke that lasted a second.

The girl's back didn't explode, more like collapsed inwards. A patch of skin on her right side, just above the hip, and no more bigger than a fist, simply disappeared into a black hole.

"AH!" came a quick gasp in a high-pitched voice. The girl stood up straight, and the wound began to bleed. The red blood leaked over the blue jeans. It was then Jif noticed the girl had short light brown hair. It wasn't Naomi, it was Foxy!

She smacked her right hand over the wound and put the left hand on the chest of drawers to steady herself, and she turned around. Foxy's eyes were wide, for the first time. Her mouth was pulled back, almost smiling; and she was gasping desperately, as if she couldn't breathe!

"WHAT THE FUCK ARE YOU DOIN' HERE?" screamed Jif angrily. He was pissed that he'd lost the element of surprise and gotten the target wrong. Foxy didn't respond; she was turning white.

"What's 'aptning? What's 'aptning?" came an Indian accent yelling down the corridor, accompanied by heavy footsteps. He knew who it was as he cocked the gun in front of Foxy, ejecting the empty shell on the floor with a dull ringing sound.

He leaned out of the doorway and took aim. Rajah was about two meters away and dressed in her school uniform: blue skirt, sailor-style white blouse, red bow tie. She wasn't wearing shoes. Once Jif had her in his sights, her legs stopped. She skidded along the polished wooden floor for about a foot, when Jif felt his finger pull back until his fingertip connected with the coldness of the handle.

Bam!

The corridor did nothing to minimize the sound, but he didn't feel it go to his ears. He heard a gasp of breath and a splatter of something liquid as Rajah's throat exploded on the left side. She threw both her hands up to her neck as blood oozed down onto her blouse. The room suddenly brightened up as a dull sunlight shone its way through the window behind him. Rajah slumped to the floor. He looked back at Foxy and saw she was on her ass as well. Her back was to the chest of drawers, the top one still ajar. Her eyes were closed.

He felt himself panting. Where was Naomi? If she wasn't in her room, where was she?

He heard a sound of something breaking. Something brittle. Glass? Porcelain? It came from the far right. The kitchen!

He stepped over Rajah's still body and caught his right shoe in the pool of blood emanating from her throat. He looked down at his heel as he took another step and cursed himself.

Ten paces. He reached the kitchen. A single white plate was lying in pieces on the tiled floor. It was along the plinth of the low-level cupboards. The air smelt of perfume; a girl was in here recently! He approached the cupboard door, gun ready! He knew she was inside! She had to be!

He yanked the door open. Naomi had tried to grip it shut with her fingernails but to no success. He could see she was curled up in the tight space, knees up to her head, and feet against her bum. She had on her trademark purple tights, green skirt, and blue denim jacket. She held her hands up to show she meant no harm, sucking air through the teeth of her clenched jaw.

"GET OUT!" yelled Jif, waving the gun to the right. She complied, with her eyes closed.

Exiting left foot first, she kept her hands high in the air, and her eyes closed. As she stood up tall, she looked up, opened her eyes, and dropped a tear.

"I DIDN'T KILL CHARLIE!" she cried on protest. She was using her eyes to plead with him, and it only infuriated Jif! He clenched his jaw and drew a breath.

"YOU PUSHED HIM INTO IT!" he yelled back in reply. He cocked the gun and aimed at her heart.

Bam! The blast deafened his ears, and he suddenly became aware that his heart was racing.

Naomi slammed to the floor like liquid. Her bum made a sound like a sack of potatoes being dropped from a window; her back rammed the cooker behind making a dull rattling, metallic sound. Her mouth dropped open, surprised. Her eyes half open, pupils wide, unflinching. Dead! The track of her single tear left a haunting feeling in his body.

But he wanted to end that face. He wanted to wipe it from his mind and from this world. He stood up next to her, to her left, and raised the gun to her head. Sideways, aiming inwards to her left eye socket. At point-blank range, he pulled the trigger. *Bamm!*

Her face exploded! A fine mist of blood sprayed up. Flesh flew in a circle over her body, onto his pant legs and his shoes. It looked like a flower of blood. Tiny bits of white bone shone over her body, and bits of skull stuck out like the jaws of a tiger. Only one eyeball was recognizable. And when Jif kept staring, he realized, her jaw was still there. No nose, no mouth; the front half of her skull was obliterated.

He took a breath, and his shoulders relaxed. A massive weight had been taken off his shoulders.

He was relieved. He was relieved it was all over!

But he also felt hateful and sick! His stomach began to burn, and he felt gases gurgle up his throat.

"Jesus Christ, what have I turned into?" he muttered to himself.

Just then his heart snapped into overdrive. A light tap emanated from a corridor. He spun round to the doorway and stepped forward. He was certain he could hear breathing. He eased himself on one side of the arch and saw black skin. A soft, smooth clenched hand was shaking. Just outside the edge of the doorway. Working out who it was, he reloaded the gun and stomped into the corridor.

"AH!" screamed Chelsea, throwing her shaky hands up to her head. She'd been crying, and she still was! Tears rolled down her wet red face. Her lips were pulled back, and her teeth were exposed. Her hair was loose, and her beautiful dreadlocks draped over her shoulders. Her white nightdress with its Barbie motif aroused a stirring feeling in Jif's groins, which he tried to suppress.

He pointed the gun at Chelsea and hesitated. He'd killed three people already, what did one more matter? She was a witness; she would rat him out. But he liked her. She was the only one he could relate to out of the whole residence, the only one who didn't take Charlie for granted. And with a shaky breath, and a tear in his eye, he made up his mind.

"Go home!" he screamed. Chelsea's hands stopped shaking, and her face muscles relaxed. She was surprised as well as relieved. Jif eased his trigger finger.

"Go and get help and tell the cops what happened, and everything will be all right." On the last word, he started to get a lump in his throat. Chelsea took two quick breaths and blinked several times to hide the tears in her eyes, before spinning round and racing towards the stairs. After two meters, she slipped on the shiny wooden floor; it must have been recently polished. Her white nightdress flew up, and she wasn't wearing underwear, exposing her beautifully smooth black bottom. She fell flat on her ass, making a low thudding sound, her nightdress taking almost a year to flop down to cover her up again. She swiftly pushed her arms into the floor to prop herself up, and Jif noticed the nervous shake in her hands was back; he was still pointing the gun. She took two paces before reaching the handrail of the flight then charged down the wooden stairs in a dozen loud stomps, for all her life, till her head vanished from view. The stomps continued until they became faint, accompanied by the loud metallic clunk of locks and the front door squeaking open. Jif didn't hear it slam shut.

"SHIT!" he cursed himself. "How could I have forgotten!" He'd only planned on executing Naomi, but he'd killed two other girls. And there were two other girls he'd forgotten about: Chelsea and Motoko.

He wasn't going to kill her. But she was a martial arts expert. If she heard the blasts, she would have fought like a lion. For her friends.

He didn't know which room she was in. So he checked the room next to the kitchen. Uniform draped out, Chelsea's.

He marched to the last room at the end of the passage. Open. It had a bed that hadn't been slept in. Sword and knives were nailed to the wall. It was her room, and she wasn't in. She must have left yesterday.

Jif eased himself, taking away his left hand, and lowered the gun till its barrel was an inch above the floor. He took a deep breath and felt a shudder of emotion in his body. His eyes watered, and tears streamed down his face. But unlike all the times before, he didn't blubber. He could feel a smile playing on his lips, but he tried to suppress it; he didn't want to be happy. He knew what had happened just now was wrong, and he was going to hell for it.

He had not done it for himself; he did it for Charlie. Now that Naomi was dead, she couldn't hurt anyone else anymore. But then, if Jif would die or go to prison, Yuzuyu would be hurt. He knew that! But he believed she was gone.

The fire exit! The fire exit to his office was on the floor above! Why didn't he think of it before? It could only be opened from the inside, but anything can be broken into. Gripping the shotgun handle, he stepped over the corpses and paced along the corridor. At the stairs, he suddenly felt dread. He didn't have to do this! He could have had a chance! He shuffled up the stairs, feeling his face burn up with anxiety. Approaching the next floor, he could see the window. The sky was cloudy. And a rag waved its way in front of the window. It was the union Rock from next door.

Jif raised the gun, barrel level with his head, ready to break the glass as he approached the door. Even in the dull light, the industrial rectangular sign, Fire Exit, Keep Shut, still shone like a star.

He was about to whack his gun, when he saw something he never saw before. A push handle. There was a horizontal push bar of metal along the width of the door, just below the glass. But that was illogical and insecure. It was supposed to be opened on one side. Even so, Jif felt compelled to try this new thing. It would work, wouldn't it? He had nothing to lose, except shards of broken glass on the floor.

He lowered the Winchester yet again and put his left hand on the push bar. Stiff. Quite resistant. Straightening out his arm, he thrust his whole body down, and the lock on the bar gave way. The door slowly creaked inward to the right.

There was light inside. Brilliant white light. And voices. Was someone in there? And why hadn't he seen this light through the window?

"What's going on?" he yelled. His eyes dried up, and the dread and sadness were replaced by curiosity and anger. Who was doing this?

The light spilled out onto the floor next to Jif's foot, and all of a sudden, he felt hot. His skin was getting brighter. He was illuminating! The door swung open fully, and the white light engulfed him. He threw his arms across his face to shield his eyes, and he felt the gun go from his hand. His shirt felt wet, and he started sweating. His stomach told him he needed the toilet, and he fought to control his bowels. But even with his eyes shut, all he could see was white!

Then black.

TEN

Shafts of white pierced the blackness. He was facing flat surface. Dark. It had something white in the middle.

It started to move. Outwards. He saw was looking at a door. Not the fire exit door, another one he didn't see before. Black door, wooden. The door opened outwards. Grey sky flooded in. And red carpet. It was the roof garden!

He felt himself move forward. He could hear a party was going on.

"WHAT IS THIS?" screamed Jif. There was a dozen people in this space, and no one noticed him.

His vision started to move sideways. He could work out why. Jif realized he was not in control of his body. Was he having an out-of-body experience?

Then he recognized it. He saw Mayor Transit Van gossiping to a blonde. This was the party where Charlie was shot! But it felt real, not dreamy. Then, he saw himself. He was patting Charlie by the fruit bowl. "Try an orange," he heard himself say. He turned away with a smile, the jacket of his tuxedo waving about.

What the fuck are you doing! he heard himself think. This was a flashback or a reconstruction of what happened, and he knew there was nothing he could do, but his brain was showing it, a play of mistakes that were made so that Jif could learn from it. He had these things before, but he never thought he'd see Charlie die again; he didn't want to see him die. *Don't let him die! Don't let him die!*

He was seeing himself come towards the stereo system. "Let's put some feeder on." Jif's vision took a step back, to where the stereo was set up, just where a man in sunglasses and black suit was standing. There was a small bulge in the side of his pants. Jif's vision scanned around this new man and saw his face!

"SHIT!" he screamed. It was Rock!

Rock spun round, gun in hand. Jif saw himself frown. He didn't turn and run. He didn't scream. He just closed his eyes and bowed his head, resigning to death. *Fight him! Fight him!*

Rock cocked the gun and eased the trigger. Then he could hear someone's heavy footsteps. Jif's vision scanned left. Charlie.

No, Don't do it!

Charlie leapt into the air, arms out, mouth open.

There was no flash from Rock's gun. Just a sudden appearance of a bullet.

Everything went into slow motion. As Charlie's head came level with Jif's left shoulder, Charlie's left temple exploded. His glasses flew off and shattered to bits in the air. Globules of red blood flew towards Jif. Charlie's eyes were now shut.

Back to real-time motion again. Charlie's limp body slammed into the floor. Dead! Jif's vision went over to the body. An aerial view. The blood in the boy's head was unbearable to look at.

No! No! Not again!

He saw himself come into view. Everything like before: he checked the pulse and pushed on the chest. He could the guests crowding around him. Yuzuyu ran up to him and clenched his arm. The flat head of Foxy appeared, and she just gawped around. Jif held the body, unable to do anything. Just like before. It was torture witnessing this event again. The feeling of helplessness. The self-hatred. Loss.

"Help me," he heard himself say.

He saw himself collapse over Charlie's body, his head nestled under Charlie's chin. Then, the unthinkable.

Charlie's right eye opened.

It wasn't blown out; it was masked in blood.

"You're alive!"

Jif's vision started to pull back, like he was on a rope.

"No, wait."

He saw Charlie's right arm bend up, hugging what was on his chest. He saw Charlie's breath hang in the air. Then everything started to go white again.

"CHARLIE!"

ELEVEN

May 18, 2006, 0901 EST

The white cogs started spinning again. The brain did its thing, and Jif opened his eyes, dreading what he would see. He felt himself lying down, on a warm bed, facing a white ceiling. His back was warm, but his body was cold; he felt naked. He was lying on top of bedsheets! Was he in prison? Before he could react, something rustled to his right and touched his shoulder.

He gasped, and his heart pumped all its blood into his arms and legs. He threw his body forward and stumbled off the bed, turning round. It was only then that he realized he was back in his bedroom. The Bratz duvet, the cupboards, the vanity, the carpet. Sitting up on the bed in front of him was Yuzuyu. She was only wearing a diaper and a bewildered, almost tearful face.

"What's wrong, Jif?" she said in an unstable tone. Her blonde hair had waved in front of her face and seemed stuck to her cheeks. There were tracks of dried liquid on her cheek that shone in the daylight where her hair was stuck. She'd been crying.

Jif looked down and confirmed what he knew; he was stark naked.

"Did I do this?" he said, looking down at his penis. It was hanging limp, partially obscured by a mountain of curly hair between his legs. He finally looked up. "I shouldn't be naked in front of you!" He panted twice, waiting for her to say something, when he realized, if she was here in the bedroom, Lime.Inc was still here.

"What happened? I thought you'd all gone!" He felt his throat wobbled. Yuzuyu sat where she was and began to crush up her face in sadness.

"I'd never leave you, Jif!" she shrieked. Her eyes narrowed, and her teeth exposed as if to break into a sob. She thrust herself forward and leapt off the bed towards Jif. Head down, she threw her arms around his waist. "I LOVE YOU, JIF!" she whined, her head in his chest. She looked up to make eye contact. Her pupils almost showing stars. "Why you say that?"

"I had a—"

"I need you to be with me!" Yuzuyu interrupted. "To change my diaper! Don't you know how many men would do housework? Tolerate smells? No man ever changes diapers! I want you always to clean me!"

128

He panted, a tear forming in his eye, from happiness. He felt relived that the love was still there, that he had his purpose.

"Is Charlie dead?"

"Yes, Jif. Charlie is dead."

The sadness came back.

"What's wrong? We went to the funeral office yesterday, remember?"

"No. His dad told me to piss off."

"What? He didn't!"

"Then . . . what happened yesterday? Hang about, I didn't see you at all?"

"I went to school, remember?"

"No."

"But I didn't want to stay for lunch, so you picked me up, and you and Vin and Charlie's dad had to go the funeral home to make all the arrangements."

"I didn't remember a thing," Jif stated. He felt his knees shaking, like a little boy after being told off by a teacher. "I woke up, got a phone call, then Vin brought me over to the embassy to tell me I was fired and . . ."

"And what, Jif?"

"I shot Naomi!"

"You . . . ," Yuzuyu exclaimed. He breathed deeply and pulled a reassuring face. "Jif, you're not a bad man."

"I know, but . . . I hated her so much. She's alive, ain't she?"

"Yes, she is. She was here yesterday. Let's go . . ."

"I heard a shout, and when I got back, the building was shut. Everyone was gone! It was like I'd been forced out, and there was nothing I could do. But . . ."

"Let's go, get dressed. You can change my diaper for me."

"You . . . diaper. Oh, man, I haven't done that since . . . how long has it been?"

"Since what?"

"Since Charlie got shot?"

"It's been a week, Jif."

"A WEEK! I don't remember a thing."

"Vin's been helping you. And Naomi."

"Man, what's wrong with me?"

"Tell me all about if, Jif," coaxed Yuzuyu. "You've listened to me, now I'll listen to you." She led him to the bathroom, where a plastic baby-changing mat was laid out.

"The diapers are over there," she said, pointing to a stack of pink girl's diapers. She sat on the mat and laid herself down, propping her legs up.

"Yuzuyu," greeted Jif with a smile as he knelt down at her feet, "everything about you is wonderful."

"Oh, Jif," sighed Yuzuyu. He unfastened her diaper and opened it up. A stink of shit filled the room.

"This is a big one," exclaimed Jif.

"Yes, it is," she replied.

"I love wiping your ass, Yuzuyu. I love looking at your pussy. I learnt new things about it every day."

"I know you do. I know you haven't abused me, Jif. You got nothing to feel sorry about. We haven't had sex. You haven't touched me anywhere I don't like." She let out a sigh as he pulled the diaper away. "I love you."

"Thank you, Yuzuyu."

He put the soiled diaper in the trash and pulled the new one out. Placing her bottom on the new diaper, visions of Charlie came back. The body, the open eyes, the hug.

"In my dream last night . . . it was as if Charlie was still alive."

"I know. I think of him too."

"How can I dream a whole day? A whole week?"

"He was a good friend. I loved him too. You and he were so happy together."

"Did Charlie really die?"

"You think he didn't?"

"I could have sworn . . . it was so real! I blew that girl's face off! The blood, the smoke. I could smell the iron in her blood. I could even smell the cordite!"

"Jif, don't say that! It'll upset Naomi, and she won't let you go to his funeral today."

"Today?"

"You forgot?"

"I didn't know!"

Fully changed, Yuzuyu led Jif back into the bedroom. Jif's funeral suit had already been laid out for him, draped up on the back of the chair next to Yuzuyu's vanity. He dressed hastily and struggled with his tie.

"Uh . . . d'ya need a hand, love?" he said to Yuzuyu as she fastened a long black skirt to her waist. She looked up and pulled small smile.

"No, thank you, Jif. I'm OK this time." Her voice sounded so sweet.

The couple walked hand in hand to the elevator, where Iffy was still.

"Hello," Jif said to him. Iffy made no reply. They rode down the elevator to the ground floor, where Shiffs and Mitzvah were sitting at their desks, looking bored and tired.

"Jif," began Mitzvah, "can we please have the day off?"

"Uh . . ." Jif struggled as he exited the elevator. "You gonna have to bear with me. I got a little amnesia."

"How come?" asked Shiffs. Jif approached the desk.

"Did we talk yesterday?" Mitzvah looked up, with a dirty look.

"Of course we did!" she replied through her veil, her eyes narrowed as if insulted. She must have thought it was a dumb question, an insult to her intelligence.

"'Coz I can't remember sorting this funeral!" said Jif.

"It is a bit quick!" yawned Shiffs.

"What is?"

"A week. From death to funeral." Jif sighed and thought. He recalled his dream. Naomi said it had been a week!

"If, uh . . ." He struggled again. "If I'm gone and all of Lime.Inc is at this funeral, then really, the company isn't really working today!" Jif said out loud. "So did Vin tell you to say?"

"Well," sighed Mitzvah, "we weren't invited, so we thought we should go back to work." Jif sighed again.

"Since you ask nicely, have the day off, all of you!"

"Cheers, Jif," Shiffs said as he scraped his chair behind him to stand up. Mitzvah followed suit, and Jif turned around to leave. Down the grey footpath, Jif suddenly felt like a king. And completely forgot that Iffy was not with him.

TWELVE

May 18, 2006, 0911 EST

"Is this the car?" asked Jif as a black Mercedes E-Class sedan with tinted windows pulled up.

"Yes. This is the car," replied Yuzuyu. "Vin paid for it."

"Hello, Mr. Kitchen," called a Latino voice. The driver got out. A thirty-year-old Mexican with stubble. He smelt of grease; maybe he did nights in Vin's kitchen. He offered his hand.

"Antonio Vancu. Private car hire."

Jif gave the man his hand.

"Do you know where to go?" asked Jif.

"I have location but not route." He started pointing in both directions as he spoke. "We can go this way or that way."

"Can we . . . ," Jif stuttered, "can we stop somewhere before?"

"Where to?"

"MIT."

"Right now?"

"Just for five minutes. I haven't been there and—"

He hesitated. He was about to say Charlie and cut himself off before he made himself upset.

"Look, just do it. I'll pay you extra." The Mexican brightened up, raising his bushy eyebrows.

"Real money?"

"Yea."

"OK. MIT it is."

The Mexican spun round and pulled open the rear passenger door. Jif stood to the side and avoided eye contact as he released Yuzuyu and gestured his palm into the car's interior.

"Arigato," squeaked Yuzuyu as she climbed in. Sidestepping on the floor to the right side of the seat, her diaper rustled as she sat herself down on the black leather seat. Jif followed suit and plopped down onto the seat before slamming the door shut behind him.

132

He twisted his back trying to find the seat belt before Yuzuyu leaned on him, thrusting her arm behind his neck, and pulled the buckle from the tiny slot in the pillar of the car. She offered the belt, waving it at his chest, as he gently took it from her dainty fingers. He thrust the buckle into the catch by his left hip, and Yuzuyu placed her hand in his. She felt warm.

He looked up at her. She was smiling. He loved her smile. He never took her for granted! Never! He knew, especially from his dream, that she could disappear at any time. But he knew he mustn't be possessive of her. He didn't want to be like any of those men he'd read about. The pedophiles! Rapists! Terrorists!

"I love you, sweetie!" he croaked, beginning to cry. Yuzuyu drew her hands to his shoulders to support him as he leaned into her.

"Shhh," she hissed as he spluttered a few tears on her shoulder. He would never be amazed at how strong she was. "In o wa," she said, meaning "It's all right!"

"I'm sorry," he apologized as he pushed himself off her to dry his eyes. "I just . . . I'm so messed up."

"I'm sorry about your friend," called the Mexican, who had gotten into the driver's seat. "Personally I hate wakes. They remind me of my mother." Jif sniffed and batted his eyes again.

"Best not to think about it, mate. Anyhow, you appear older than me. You should be a bit more used to it."

The Mexican didn't reply. He put the car in gear and joined the traffic.

The Mercedes drove along Federal Street and turned left onto Franklin Street, heading towards the downtown crossing. He turned left again and trundled along the massive grey building then made left and immediately turned right, passing the Hyatt Regency.

Chauncey Street had a lot of Chinese-looking people today; after all, this was Chinatown. One stocky chainman leaning against a battered old van stood to attention and doffed his red baseball cap. Maybe he thought an official was driving through. The smell of Chinese food was seeping in and making Jif feel hungry.

"I'm sorry we had to go through here, Yuzuyu," Jif said.

"It's for Charlie, isn't it?" she asked. Jif didn't have time to respond. "Why did it have to be MIT?"

The car suddenly made a sharp right as it emerged into Essex Street. Jif had to lean against Yuzuyu for support.

"Sorry, homes," apologized the driver. "There's a DUCK coming up the street. Trust me, you don't want to be stuck behind that today." Jif knew what he was on about. DUKW was a military amphibious vehicle from World War II. But in Boston, it was a great tourist attraction, driving on roads and in water. He turned his head to spot the green "truck" trundling behind at a distance.

Up Charles Street, it was quite busy. Cars, buses, and trucks were grinding to halt in a gridlock. A new-style yellow VW Beetle was in front of them. The driver wound down his window and poked his head out, to look at Boston Common. Jif didn't want to look; he knew what was there.

"Yuzuyu," he began, staring into the back of the front passenger seat, "you're the purpose of my life." The car suddenly felt as though the oxygen had been sucked out. His heart felt like lead.

"Jif, I feel . . ."

"I love you!" he spluttered, gasping a breath. "And Charlie had a love. His first love." He sat up straight and turned to face Yuzuyu. She shuffled close, rustling her diaper. Their legs connected. He drew his arm over her shoulders as she hugged his chest. "He and this girl made a promise that they'd meet again at MIT and get married."

"But they didn't," she stated, looking right into his eyes. "How could he be certain she was still there?"

"He couldn't, but what did he have to lose?"

They were already halfway down Beacon Street when Jif noticed. He looked across the Charles River and saw the Longfellow Bridge behind him, shrinking as they drove away.

"I offered to help him get into MIT," he explained, gazing out of the window.

"I know," replied an annoyed Yuzuyu. "I was there, remember?" He turned back to face her again.

"But I also tried to find her, the girl."

"The . . . did you find her?"

"Yes."

And as he told her who "the girl with the strawberry panties" was, the car turned right and started crossing the Harvard Bridge, almost free of traffic. The gleaming white dome of the MIT building was in sight beyond the row of trees in the riverbank.

"Jif, you've got to stop tearing yourself apart like this!" cussed Yuzuyu, shaking Jif's hand in her grasp. The car hit a bump, thrusting Jif up, then down again, sending his intestines into orbit. Yuzuyu was unfazed. "I love you too, Jif, and it really hurts me to see you work your heart and soul for things where you don't get rewarded or appreciated."

A university canoe punted its way under the bridge as the Merc left the bridge and entered Cambridge, greeted by the four-lane highway. The car turned left onto the inside lane of Memorial Drive, at a moderate speed, where the driver started looking around.

"Uh . . ." He struggled. "There's MIT," he said, pointing his right hand diagonally at his window. "But I don't know how to get in. I think we . . . got to go long way round." He returned his right hand to the steering wheel and gestured a circle with his left hand.

"You mean a U-turn?" asked Jif.

"Uh . . . yea," replied the Latino. Killian Court was right outside Jif's window. He pondered what to do. Time was running out to get back to the funeral. There was no way the driver would risk cutting across four lanes of traffic. The two lanes were about to merge as the Charles River Reservation grew out of the ground. A flat patch of earth with tired-looking grass and a few streetlights.

"Pull up onto the reservation, mate!" called out Jif quickly.

"Uh, are you sure?" questioned the driver reluctantly. He cocked his head a little.

"Just do it, mate! I'll pay for any damages you get!" The driver raised his eyebrows as if saying hello to extra money.

"All right," he replied as upbeat as possible. He switched on his emergency turn signals and steered toward the reservation. The car lurched forward over the curve and narrowly avoided a streetlight before turning slightly to make a straight line. He put the Merc out of gear and pulled up the emergency brake.

"You better be quick," the Latino said, turning his head.

"So as I can," replied Jif. He pulled the pick handle, and the door clunked open. He shuffled out of the car, Yuzuyu following him rather than opening her door. Closing the door, Jif tapped the glass.

"Five minutes, tops," he called. The driver nodded, the engine still rumbling. Jif prayed that this guy didn't drive off without him.

Jif walked around the car, Yuzuyu by his side, pacing up to the westbound lane. Cars were roaring past this morning, and the metallic clouds made him feel as though lead was going to fall from the sky and smack him.

"Jif, can you pick me up?" begged Yuzuyu. Jif didn't even pause. He smiled and scooped up the short girl into his arms. She hugged his left hip, placed a leg on his back and stomach. The road went quiet, and Jif dashed across to get to the other reservation.

"You feel so warm today," Jif said to her in joy.

"I know," she replied. There was another break in the traffic, and they made it across to the sidewalk.

"Well, this is what we tried to fight for," said Jif as they entered Killian Court. From the air it looked weird. Like LED display of a nine, on the right, and its mirror image on the left, connected by a huge dome at the end. The building blocks were white and about two stories high.

Jif set down Yuzuyu and slowly walked along the mass of green that was the size of a football pitch. Crossing a concrete footpath, the grass felt crisp under his feet. There was a flagpole either side of them and twenty trees, though in the Boston coldness, they appeared quite naked and dead without their leaves. It felt dead without Charlie here.

Jif stopped walking, about two hundred yards short of the giant white dome.

"I wanna stop for a minute, Yuzuyu," he said, looking down without facing her.

"OK," she complied. Jif felt cold and shivered. He could go into the building, not now. He thought he could, but not now. He closed his eyes and thought about that night. The night before the party. The shooting. The chance he had to tell Charlie the truth.

May 8, 2006, 2048 EST

"Fuck!" Jif cursed himself. "Fuck!" He was staring into the A4 sheet of paper, held in his right hand, shaking slightly. The large brown envelope which it came in lay facedown at his desk, with an ugly torn opening at the end where Jif had done what he had to.

"I've been workin' for this blood-e thin'! All day and all night!" He threw the letter onto the desk in frustration, causing it to float and slide across his desk. Even though the problem was not his own, he still felt responsible. And on company time, he was putting himself at a big risk.

"JIF!" called Charlie from behind the fire exit door. He put his head against the glass before tapping the wood, making a hollow noise. He looked the same as ever: insecure, dishevelled, geeky. The wire in the glass made him look like a prisoner.

"Come in, mate," Jif said, before walking his chair over the door and pushing down the bar. Charlie pulled it open and stepped into the office. He had a green T-shirt and cream shorts that day, even though it was still quite cool.

"Office blues?" asked Charlie. Jif caught on but quickly spun the chair round to pick up the paper and hide it in an open drawer under the desk.

"No more than you, mate!" he replied, failing eye contact. He realised his mistake and pulled a smile as he reached the opened bottle of vodka.

"Russky drink?" Jif scoffed, mimicking a Russian accent. He held the bottle to his face like a trophy.

"No, thanks," replied Charlie. "You wanted to see me—about work." Jif frowned and put the bottle down and waved his hand at the empty office chair in front of him. Charlie quickly slumped down.

"Several things, Charlie." Before he could say any more, Charlie cut him off.

"Jif, you really have made it so much better!" Jif looked up and gulped. He was touched. "All these jobs . . . no one has ever . . . cared as much . . . shown as much interest as you have!" Charlie was also avoiding eye contact, thinking up words. It was his way of saying thank you.

"You're welcome," replied Jif.

"But has . . ." Charlie hesitated. "Have you found out anything? About my strawberry girl?" Jif looked straight into Charlie's face and drew a breath.

"I have a hunch, but I'd keep that to myself for the moment."

"What? Why? You've never held anything back before!"

"I'd rather you paid off ya debts before you hear the information." Jif started feeling sick. Why did he have to say it? Why couldn't he have kept it to himself and tell Charlie to fuck off?

"But . . . this could be . . ."

"It ain't Naomi!" stated Jif. "And that I'm proud to say! But even though I hate her, you don't! I know you love her."

"If it's not Naomi, why are you telling me this?"

"You've come all this way, to get into MIT, just to find this dream girl. You got bills for the apartments to pay. And an exam to do. If I drop this bombshell now, I'm certain that you'll drop everything and give up 'coz you won't like the results."

"Who is she?"

"Just do this one job, and I'll tell you!"

"I've got . . ."

"Ten grand!" Charlie's jaw dropped.

"Lump sum, for one day's work."

"It's the party tomorrow, isn't it."

"Yep. And I want you as my bodyguard."

"What, but you got Iffy!"

"I know. And he sucks. Look, just do this. Vin won't give a toss. All you have to do is follow me around, and you'll be home free."

"Say no more. I'll do it."

And that was it. His fate was sealed.

May 18, 2006, 0942 EST

Jif opened his eyes and looked at the dome again. He was getting sick of it. He sighed and started explaining to Yuzuyu.

"I never told Charlie about his girl," he said to her.

"Would it make any difference?"

"Yes, it would. He would have dropped everything. And . . . he would have gone off with Naomi, and I didn't want that. 'Coz I knew that even though she was a bitch, he loved her, from the attention, even if it was slaps and punches. And she loved him 'coz he kept coming back."

"But why? How could this girl make him . . ."

"They wouldn't be compatible! That simple! Think you and me but even more controversial. Sounds snobbish, doesn't it? But it is that fact. And . . . he only wanted to do this . . . go to MIT to find her. I thought he'd throw his degree away."

"You loved him, didn't you?"

"Yes, I did."

"He loved you too."

"Thank you."

"That's the thing about you, Jif, you're so nice. Too nice! I didn't stay 'coz there's no one else. I knew you'd be a good person! And I knew you'd be a good dad."

"Yuzuyu . . ."

"You're not unhealthy! You're not fat! I know you'll give me wonderful children. I just wanna be a mommy. So please, Jif, let him go. I know he was the son you never had, but you can have your son with me."

He picked her up.

"Yuzuyu, you know there are too many boys in this world. I want you to have a daughter."

"Oh, Jif. Stop it, you're making me drool."

"Mate! You see, you can make me smile! Now, you had enough?"

"Let's see this board."

"Board?"

"The notice board, like they used in *Good Will Hunting*." Jif knew what she was on about. *Good Will Hunting* by Matt Damon and Ben Affleck. A thug cleaner in MIT with a superior mind. In the film, he solved an equation on a notice board.

"Nah, Yuzuyu. They filmed that bit in Vancouver."

"Vancouver?"

"Yea. It was cheaper over there." Jif wanted to go inside the university as much as she did, but he knew time was short. And he didn't know the first thing about the layout of MIT, despite having tried to get Charlie in there for over a year.

Jif felt more eager to leave when Yuzuyu turned her head. A car engine was rumbling quite close. Jif did as his wife did and saw an MIT police car creeping up to him along the grass. It was an old-style white Chevy Caprice with a red light bar on top and MIT police in black along the doors. A fifty-year-old bald cop in a standard blue uniform behind the wheel wound down his window.

"What cha doin', sir?" he asked. His voice was husky, and his throat wobbled as he spoke. Jif thrust Yuzuyu up again and repositioned his arm under her bum.

"Just admiring the court," replied Jif.

"You a student?"

"No."

"Are you, little lady?"

Yuzuyu shook her head at the cop.

"Then I'm gonna have to ask you to leave!" ordered the cop as a low electric whine drowned out the end of his sentence.

"Leev 'em illeee!" mumbled the cripple as he rolled up alongside the car. His name was Shaz, and he'd been at MIT for four years and was Jif's inside man for info on the course Charlie was after.

"Do you know them?" asked the cop.

"Air with me!" replied Shaz.

"OK," deflated the cop, and he accelerated away in a circle. Shaz pushed a closed fist against the joystick on his electric wheelchair. He drove towards Jif and swerved slightly to come alongside him.

"Shaz," introduced Jif, "I don't think you met, Yuzuyu."

"Na . . . no," struggled the Arab cripple. He had black jeans, green sneakers, and an MIT T-shirt under his Sundance jacket. "Ah 'eard wa . . . ya friend ot it!" Jif frowned and nodded.

"Yea, he did," answered Jif. He looked up again. "I never actually been here. I just thought it was appropriate. For him."

"You a student?" asked Yuzuyu.

"Yea . . . buuuut . . . I gone get scholarship. I be professor!"

"Here?" she asked, pointing at the ground. Shaz nodded.

"Sorry to interrupt," cut in Jif. "But . . . do you have any wisdom to share?" Shaz shook his head. "To be honest . . . I've been . . . flat out of ideas lately."

"Can't help you!" answered Shaz. "You figure out for yourself!"

Silence. Jif bowed his head in sadness as Yuzuyu dragged a hand over his cheek in comfort. He thought about how he'd made her comfortable as well, at the island.

In the rescue chopper, Jif would learn a little more about what happened in that building. Atlas had given him a Japanese translating book, and he tried to connect her words the words in the book and connected what little Japanese he knew of by heart with English-sounding words to make sense of what Yuzuyu was saying. Today, he could remember exactly what she said in her native tongue that night; only the translation that he found.

"They took us to a giant building," she said, crying. She continued to mumble her story in between yelps of crying as Jif did his best to comfort her, stroking her hand and hugging her. He'd learned that Yuzuyu and Keitaro were separated after being taken up in the elevator and that a man wanted to speak with her, to the annoyance of Rock. She was taken into the room on the fortieth floor, the room Jif had crashed through in the power cut, and she had come face-to-face with a man she did know.

"It was my daddy!" she cried to Jif. "It was my daddy!"

"Did he say anything?" asked Jif. Yuzuyu nodded.

"He said he was glad to see me again and that I . . ." She struggled to say anything. "I wasn't human. HE TOLD ME THAT I WASN'T HUMAN!" She wept a little more as Jif stroked her shoulder. One of the guys in the chopper offered a bottle of water, and Jif gave it to Yuzuyu who took a long swig. "He said he was going to take away my emotions and that I would be part of a computer system they were making!"

The whole thing was an experiment! Not just to control the island but to use a WMD. A weapon of mass destruction. That was the point of the microchips in her head. Everything was far-fetched, but they'd tried! By connecting a human to the communication link, the Internet, millions of calculation would be done faster than any computer. She'd be able to hack into top secret systems and control defense systems. Missiles!

After that, she wept uncontrollably! Much later, she said that Keitaro had managed to break through and was trying to lead her out through an airshaft when Rock appeared again. He argued with Yuzuyu's father then ordered the kids into another room at gunpoint before shooting Keitaro. Jif realized he'd arrived a few seconds late, or he would have been able to save Keitaro as well.

What a fucked-up day!

May 18, 2006, 1040 EST

The car trip back was unremarkable. Except for the huge traffic jam at Boston Common. They had somehow ended up on Charles Street, sandwiched between the common and the public garden. Why it was busy, Jif didn't know.

"It's terrible," exclaimed the Latino driver as they pulled behind a blue Chevy Cavalier in a solid line of cars. It looked nothing like the Cavaliers Jif was used to in Hull. "It's one more traffic jam every day!" complained the driver, shaking his head. "Gets worse every day!"

Jif was gazing out of the window, looking across Boston Common. A mass of carefully manicured lawn and pathways, the white bandstand in the centre. He could see the top of Park Street Church in the distance. Its giant white spire scraping the sky as if it was trying to touch God. He could get to it from here. Maybe walking would be quicker than this jam.

"We'll walk," stated Jif, leaning forward till his head was next to the driver's headrest. The Latino turned his head, a little surprised.

"Are you sure?" he asked.

"You really want to?" asked Yuzuyu, placing a soft hand on Jif's arm. Jif wanted to answer her, but he had to finish his talk with the driver, out of respect for his work today. He gave Yuzuyu a smile and tapped her hand before turning the driver again.

"Don't worry," reassured Jif. "I'll tell Vincent that you did your job, and there were no problems!" He knew the guy was bothered about his orders being broken. But the guy resigned to it.

"OK," he said in resignation. Yuzuyu was shuffling to the door while Jif riffled through his pockets. He found his paper. A lot of it; he wouldn't have much use for it the rest of the day.

"A hundred-dollar tip?" asked Jif, offering the bundle of bills in his clasp over the driver's shoulder. The Latino smiled.

"Oh, no no no," he replied, almost laughing. "You no give me that much. I get paid today anyway!"

"Look, just take it, man!" Jif went of, a little angry. "Use it to better your family!" He took a breath. "Raise your son to be better than me!" The driver raised his eyebrows, surprised, almost thanking him.

"OK," he replied, deflated, encasing the money in his palms around Jif's as the English guy raised his grip on the cash. Jif sighed and shuffled along with Yuzuyu. He pulled the pick handle, and the door clunked. She swung it open and stood out. Jif followed.

They stood out in the chilly air, and straightaway Jif had to thrust his hands into his pant pockets. The sidewalk was unusually empty, yet the blasts from car horns were continuous.

"Yuzuyu, could you shut the door?" asked Jif as he sidestepped to the front passenger side. Yuzuyu nodded and complied, pushing the door back with a *shlok*. Jif bent over a little to level his head with the car window, to see the driver. He tapped the glass with his knuckle.

"Cheers, mate!" he called out. The driver gave a thumbs-up. Jif stood up again and rejoined Yuzuyu at the back of the Merc. "We gotta cross here," he said to her, threading a hand into her own. She gently wrapped her fingers around his palm. There was no need to wait, or look, because the traffic had stopped on both sides, although Jif knew a motorcycle could come shrieking down the middle at the worst possible time.

They walked as one, waltzing around the Mercedes and old blue Buick in the other lane while constantly looking around in case a dumb driver should come down the middle. They got to the other sidewalk and started their trek into the common.

"Boston Common is enormous," exclaimed Yuzuyu as they pressed on along the grass. "Feels like Central Park."

"Yes, it does," replied Jif, with a smile. Jif loved this sort of talk with Yuzuyu. It was sometimes stupid, stating the obvious. But it made him appreciate the beauty of thing, the beauty of life. She made things bright and pleasing because that was the sort of person she was. Being with her gave him something to live for.

They were about an eighth of the way into the common when they got onto a wide footpath, partially covered with dead leaves from the branches hovering over them. By now the sound of the traffic had died behind them. There was no one else around, except for a cycler heading the opposite way.

Orange mountain bike. The dude had no helmet and had blue jeans and a grey T-shirt, even in this cold weather. Jif didn't dare look at him as he passed by.

It was enchanting in daylight, even in winter. But to a person who's already edgy and sluggish and overstuffed, it's a different story. The wind began to die down, and it was quieter; quiet enough for Jif to hear a branch crack behind him. He spun round. Did he really hear it? For Jif, it was hard enough to hear anything with the pounding torrent of panic in his ears. Yes, someone was there! He could feel the presence, even without seeing him, or her.

"What is it, Jif?" asked Yuzuyu.

"Nothing," replied Jif in resignation.

He kept on walking, and a sudden breeze caught some of Jif's exposed skin, sending a wicked shiver underneath his suit. He knew the follower could be anywhere. And he felt the park close in on him, while also feeling naked and exposed.

He stuck his head down in his chest and walked faster, trying to blow some of his exhaled air under his shirt to warm himself up. He listened hard and concentrated so much, he almost knocked his head with happy couple coming towards him.

"Careful, Jif," exclaimed Yuzuyu. The man and woman were in their thirties and wearing light-coloured fleeces and beanie hats. Jif made an abrupt stop and insecurely stepped out of their way. He watched as they passed by. They were arm in arm, smiling and pushing together for the warmth. Seeing them made Jif think about his wife, and Charlie. Even with Yuzuyu by his side, he felt even more cold and alone. And angry!

He paced another three steps when a voice came out of nowhere. "You couldn't win an egg-and-spoon race!" he said. Jif knew the statement was aimed at him. Jif stopped and could walk no more at all. He couldn't see Yuzuyu behind him. He knew not to move his head. He kept still and gazed with his eyes, trying to see any movement ahead of him. Nothing, so it must be behind him.

"Jif," asked Yuzuyu, "what's going on? I don't like this." He knew how she felt. But why couldn't she use some of that strength that she had? He wanted to run. What if the other guy had a gun? Instead, he spun round.

Nothing! No one was behind him! He tried to swallow, but the cold air had robbed his throat of all moisture.

Then he saw him.

At least his outline. In the shadows of the trees. Bulky, solid, dark clothes. His head looked flat, maybe be he was wearing a hat. A peaked hat.

"Where do I know you?" called out Jif. The voice was slightly familiar. Dark and powerful. The figure moved forward out of the dark, and at last Jif recognized the clothes. It was the army officer from the interrogation. Exactly the same, his every step showing power and pride.

Jif was still considering running away but was locked like a statue. He wanted to know what was going on. He drew a breath as the black man finally stepped onto the path. But before Jif could say anything, the man spoke.

"Where is your RV?" he said without emotion. Jif didn't respond. He didn't know what the word meant.

"What do you mean RV?" questioned Yuzuyu.

"It's the hospital, isn't it?" went the black. He drew a breath and leaned back, rolling his eyes at the sky. "I'm not gonna stop you." Jif grimaced!

"THEN WHY ARE YOU HERE!" screamed Jif.

"You have a lot of nerve speaking to me like that," replied the black.

"Nothing is right anymore! And I know you've been fuckin' with me! You have a lot of nerve, trying to gate-crash a human being's funeral! Are you not a human?"

The man smiled. "I don't fuck anyone."

Jif studied the man for the first time. He gazed at the stitch-on badge under the lapel, US Army. He looked up at the hat again and finally asked, "What section are you?"

"Intelligence corps," replied the black.

"Slime," replied Jif. Slime was a nickname for anyone who was involved in intelligence.

"It's not what we're doing, it's what you're doing."

"I just want to be a father figure to my girl. I haven't fucked. I don't do mind games. I don't play with her pussy! She just loves to be pampered. I'm not a pedophile! And I didn't kill my friend!"

"How come you don't remember coming down that elevator?"

"What are you talking about . . . mister?" Jif thrust his head forward to annoy the black. He genuinely didn't know what he was saying. What elevator?

"After the boy got shot, what happened?"

"I fainted!"

"And then what?" Jif was getting impatient. After being scared for so long, he was pretty fearless.

"Look, why am I talkin' to you? I don't wanna talk about this! You don't know anything about me!"

"There's more that connects us than you think!"

"Besides being fat?"

"How did you end up two stories down without remembering? How did you get to the ground floor and not know how you got there?"

"I just . . ." Jif racked his brain for a reply. Then a switch flicked in his head, and disgust filled his face. "Are you saying I'm losing my memory?" he said as angry as he could get.

"Don't you feel as though this isn't right?"

"You're not makin' any sense!"

"You want to kill your enemies and be happy ever after, but you know you can never be happy without people to be with you. That is why you are here now!"

"Come on! Stop fuckin' around!"

"Follow the light, Jif! Go to the hospital."

"Why?" asked Yuzuyu. The slime didn't react to her, as if she wasn't there.

"But watch out for the other men," the soldier went on. "I'm not after you, but they are!"

"Then you should try to be careful who you hire! Mate!" reacted Jif. His eyebrows were so low in his anger, he could barely see.

"And ask for yourself," said the slime.

"What?"

"At the hospital, ask for yourself. Ask for someone with your surname. Trust me, they'll know." The soldier turned round on his hell and walked away.

Jif grasped Yuzuyu's hand, lightly, trying not to frighten her. He paced forward, slowly, refusing to look back. But the thoughts of curiosity burned in his brain. As he took several steps, he spun round again. The slime was gone.

"What was that about?" asked Yuzuyu. Jif continued to walk, gripping Yuzuyu. He stared at the green, unable to make eye contact.

"I honestly don't know," replied Jif. "But it's something to do with Vin and Charlie."

"But you knew him! And he knew you!"

"Yea," replied Jif. He breathed heavily. "I can't be certain anymore. I can't be certain if it's a dream, if it happened, if they drugged me . . ."

"What are you saying?"

"He and two guys interrogated me about the island!" Jif finally said in a flat tone. He stepped over a horizontal footpath in front of him. He figured they were getting near to the Shaw Memorial.

"Yep."

"What did you tell them?"

"Nothin' really 'coz they already knew about it!"

The sounds of traffic erupted again. He looked up and saw they were at Park Street. The Granary Memorial Ground once upon a time used to be part of Boston Common. And then one day someone decided to build a road across it, cutting it off from the opening.

"Some project, huh!" said Jif to himself. The church was on the corner of the street; they were a few blocks up. Obnoxious diesel was in the air, but there wasn't much traffic. Sedans and vans were parked up against the sidewalk opposite, alongside dozens of redbrick 1960s buildings, all of them at different height but still in the line on the sidewalk, never sticking out or recessing.

The street went quiet with no cars, so Jif and Yuzuyu crossed hand in hand. On the other sidewalk, they passed a set of propped-up motorcycles before Jif spoke again.

"I'm still nervous about this," he said. "But even more with meeting that slime today. If he'd corner me in the common, what to stop him coming to a funeral?"

"I'm sure Vincent has seen to everything," reassured the girl. They passed a three-story building with huge windows before coming alongside the church. The windows looked Victorian, six-foot-high white frames with a curve to the top. Jif counted seven windows along the sidewalk until they got to the corner.

The front of the church looked Roman, a quarter of a circle holding four white supports and six windows. There would be another one of these on the other corner, but it was obscured by the tall flat wall of the front entrance that held the tower clock and the spire. A set of steps and four white posts completed the picture.

Jif still hadn't noticed the three thickset men in black standing around on the sidewalk. A Ford Crown Vic was parked on the sidewalk. It was a police car, its blue light bar still flashing. It was finished in ocean blue with grey trim in the centre and a white dumper. Police was written in blue against the grey.

A cop was pacing around. He wore a midnight blue uniform with a light blue match on his arms, the standard peaked cap, and an orange vest. He was making along his car, heading toward the couple. Jif stopped, expecting a telling off.

"Mr. Kitchen," started the cop. His voice was gravelly; a service veteran maybe. His thick moustache made him look more a fireman than a cop. In fact, he looked a little like Fido.

"Yea," answered Jif, staring straight through him. If he was going to be ordered away, he didn't want to act surprised or plead with this guy. He was tired of begging.

"Just wanted to say this is a sad day," finished off the cop. He directed his hand towards the open burial ground, teeming with people. "Go, go on."

Jif turned on his heel and pulled Yuzuyu's arm slightly. The suits nodded and stepped aside to invite him in, hands behind their backs. Vin's not-so-plain security. They certainly looked like cops. Jif paced through them, a little nervous in his step.

The cortège of three hearses was parked in the twisting pathway alongside the church and next to the open green. What looked like the undertaker was leaning against the passenger door of the middle hearse, puffing out breaths of mist around his head. Jif gazed around. There were dozens of people. Charlie was certainly popular; he didn't recognize anyone. He wanted to talk with someone he knew. He thought he saw Vincent in the distance by a tree. He was obscured again by a fat woman in black.

Then he saw Naomi. She was with the whole gang of Babylon Zoo. Motoko, Rajah, and Chelsea were all in black dresses and panty hose. Naomi had gone one step further and added a beautiful hat with a bow and a veil. He paced up to them, pulling Yuzuyu with him. She'd been very quiet; Jif was too preoccupied to notice.

"Hey," he called. They all turned round. Naomi stepped up and approached him in turn. She nodded to him and pulled up her veil. She looked lifeless without her makeup; he never noticed before the power of her blush or mascara. A good job he didn't need any of that on Yuzuyu.

"Jif . . . ," she began. He wanted to scream at her, but he knew he had to ask about the slime. He closed his eyes and pondered over what to say. Then he said it.

"Has anyone been askin' about Charlie?" he questioned.

"Of course. Everyone . . ."

"No, I mean, like . . . personal stuff. His bank accounts. MIT. His jobs, his relationships!"

"What are you thinking?"

"I think Vincent might be covering his tracks. Three guys were asking me about Charlie and some thing in my life that I can't say."

"So?"

"I had a feeling they might be talkin' to you next. They might think since I was so close to him, I might have said some things to 'im . . . and to you."

"Fuck, man, what did you get us into?"

"Deep shit, all right! It's no different from what happening now."

"Jif, why haven't we spoken? We were all peachy doing the funeral, and then you stopped talking for a week."

"Did I?"

"Well, yea."

"I honestly can't remember. I don't know if I had amnesia or if I was mad . . ." He let the sentence hang in the air.

"All I can see is it happened." She unclenched her fist then lowered her head to hide her eyes behind the brim of her hat, creeping it up slightly to remain in eye contact, like a naughty schoolgirl about to be spanked by the teacher. "But . . . ," she sheepishly spoke, letting the sentence hang in the air.

"What?" he quietly barked, chattering his teeth as he took a breath.

"Don't bring out the things I said about Charlie, OK? Not here!"

"Naomi. I know we ain't got along . . . honestly . . . I fuckin' hate you!"

"You pick a hell of a time to say that!"

"Well . . . you attacked my friend . . . I think I have a right to say that."

She drew a shaky breath, and Jif knew she was going to cry. He was surprised and somewhat pleased. He felt he had pierced the shield of the monster. But he knew he had to stop thinking like that.

"I think you know that despite everything . . . Charlie loved you! Tons!"

And that was the clincher. Naomi threw her palms into her face and blubbered.

"I just hope you can throw the dirt. I don't think I can."

She looked up. Foxy approached. She was in a black pantsuit and staring straight at Jif. She stopped dead a few steps from behind Naomi.

"Mister . . . we all loved him," she stated, rotating her head as if she was representing everyone on the green. "Maybe you can't see that, but we did. Even Chelsea over there. Why else d'ya think she made all the food today?"

"'Coz it's the only thing she's good at? I'm not gonna be nice, man. I honestly think I'm goin' mad."

"Well, you are," sniffed Naomi. "Now fuck off!"

"You know, I have great respect for you guys. But I hope to God that you're wrong. That the world won't see through your cynical eyes!"

Naomi was already turning. She had her head bowed and her arms to her face. She was playing it, he was sure. He knew a fake crier when he saw one. He'd seen them put it on his whole life. Only Yuzuyu never pretended to cry.

Naomi and Foxy paced up to a middle-aged couple. A woman in black and a man in white. Dress whites. Military. Not American. Foreign. Jif made out the cluster of badges on his chest. IDF, certainly. Israeli. It was her father. She'd always said her dad was some big shot in the Israeli Defense Force.

"Hey, do you wanna speak to Charlie's friends?" asked Yuzuyu. She was tugging his sleeve and pointing to a group of boys gossiping by a dirty gravestone. One was black, short hair: Alan. The other had his back turned. The other wasn't dressed for a funeral. He wore a yellow jacket over a corporate blue tartan shirt, midnight blue pants, and dirty solid black shoes.

"Yea," replied Jif and started walking toward them. As he did, the two boys in black parted, leaving the dude behind. He wandered in a circle as Jif got closer to him.

The busboy had his back to Jif and was peering over his shoulder. He turned around and nodded to Jif. Jif nodded back; he knew who it was.

The guy had a face that looked like the skin of the moon. His black Adidas ball cap covering most of his ginger hair. Jif knew a Ronco uniform when he saw one; Charlie wore one for nearly two years.

"Why does everyone say they're sorry?" he asked Jif. "Why can't they just say it sucks that a good friend is dead?"

"Oh, fuck off, Ginger!" snapped back Jif. "You never went to see him after he left." Ronco's was an out-of-town supermarket, recently built, competing against Wal-Mart. It was Charlie's first employer, where he worked as a trolley boy, along with Ginger.

"Hey, he just disappeared!" replied Ginger. He didn't know the full story. Charlie was forced to leave after Shiffs got him involved with some deep shit.

"D'ya know why?" stabbed Jif. "Did they tell you?"

"Hell no."

"Shiffs said hello to him."

"So?"

"Shiffs said hello and showed him the bathroom."

"Was it that . . . Peeping Tom?"

"Yep."

Ginger turned on his heel and threw his open palm out in the direction of the floor. He spun back at Jif.

"Why the fuck is he still workin' for you?"

"He's a perv and an outcast, but no one else wants his job. He's irreplaceable. And anyway, my hands are tied by that nigger over there."

"Over where?" exclaimed the dude, throwing his arms out in frustration. Vin was nowhere to be seen.

"Fuck, I thought I saw him," replied Jif.

"He's over there," pointed out Yuzuyu to a group of six or seven guys mingling among the gravestones. He spotted Heseltine—her spiked-up hair! It was them lot all right!

"I gotta go," Jif said to Ginger, leaving the dude with a bemused face, as he pressed on, waltzing around the aging gravestones.

"Why do you need to speak with him so bad?" called out Yuzuyu in between her stomps.

"'Coz I gotta tell him what's been going on!" replied Jif. He felt dumb, crazy for doing this. He'd end up embarrassing himself. But he had to try.

He could see Vin and Transit. With his back turned, Jif could see Vin had black pants and smart shoes under his long green overcoat. Transit was pell-mell in funeral suit, his balding head showing signs of sweat, even in this coldness!

He approached the board. Dill was shaking his head towards Transit, probably warning them all that Jif was approaching. They all turned around to face him and gave looks of sorrow and pity; Vincent pulled a solemn smile with his hands behind his back.

"Vin, I would like a leave of absence from Lime.Inc."

"A bit short notice, isn't it, Jif? After all we said yesterday!"

Jif tried to think what he might have said, anything at all, if it happened. And he couldn't.

"Whatever we talked about, I can't remember."

"What are you saying, Jif?"

"I think I'm losing my mind. I'm having blackouts."

"You said you weren't having any—"

"Then I must have lied, or I simply can't remember."

Vin looked around, probably expecting a pie in the face or a camera. Then he turned back to Jif and shrugged, pulling his lips tight across his mouth. He jerked his head to the right, and Heseltine crept in front of Vin. She was dressed aggressively in a retro dark uniform jacket and leather pants along with black high heels. Her black lips gazed the dull shine of the clouds. Her beautiful eyes were the only sign of friendliness, other than her voice.

"If you are doing this to scare us, you made your point. Next time someone dies, I promise to see to it you only do the paperwork."

Jif was unimpressed. He pursed his lips before he gently pushed Heseltine aside and stepped up to Vin again.

"I'm serious, man! I've been daydreaming this past week. I believed you guys had left me and I'd gone and shot my neighbours!"

Finally the group pulled stares at each other.

"How?" butted in Dill.

"I just did, all right. I dreamt I bought a gun and killed Charlie's girlfriend for putting him in the situation!"

"You still hate her, don't you?" said Transit quietly. Jif paused.

"Yea," he said under a breath and a nod.

"Well . . . ," Vin was beginning to say.

"How can I tell what's real and what's not?" Jif drew a breath. "Everything looks the same, sounds the same, and tastes the same. I could smell the cordite on the shotgun I used!"

"Seems like I'd be the last person you'd want to ask!" replied Vin, his eyebrows now in a line. Transit finally intervened.

"Look, he's not as old as us," he said this waving a hand in front of Vin's belly. "Just put Dill in charge of the building! It's not like anything worse can happen!" Vin sighed and looked back at Jif.

"All right, you have your holiday," resigned Vin.

"It's not a holiday!" replied Jif, gripping his girl's hand a little tighter.

"Just give a two weeks' notice before you pull a stunt like this again!" commanded Vin. "Now, I paid for this funeral!" He pointed his boney finger at the grass. "I want to see it put to good use!"

He turned on his heel, and the politicians darted out of his way. Vin stuck his hands into the pockets of his overcoat and pressed on over the grass as the group followed him, like dogs on a lead. Jif drew another breath and felt his knees shake.

"You shouldn't have said that," said Yuzuyu. "He'll think your crazy!" Jif didn't look but focused on Vin as he reached a limo and started gossiping again with the group. They seemed to be arguing. He knew it was no longer his business, so he decided to answer Yuzuyu.

"I think this job is making me crazy!" he said to the open air. He finally looked down on her. "They're startin', aren't they?"

"Yes," she replied. He bent his knees till his head was level with her stomach. Placing his arms around her shoulders and bottom, he hoisted her up, welcoming the feeling of her arms around his neck as he did so. She smiled again. Sliding her to his left, he made his lonely walk to the church. He negotiated around the hearses and found the entrance, submerged with dozens of bodies scrabbling to get in, orderly but still chaotic.

He entered. A vicar stood at a small podium, in white drapes and a Bible in his hands over his crotch. He smiled beneath his horn-rimmed spectacles at Jif. Behind him was an oak casket. Charlie's oak casket. Jif wished it was open so he could see the boy one last time, but he knew that was impossible. And behind that was a small podium for the vicar. Jif could only nod, before approaching the noisy mess of people.

"Before we begin," began a New York-type male voice, "I'd like to thank everyone who actually got to know Charlie." He knew who it was, but he had to see his face. He fought his way through the crowd of black, before greeting an open circle of grass.

There were several faces he recognised. Naomi, in a black pantsuit, Next to her, Tim, Charlie's friend, and they were both looking at a man in a dark grey suit who had his arms out. Six feet tall, slim build, balding black hair, heavy rings of skin around his grass green eyes. He'd only seen him once, but he knew it was Charlie's dad. Then, their eyes connected. The man took a step forward.

"And I'd like to thank you, Mr. Kitchen . . . ," the man said as his eyes began to fill up with water. As he approached, Jif felt like crying too. But he had cried too much in his dreams, and with everyone around him, he knew he had to be strong. He lowered Yuzuyu to the floor and released his grip. He felt her grab a handful of his pocket. Jif felt the man take his hands; they felt warm and inviting.

"Thank you . . ." The man paused to take a shaky breath. "Thank you for letting Charlie work one day in his life and prove what he was worth."

Jif felt his heart sink. The old man was right. Charlie was a hero, but not the hero Jif wanted him to be. Nevertheless, he knew the father was at peace and had to make certain that there was no difference between them or risk causing an argument, which he did not want in a time like this. He drew a breath and twisted his throat to find a clear voice. And smiled.

"He was a brave lad," Jif said as clearly as he could.

"He was a . . . ," the man began, before breaking into an uncontrollable sob, blubbering into Jif's shoulder. His smile shrank. He felt like crying too but fought against it, feeling his eyes burn. He closed his eyes as he tried to support the crying father, hearing whispers and footsteps behind him.

Jif found himself in a white open space. Nothing but white. Either he was imagining it, or he was in a studio.

"Hello," he called out. No reply. He found he was standing up, and his knees were aching. He turned around; there was nothing else to see, nothing to tell which direction he was in. He turned a full 360 then noticed a tiny dot of green ahead of him.

"Uh . . . anyone there?" he called. He didn't have to wait long as the green dot got bigger. It was a figure, moving towards him at incredible speed. As he got closer and closer, he could see it was a man, in a green uniform. Jif's first thought was that it was the general he'd seen in his dream earlier. As he got closer, he realised there was nothing to fear.

Charlie zoomed in to a sudden stop, just an arm's length from where Jif stood. He was wearing his grandfather's RUC uniform. His arms were straight. Charlie looked more manly than ever before, even Jif felt to stand to attention.

"Jif," Charlie finally said.

"Charlie," replied Jif. He looked down and shook his head as he paced forward. He couldn't make eye contact. "This is weird. It's getting to a point where I can't tell what's real anymore." He returned to face Charlie; his eyes were on Jif.

"You gotta let it go," Charlie said robotically. Jif got the gist.

"I know! I know!" He nodded in agreement. "I gotta stop hating Naomi. It's tearin' me apart!" Jif stared at Charlie for thirty seconds, doing nothing. The silence was driving him crazy.

"I found her, ya know!" he said.

"Who?" asked Charlie.

"The girl of your dreams. The reason why you wanted to go to MIT."

"Was it Naomi?"

"No, but would it have made a difference if it was?" smiled Jif, shaking his flat open palms at his chest.

"No," replied Charlie. Up until now there was no emotion in his voice.

"I blame myself for what happened," went on Jif, looking down again, into the white. His throat was clenching up.

"Then don't," replied Charlie. Jif looked up and dropped a tear.

"I am so glad your face is back to normal!" he sobbed on shaky breaths. For every shudder, another tear fell down and burnt his checks. Charlie didn't reply. Jif wiped his face with this jacket sleeve and recomposed himself.

"How am I supposed to know what's real and what's not? Everything looks the same, tastes . . ." He let the sentence hang in midair. "I even smelt the cordite when I shot those girls!"

"Who did you shoot?" asked Charlie. Jif shook his head; he didn't want to upset Charlie. And then an idea hit him. He blinked multiple times to hold his tears and looked straight into Charlie's eyes.

"You're obviously not here," Jif began saying, gazing around. "I'm obviously not here." He drew a deep breath, closing his eyes and slowly opening them. "Which means this is a creation of my mind, which means I'm really just asking my mind."

"You're talking to yourself. There's a lot of unnecessary explanation."

"Hey, I'm trying to work this out. That means I need give and take, even in my own mind."

"All right, what was the question?"

"How can I tell what's real?"

"Does it matter?"

"That doesn't sound like something I'd ask."

"All right, your worry is that if you act in the real world based on info that's not real, the results can't foresee." Jif became statue, not moving, his mouth open. He felt a trace of dribble creep over his bottom lip, closing his mouth just in time, sucking it back in.

"With you so far . . . ," he replied.

"But data doesn't do harm. Ideas are neither good nor bad! They're useful as what we do with it. Only our actions can cause harm."

"You're saying I should do nothing?"

There was no reply. The light brightened, and Charlie faded into white. But this time, Jif didn't react. If anything, he was expecting it.

May 17, 2006, 1204

"Mr. Kitchen?" asked a smoky voice. Jif found himself waking up again and felt a hand on his shoulder. In blurred eyes, he gazed around. His head was bent down, facing the floor, and collection of black shoes and pant cuffs. He looked up; the father had darted back and was wiping his face with his hand. A crinkly brunette woman in thick-rimmed glasses held the father, her mouth open. Charlie's mum. A dozen faces were on him now; Jif felt blood rush to his face in his moment of embarrassment.

"Sir" came the voice again, a little more aggressive. He looked to his right, where his shoulder was being touched. A young black male with short hair and brown eyes was nodding at him.

"Yes, Alan," replied Jif. He quickly put a finger to rub his sore eyes.

"You nodded off, we thought you'd gone into a coma!" exclaimed the boy. Alan was another of Charlie's small group of friends. Jif laughed at the boy's comment.

"Ain't no chance of a coma with me, mate!" he replied. "I'd 'ave gone to it straightaway and not have to go through all this pain."

"Hey!" snapped the Negro. Jif knew he'd caught a nerve. He knew Charlie would have wanted a good send-off. "He was a good friend of mine! And he'd be damn insulted if someone he'd been peeking to for nearly two years couldn't be bothered to come to his funeral!"

"I never said I wouldn't come!" replied Jif softly, his smile now gone. "But fucked-up shit has been happening to me lately!"

"Yep?" replied the boy. He thrust his hand in his pockets. Cocky. Angry. Defensive. Jif knew what he had seen or dreamt couldn't compare to seeing a mate die and not give the last word. Maybe that was why Alan was pissed. Because Jif got to have the last word, and he didn't. Jif looked around again. It was as if the whole world was on him. He even saw Lime.Inc staff gawping at him. Jif thrust his left arm forward to tell the lookers where he wanted to go, and an open line formed as several men and women scuffled to the side. Jif paced on, Yuzuyu still clutching his jacket cuff.

"If you wanna know . . . ," Jif began speaking to no one in particular. He found an empty black pew and turned into it. He banged the side of his knee on the wooden seat, and he shuffled to the end. He steadied himself against the white wall of the church then turned around. He saw a dirty green hymnbook on the back self of the pew ready to be picked up. Yuzuyu had let go of his arm and was looking up at him with eyes full of admiration.

"I . . . I been havin' problems lately," Jif called out. Half the procession looked at him. "Mr. Ronshoe," he pointed out, "didn't mean to nod off, but it's been happening since—" He cut himself off. He was about to say "Charlie's death." He didn't want to start tears rolling again. For all he knew he could start crying as well. He shook his head. "I feel terrible!" he finished off.

"Please be seated," called a thick old Bostonian voice. Certainly the vicar. Everyone sat down with a scuffle of shoes. Jif felt the pew creak under his weight. He quietly prayed it didn't break; he'd been embarrassed enough already. The vicar continued to speak.

"In Richmond, Christ is the savior of the people. One such hymn is considered the finest form of words to praise the piece of Christ and better the human race. Please turn to page 27."

Everyone stood up to the sound of paper shuffling. Jif did the same. He found the page. He knew this song since elementary school. A few coughs echoed the chapel, and the organ started up. Everyone sang in unison. If a little flat.

"Make me a channel of your peace. If hope . . ."

Jif could only sing the first verse, then his throat clenched up, and his eyes and cheeks began to heat. He spluttered a sob and closed the hymnbook to put his right hand over his eyes. He felt as though all his sadness had been saved up for this moment, and he had to get it out. He wiped his eyes as the choir got the end of the chorus. He opened the book again but found he simply couldn't sing anymore. He looked down at Yuzuyu. She was still singing and hadn't seemed to notice Jif at all. Jif had always relied on others to look out for him, and he didn't expect much, but after years of being with Yuzuyu, he expected her to comfort him just like he had comforted her. He closed the book up again and waited for the hymn to finish.

"And in dying that we're born to eternal life," finished the congregation. Jif sighed and held back another sob. He saw Tim stand up. Turning round, his glasses reflected the light streaming through the windows. Jif had to blink.

"And," started Tim. He suddenly snapped to attention and stood straight with his arms behind his back. "The day after Charlie got his first job at Ronco's, we organized a party, and he asked for a karaoke CD of Remy Zero's 'Save Me.' We . . . had our camera that day, and we recorded the song to CD. In Charlie's will, he asked this song be played on his funeral, and here it is."

Jif recognized the first strum. Remy Zero was a terrible singer, but this was a great song. Even he listened to it. A heartwarming song of being there for someone and sacrificing yourself. Which is why it got used in the intro of the TV series *Smallville*. Jif wiped his eyes, smiled, and dreamed.

September 14, 2003, 1602 GMT

Jif had fallen asleep three times in the taxi, only to get woken up again whenever the car turned a corner. He'd tried using his right arm as a pillow to soften the vibrations of the suspension, against the plastic interior of the door of the white Nissan Serena, but it did little good.

"So you've been in the wars?" said the brown-skinned taxi driver. He said his name was Iffy and his "old man" came from Yemen. Jif could only concentrate on the man's short black hair, tidied up into a flat cut on all sides, as if it had been sanded from wood.

"I guess," replied Jif. "Can't say much though . . . my boss's orders . . ." He let the sentence hang in the air.

"How 'bout you, li'l girl?" he was addressing Yuzuyu. "What's ya name?"

"Yuzuyu," she replied automatically.

"That's a beautiful name," replied Iffy.

"Punto?" she replied. Jif knew she was saying "really."

The taxi had been arranged by Vin to pick him up from the airport and take him home. After hours of sitting on a lurching helicopter, ferried on a busy passenger ship, and sitting in a private plane, there was no strength left in Jif's body. Having been rescued, he was ditched in Tokyo, where he managed to find a pay phone and contacted Vin. Vincent was amazed Jif had survived and pissed off that he'd been betrayed by his investors and that the island was gone. Vin was able to get Jif and the girl onto a plane, which sent them to Gatwick.

No one paid attention to the sudden disappearance of a Japanese island. At best, it got a ten-second summary on BBC news. The world was more preoccupied with the ongoing war in Iraq, soon to become a quagmire of government scandals, and the downfall of Tony Blair and George W. Bush.

The taxi turned into Jif's old neighbourhood. The Orchard Park Estate. Taking the girl, holding her close, he reached for a door key, concealed in an envelope under a rosebush below the lounge window. Opening the door, he felt relief fill his body, and his eyes welled up. Slamming the door, his body gave in, and he started crying into her shoulder. And she started crying too. Collapsing to his knees, he buried himself into her chest. She felt warm and comforting. And the crying became hysterical.

May 17, 2006, 1229

The funeral was over as soon as it began. Some lines of the Bible were read, and a few more songs were played. The congregation stood from their pew and bottlenecked the gangway. Jif caught the undertakers picking up Charlie's coffin with the utmost respect and leveling it on their shoulders. They goose-stepped out through the doors as the family and onlookers followed.

Jif picked up Yuzuyu and fought to get to the front. He wanted the best view to say goodbye. As the cortège paced gradually through green path between the tombstones, the undertakers seemed in trouble. The casket appeared to be wobbling. Jif could see the men's head turning, with looks of bewilderment on their faces.

"What going on?" shouted Charlie's father.

"The casket is shaking!" yelled one of the top hats. The procession swarmed around the group as they lowered the casket to the floor. Jif's heart pounded. Was Charlie really in there? Had he been replaced? He fought through the crowd to get to the front. The casket was indeed vibrating.

"Is this some sick joke?" shouted a woman's voice. Charlie's mum.

"Jif, I don't want to be here," Yuzuyu whined. For the first time, Jif ignored her. He crouched down and placed his hands on the smooth oak. He wanted to feel where the vibration was coming from, in what part of the casket.

"Charlie!" he called.

Plank! There was the sound of wood splintering out of nowhere. Women emitted low cries of shock and surprise. Jif just kept his eyes in the lid of the casket. With a horrid slitting sound, it ripped open. Two long boney grey arms fired their way out. The crowd's moans became screams. The wood fell away, and a decaying face of what was once Charlie appeared out of the casket. As the crowd darted back, Jif stayed where he was. The face moved in his direction. Fast.

"Charlie," Jif said softly. He hoped the boy would stop. He didn't believe in zombies, but he was looking at one now. He felt Charlie's cold hands dig into his chest. His strength left his body. "Fuck he through to himself," as Charlie's face contorted into the ugliest thing he'd ever seen. "I allowed my feeling to make me weak. Friends always betray you!" His head started aching and felt like it would explode. A beam of light emitted out of the casket and dazzled the area around him. And everything went white.

He couldn't see anything else! He felt so helpless, like he was dying. The light faded into black. And then, he became aware he was breathing, heavily.

He tried to move but couldn't. He felt his eyes were closed. He tried to open them, but they felt heavy. He could hear his heavy breathing and his heart beating. Then he could see a tiny ray of yellow light in the bottom left corner. He tried to focus on it.

"What's happening?"

He tried to talk, but his lips felt dry and stuck.

"Where am I?"

The ray increased, and suddenly he felt his eyes open. He could only peek. Something was over his eyes. White and fabricy. A bedsheet maybe?

He heard sounds! Footsteps. A low hum. And breathing, not his own. There was clunk. And a metallic voice pierced in the distance of wherever he was.

"Dr. O'Hare, please report to the hospital admissions office . . ."

"Doctor?" questioned Jif. Was he in a hospital?

His vision became slightly clear. The light was coming from a penlight, penetrating the darkness. He felt his breathing go short and anxious.

"Is she sure she saw the arm twitch?" a black woman's voice said in the darkness. He tried to focus to see if anything was there.

"Who's there?" Jif tried to say.

"Won't take no for an answer" came a reply from a heavy-sounding male.

"Am I in a coma?" shouted Jif into his darkness. There was no reply. Just then, he caught a glimpse of cheek and the penetrating light. A young black woman with thick lips and curly black hair down to her neck. He saw her lips move as she spoke.

"It's probably a temporal lobe seizure."

"What was she talking about?" hissed Jif. There was still no reply. He wanted someone to shout out, "LOOK! HE SPOKE!"

The woman's face faded back into darkness, and the penlight disappeared. *This can't be happening!* Jif trembled. He could feel his forehead begin to heat up, and his heart shrank in the grip of fear. "Help me!"

"Increase his Valium to ten milligrams" came the voice of the black woman. "That should put him into a deeper state of consciousness and alleviate the tremors . . ."

"No!" screamed Jif in his silence. "No . . . no. It'll put me to sleep. I gotta get off here!"

"Let's go!" said the heavy-sounding man. And Jif felt his heavy breathing become light. The Valium was taking effect. He drew a panicky breath!

"Help me!" he yelled. "Help me! Help me!"

THIRTEEN

He opened his eyes. He was facing the ceiling again, in his bedroom. The bed he was on felt warm all over his body, almost engulfing him. He thrust his arms backwards and elbowed the mattress to prop himself up. Cold air rushed over his back as the blanket on top of his chest began to drop from him. He looked around. Everything was normal. Except he was lying by the bedroom door, this time.

He looked to his left. Lying next to him was Yuzuyu. She was lying on her left side. The blanket now around her knees, exposing most of her body. She was wearing pajamas today: pink, with weird grey scribbles of vertical lines. The top half was raised slightly, exposing a glimpse of her bare stomach. The bulge of her diaper visible under the pajama pants. Her mouth was open, and her stomach raised and lowered as she breathed. She looked so peaceful, and he didn't want to end that beauty, but so much stuff had happened. He had to do it.

"Yuzuyu?" he said softly, leaning towards her. Her arm slid from under the sheet and over the pillow, resting next to her mouth. But she didn't wake. He tried again.

"Yuzuyu?" he spoke more forcefully. She opened her eyes and drew a long breath.

"Jif?" she replied, pushing her arms backwards to uncover herself from the bedsheets. The silky skin of her bare stomach looked tempting, and Jif fought off an erection.

"What day is it?" questioned Jif.

Yuzuyu hesitated in confusion. Her eyes narrowed, as if it was a stupid question.

"It's Monday!" she replied in an authoritative tone. He'd never heard her like that before; she was always submissive and unsure.

He was drawing another breath for another question, when there was a sudden sound of the door opening.

Plank! The bedroom door flung open and slammed into the wall behind. Dark grey pants legs emerged from the doorway before an entire figure stood into the room. Vin Bird gripped the brass bedpost and leaned over the couple. Yuzuyu thrust her legs up to her chest to hide her modesty.

"JIF!" screamed Vin. His head was shiny again. The thin brows had sunk and gone into a line to display his anger. "Stop moping around and get back to work!"

Drawing a breath, Jif fought to keep in his anger. He wasn't certain this was real anymore.

"WHAT THE FUCK HAPPENED, VINCENT?" shouted Jif. Vin backed off a step, palms showing up at his chest, defensive. He'd never done that before. His brows went back up again, and his eyes were wide in surprise, but his mouth didn't change.

"About what?" replied Vin.

"Has Charlie been buried?"

"Yes!"

"Then why can't I remember it?"

"Because you don't want to believe!" came the reply. His words felt cold, and Jif felt the room fill with hostility. He gulped, pushing his nervousness to the back of his head.

"Shit is happening, Vin. I thought you sold me out to protect yourself, and then I see Charlie come back to life! Somebody's got to tell me what going on!"

There was a pause in the air. No one spoke, just all eyes on Jif as he gazed from face to face.

"I know a therapist . . . ," began Vin. The nail was in the coffin as Jif's eyebrows raised.

"Since when did you care about counselors or therapy?"

"Since now." Vin nodded. This was not Vin's usual self.

"Why did you back off like that, man?" blasted Jif, throwing his arms in the air. His nose started to become irritated as it got colder. Jif stammered, "You never back off! Ya . . . you never answer questions from . . . insignificant employees like me."

"You're not insignificant, Jif!" pleaded Yuzuyu from behind. Jif felt the mattress sag behind him as if Yuzuyu was moving around. He felt her soft, warm hand slip onto his shoulder, caressing his neck. It felt almost good, but Jif didn't turn around; he kept his eyes fixed on Vin.

"How come you were so pissed off? You were authoritative. You never are. Something ain't right!"

"Yes. Something isn't right," said Vin, in reply. It was a genuine answer.

"Since when do you agree in what's right and not?"

"Since now!"

"No! You always think rationally! Ya . . . you reckon that there's always something to screw up, like. You're what I'd like you to be . . ."

For the first time since he remembered, Vin pulled a toothy smile. It was a chilling smile. So much so Jif couldn't look into it. He had to turn around. He faced Yuzuyu. Her face looked innocent: open mouth, wide eyes. Something wasn't right. He had to break this illusion.

"Forgive me!" he hissed through his clenched jaw, staring straight into Yuzuyu's eyes. He crushed his fingers into a fist and threw his knuckles into Yuzuyu's jaw. He felt his wrist sink in a little, and a sharp pain filled his knuckle. He heard Yuzuyu's jaw click, and her face crushed up into a crying mode. She began blubbering.

"Ahhh!" she howled in pain. "Why! Why!" She drew a breath as she threw her hands to her face. Blood dribbled out of her mouth and onto her pajamas. "You're crazy, you're crazy!"

Her words were chilling to Jif. This was a person he loved more than himself. She was his only purpose to life. And yet he'd harmed her. Maybe this was reality after all. He felt a warm hand grab his right shoulder. He was spun round and came face-to-face with Vin.

"You're unbelievable!" screamed the black man. His face was crushed up in anger. "Are you hallucinating?" Jif felt all his fears drain away. He was no longer afraid of the boss; he could do nothing that hadn't already been done. He threw his fist into Vin's left eye. It felt wet and soft. Vin squinted, released his grip, and darted away from the bed.

"Yes, I'm hallucinating!" screamed back Jif. And then another soft hand connected with his shoulder. Yuzuyu pulled him around, and Jif complied, expecting a sob story.

"No," she began spluttering through her bleeding mouth. "He means right now." Jif wanted to apologize but felt his jaw clench up, and then Yuzuyu spoke again.

But the words she spoke were not of her own voice. They were that of Charlie's.

"Are you hallucinating?" said Charlie's voice as Yuzuyu mouthed the words.

Jif's heart began racing again, and all off a sudden the room brightened up.

"No . . . NOT AGAIN!" he screamed. The light became blinding as it engulfed Vin, Yuzuyu, and every object gradually, until everything was white, and then, black.

FOURTEEN

Jif felt himself waking up again with his arm over his eyes. Beneath his body, he felt solid wood. He could smell pine and old paint. He pulled his arm from his face and saw he was in his suit. Looking into the cloudy sky, he saw the sign for the gun shop: Hired Guns. He was on the bench again.

He jabbed his elbows into the wood, propping up his body, swinging his legs off the planks and onto the sidewalk, sitting up on the bench. He stared into the pavement of the sidewalk, trying to make sense of everything.

Had he been sleeping all this time? Had he imagined the shooting, the funeral? Something was up, but he could do the shooting now! He stood up and stared straight into Federal Street. He focused away from the glass and steel structures around the road and kept his eyes on the end of the road. He could make out the grey block of the old post office triangle. Nothing interesting there, except it would provide a viewpoint to see the river.

A UPS van trundled past spewing diesel fumes; he held his breath. The traffic was starting up. Jif pushed himself from the bench and gazed along Winter Street, not certain what he was looking for. He felt drunk; maybe he was dreaming again, but he promised himself he wouldn't kill anyone this time.

"Hospital," he said to himself. It was the only thing that kept coming up, and Jif hadn't explored yet. He felt stupid. What was he going to do? Or say? That he thinks he's already in a hospital? He'd be chucked in Broadmoor. Or Bellevue! Whichever mental hospital they had in this state!

He wiped his eyes, trying to rub out the grogginess. He pondered if he was really in control of his body. Massachusetts General Hospital was a huge compound in the West End. A mass of interconnecting grey buildings, like the World Trade Centre complex in New York. In the two years he'd lived here, he'd never been there. Except for when Charlie got his nose broken. The dreams had to mean something! Maybe it wasn't him there; maybe it was Charlie that was being kept alive and someone didn't want anyone else to know. But why?

He quickly rifled through his pockets to check he had all his things, the things he normally carried. Mobile, wallet, some spare change in a clear coin sack, and a folded photo of him and Yuzuyu. He opened the wallet to check how much cash he had. He guessed about $80 in paper in his leather pouch. He pocketed the wallet, watching around to make sure no one saw his things; he'd be a sitting duck for a mugger.

He knew he was not in a fit state to walk. The hospital was the only place left that seemed to have any significance to what was going on. He didn't know where the nearest bus stop was, and he wasn't going to risk getting a lift, so it would have to be a cab.

He stood at the edge of the sidewalk, gazing down the street at the oncoming cars on the other side of the road. An articulated truck roared by when a white Crown Vic appeared. He saw the taxi approaching and waved his arms in a cross above his head to hail it down. There were many taxi companies in Boston, and this one had Metrocab in foot-high green letters along the driver's door and an advertising triangle on the roof with a banner for Bud Light.

The front headlights flashed to let Jif know he'd been spotted, and the car slowed. It stopped, holding up an angry, horn-beeping Chrysler Voyager driver behind to let a Chevy Caprice pass in the opposite direction before steering onto the wrong side of the road and bouncing up onto the sidewalk till it was two feet away from Jif. He approached the driver's side as the window whined its way down. It was driven by a woman. Fifties, white, curly black hair, and thick-rimmed glasses. She had a South Park T-shirt on.

"You on duty?" asked Jif.

"Of course I am!" yelled the female driver in a husky voice. Jif nodded and reached for the passenger door behind the driver. Strangely, the inside of the cab felt colder than the outside. He slipped in and slammed the door behind him, and the woman turned her head to make eye contact with him.

"Massachusetts General Hospital please," he asked.

"You got it!" she stated as she floored the accelerator and pushed the buttons on her meter. The numbers started to appear on the LCD. Jif sat in silence.

"What happened to your hair?" asked the woman. Jif rubbed his head and remembered his self-mutilation the previous day.

"Argument with the wife," he replied.

"Man," she suggested, "just leave her!" Jif sighed.

The taxi cruised along High Street and into Chinatown. The traffic was light as the taxi made its way to the grey building of the downtown crossing. At the end of Winter Street, they turned right along Tremont Street, alongside Boston Common. Jif could make out the giant statue and the short bandstand in the centre. It got to King's Chapel, turned left, and went up Somerset Street, heading towards the JFK building. As it filled the windshield's view, the taxi turned left again on Cambridge Street. They passed the Old West Church and a DUKW, an old military floating vehicle, now being used as a tour mobile. Several children on the side waved as they passed. The hospital wasn't that far.

The taxi slowed down and eased right into Blossom Street. It went to the far end and steered around a reservation "garden" in the road that held a welcome sign for the hospital. The taxi bounced into the drop bay area of Boston General. Sandwiched between two brown buildings, the hospital looked like a flower sprouting out of a pot of dirt. The front entrance was a white box with three giant window sections that appeared black in the cloudy light. There were two flagpoles, parading the Stars and Stripes; and behind that was the rest of the hospital, a huge cylinder against a flat block, like a giant with its head and shoulders, about twenty floors high.

The driver negotiated around a parked white-and-red ambulance and pulled up in front of it. She put the car out of gear and pulled up the emergency brake.

"That'll be $76," she said like a car salesperson. The red LCD display in the dash confirmed it. Jif went through his internal pockets and found the eighty dollars, in cash.

"Here," he said, "here, keep the change," as he handed the money through the opening of the plastic window.

"Oh, come on," she started saying. "You don't have to 'coz I'm a girl." But Jif was already opening the door. He leapt from his seat and made for the hospital. She beeped the horn after him.

In the right corner, he found the doors. They slid open automatically as he tripped the sensor. The reception smelt heavily of antiseptic and was filled with a hundred coughs, yelps, and chatter from other patients out of view. He made up to a white-wall desk with the hospital crest in the centre. A single Latino girl with a dark brown ponytail and a white medical jacket was sitting there, eyes down at a computer screen partially hidden by the recessed shelf. She looked up at Jif and raised her eyebrows to say hello.

"Hello there," began Jif, pulling a friendly face trying to be as polite as he could. "Do you have any patients by the name of . . ." He paused. His smile faded. Who should he ask for? Himself or Charlie? Kitchen or Ronshoe? "Kitchen?" he finally said. He felt the entire possible insecurity sink into his skin as his head started the sweat.

"Are you a friend or relative?" asked the receptionist. Her voice was 100% Boston all right.

"Uh . . . ," he stammered for a good excuse. "I have the same surname. I'm just trying to trace my bloodline, my . . . relatives. If he's not related to me, I'll leave him . . ." The receptionist was already typing before Jif had finished, her eyebrows raised.

"Jif Kitchen?"

"Yes," exclaimed Jif. There really was someone here. Even he knew that Jif was not a common name, the product of a drunk typist and father with no originality.

"Floor 2. Carlton Ward."

"Carlton?" exclaimed Jif. In England, Carlton was a type of car.

"Yes," she replied. "He had his own private room."

"Really?"

"I don't think it's a problem. Just follow the signs, you can't miss it." She was pointing out to the right, toward the doors of three elevators and a flight of stairs. On the corner of the stairs was a direction board in green, pointing out all the different floors. He didn't look hard because he knew where to go. Even if she was wrong or lying, he could always go back and complain. Or just look elsewhere.

"Thank you," he said, smiling and nodding. Jif was turning to the elevators when he stopped and turned his head again.

"Uh . . . what's this ward for?" She smiled.

"Now that would be telling, wouldn't it?" replied the nurse teasingly. Jif could feel something was up but didn't want to think too hard. He wanted to get this over with. Jif nodded and pressed on to the bank of silver doors. He hit the black button on the wall, and a red light beamed out. After five seconds, the left doors pinged open. Jif entered and hit button 2. The doors didn't shut immediately, so he sighed and waited. When someone in the distance appeared.

A man in a suit. Bald. Fifties. Heavy bags under his eyes. It was the interrogator from before! Jif made for the control panel in the wall and repeatedly stabbed the close-door button. The guy started running toward him. The doors shut. Out of sight.

"Fuck," he swore. They were in the hospital! But why? Was this a trap? It was the slime who'd implied the hospital, but there was nothing really secretive that they didn't know about! If they wanted to kill him, why didn't they just do it when they had the chance in the room? Or in Lime.Inc? Or was he just imagining them? What the fuck was going? He slammed his fist into the side of the elevator as the doors opened again. Fuck!

"Where are you going?" demanded the mophead as cocky as could be. He was wearing scrubs, a far cry from his suit. As he stepped into the car, Jif placed his back against the wall and threw his arms into the solid structure to push himself forward. His head zoomed in onto the four eyes. His eyes had gone wide.

Chock! The smack caused Jif's brain to rattle. He felt it spin, not sideways but backwards. He felt the skin start to swell as they both fell down. The glasses had fallen off.

"Ah!" whimpered the mophead. Jif had landed in the guy's chest. He smelt heavily of cheap aftershave. He groped around for the floor and pushed himself to his feet, noticing a bit more of his hair flaking off onto the guy's green skin. "You need an operation!" yelled the mophead again. Jif wasn't going to interact!

As he made his way out of the elevator, he found himself in a white-walled room with green-tiled floors. Another service desk. And a black nurse was leaning against it, busy with a clipboard. Jif felt the four eyes stagger to his feet behind him.

"I need some help here," whined the mophead as if drunk. The nurse looked up and came up to Jif, taking him by the arm to calm him down. And then Jif realised who she was. She was the doctor he'd seen in his dream!

"Excuse me, sir, who are you visiting?" she asked.

"Look . . . like . . . I just need to see for myself . . ." Jif struggled to speak.

"See what?"

"Jif Kitchen."

"He . . . cannot see anyone . . ."

"Look, I'm Jif Kitchen!"

"That—"

"Tell me . . . Is he in a coma?"

"Of course, you're not in a coma. You're right here talking to me."

"I never said it was. I asked if it was him. YOU SAID IT WAS ME!"

"Are you on any medications?" He didn't respond. Out of the corner of his eye, he saw a male nurse in green overalls rush over. His brown hair doffed forward as if in question.

"Five milligrams of Valium," the black doctor said to the nurse. Jif knew what would happen. He saw a closed door. Black. It had 67 in letters of gold in the centre. And a sliding card with blue biro scribbles just beneath it. He felt familiar with the door. As if it was in his dream. Then he realised. IT WAS THE DOOR HE'D SEEN WHEN HE RELIVED THE SHOOTING!

"I just need to see!" he pleaded, throwing his weight forward to get through their grip. He pulled free of them and made it to the door. He glimpsed the writing on the card. Jif Kitchen, he could just about make out. He turned the brass doorknob on the left of the door and pushed it open, stepping into the room.

He'd anticipated what to expect, but he still couldn't help reacting with horror. He heard the door close behind him, and a flurry of emotions quivered his soul.

"AAAGGGHHHHHH!"

He stepped forward one pace, still unable to accept what he was seeing. Himself, lying in a bed, in front of him!

The room was green: green-painted walls, green-tiled floors. A single hospital bed in the centre of a six-by-nine room. A brown plastic chair sat to the body's left, along with a hoard of hospital equipment. He took another step. The man was fat but with a slim face. Undoubtedly himself. His head had been recently shaved, leaving a blade of bristled stubble over his scalp. Different, but still himself. Thin clear plastic tubes were hosed into his nostrils. Thin white cables spiralled from a nearby ECG machine and disappeared beneath the green hospital blanket as it beeped eerily to take his heartbeat. He saw his own stomach raise and lower to his breathing.

"Why am I here?" he asked himself. He couldn't work it out. Had be been living in a coma all this time? Was every thing he'd seen not real? A lie? Frontiera Island? His schooling? Hull? Going to Boston? Lime.Inc? Yuzuyu? Charlie?

He took another step. Still no reaction. He wanted the figure in front of him to open his eyes and speak. But he knew that would never happen. Standing at the foot of the bed, he could make out something white on the man's shoulder. A bandage. Then he remembered! It was the same place that started hurting during the interrogation with the black general.

He stepped around the bed up to the chair and kicked it aside. At his own bedside, breathing hard, his heart pounding, he looked down at himself. He reached over to the left shoulder to pull away the bandage. It wouldn't budge. It has held stuck, like superglue. But why? What was it covering?

He ground his teeth and looked into his own face.

"Wake up. Wake up!"

He threw his palms down into the chest and shook himself.

"WAKE UP!"

Then, the room began to lighten up, just like all the times before. Looking up, the light invaded the room from the right corner, for no reason, and his suspicion was confirmed.

"No no no!"

He threw his hands up to his eyes but to no avail. The light went blindingly bright, and everything disappeared!

FIFTEEN

Jif woke up in his room again, like so many times before. Only this time, he knew this wasn't real. He could feel everything, the warmth of the bed, the coldness of the air. Everything was normal. Yuzuyu was even sleeping peacefully next to him.

He crept out as quietly as he could and opened a drawer. Slipping on a pair of underpants, he tiptoed through the doorway, down the corridor, to his office. He still wasn't entirely sure what he was doing, if there was anything he could do in this place. But he had to try.

Sitting at his desk, with a notepad and a pencil, he sketched the ballroom. He was recreating the shooting incident. He drew himself as a huge circle with a blood on top, Rock as a stick figure with the shotgun, and Charlie, hanging in midair, as he saw in the dream, his head level with his shoulder.

He fought off a tear and then drew a faint line to follow the direction of the gunshot. He started from the shotgun, along a centre meter of paper, into the viewer's left hand side of the head, Charlie's right eye. He circled that small spot twice, trying to think all the other possibilities.

Could he have dreamt that Charlie took that bullet when really he didn't? That he wanted to believe that Charlie was brave enough to sacrifice himself? In which case, he must have dreamt his death. But that would mean that Jif, himself, was shot, without protection. So close, Rock could have missed Jif's head. So was Jif really dead? No!

Jif always believed that in death, it would just be blackness. No afterlife, no ghosts. And if he had dreamt of Charlie, how could he rule out that he didn't dream of Rock as well?

He'd seen Charlie open his eye in the dream. But how? Maybe the bullet would have stopped in his eye, and he would have survived, but that still meant he'd be unable to open his wounded eye if there was nothing there. Could the bullet have missed Charlie? In which case, why was there blood in his eye? And why was there a bandage on Jif's shoulder in the latest dream?

He stared at the paper for five minutes, pondering and daydreaming, feeling sick with anticipation. The he felt his belly tighten up.

"SHIT!" he screamed.

Spinning the pencil, he scraped the eraser on the end over the faint line of the gunshot and drew a deep breath. Lead on paper again, he drew the line again, slightly angled. He drew it over Charlie's head and onto the fat man's right shoulder. He didn't want to believe it, but it was the only way he could explain what he'd seen.

"The bullet didn't go into his eye!" he said to himself. "It scraped his temple, and went into my shoulder." He paused, wanting to continue, but held back, trying to think of what else to add. "The blood . . ." He paused again. "The blood . . . trickled from the wound in the temple." He drew another breath. "That's why it went into his eye!"

He knew from what he was saying that Charlie may well have been alive. He knew for a fact he was in a coma. What he didn't know was why?

"Blood!" he said to himself. "Blood!"

He began daydreaming again, and his mind cast back several weeks to an incident in his bathroom.

He'd been stressed out those previous weeks over the ball and helping Yuzuyu with her school problems. He was sitting on the john in the bathroom, taking a dump. This time around, it was painful, on his ass, and his belly. Taking some paper, he felt very smooth on his ass. He looked at his own shit on the paper. There was a streak of blood. He stood up. In the toilet, his shit had a small globule of blood, no bigger than a Skittle sweet.

He felt nervous and panicky, but he was in a hurry and needed to get back to work. He cleaned himself up and flushed the john. And said nothing about it to anyone.

And here he was now, at his desk, thinking about it.

He stood up, panting, and made for the front door. As it opened, the light flashed over him again. The white abyss.

"FUCKING HELL!" he screamed. He gazed around to see what it was his brain wanted to say. He expected a slap in the face or a bang on the head. But as he did a full circle, he gasped. He was staring at his long nemesis. Rock!

"You've wasted your life," Rock said emphatically. He was wearing the assassin suit from the shooting. His shirt was bloodstained. His scary looks were as awful as it had been. His accent was peppered with American *r*'s. Jif could only think of how much hatred his being had made. He felt his eyebrows sink, and his eyes burned.

"Yeah," he replied, nodding once. He felt his eyes full of hatred. "If only I'd dedicated my life to finding someone worthy to hate! Like you hating Yuzuyu!"

"If I'd have killed you instead of Ronshoe, would it have mattered?"

Jif hissed a breath, summing up all he'd learnt in his strange life. Then he looked at the Jap without emotion.

"Nope."

"You don't care whether you live or die?"

"I care because I live," snapped Jif. The anger was returning. He didn't want to be here. But he knew this might be the only way to face his demon. "I can't care if I'm dead!"

"Don't give me no semantics."

"You antisemantic bastard," Jif said with a dry smile.

"Would anyone care that the world didn't have a funny side?" Jif didn't reply as his smile shrunk to a frown.

"That's all right. You don't have to say anything. This was weird. Just let me sink into your mind." Rock made a sigh. "You reckon the only truth that matters is your truth. Even if you live a lie, working for an arms dealer and telling everyone else you sell fruit!" Jif was trying to think out what he was saying and found himself staring at the Jap's dirty, smart shoes.

"You know, you think that good intentions don't count, just because you haven't been rewarded lately! Actually, people do care what you do, but you don't want them to care!" And then he got even weirder. "Doesn't mean that I'm not real!" What the hell did he mean? Of course he was real!

"That doesn't a fucking monkey's sense," he exclaimed. He looked up again and drew a powerful breath. "ARE YOU HUMAN?" He wanted to insult this person, make him cry for all the things he had done, trying to kill Yuzuyu, killing his friend! "What kind of person kills innocent bystanders and tries to tell me about good intentions?"

"Even if I'm wrong, you're still miserable. Do you really think that your life's purpose was to sacrifice yourself and get nothing in return? No." His gun disappeared, and his hair seemed to pull itself back.

"You have a beautiful, doting woman that loves you. She wants to have children with you! And it tears her up inside that you're scared of her. You think you're going to get arrested for touching her pussy. Because you want to touch her pussy! You are perverted! You focus too much on the sexual side of things! You want to be arrested! She's too young for you, and you know it. The one good thing in your life is killing you. You're miserable for nothing. I don't know why you'd want to live!"

Jif's jaw had already dropped. His brain was clunking. Like a jigsaw being completed. It all made sense. He knew what to do. And he smiled.

"I'm sorry," Jif said, nodding at the Jap. "I know what's wrong." He closed his eyes and felt warmth engulf him. He felt Rock disappear. And felt himself waking up.

But he didn't.

He was lying on his back again, this time in the open. There were people screaming around him, and he could smell freshly cut grass. He sat up, and he was on Park Street Church, Charlie's funeral procession.

Women in black were running towards him, away from the coffin that was dumped on the green. The undertakers were panicky startled away. He caught sight of Vin, running away as well. For the first time, he saw panic in Vin's face.

"Jif!" he screamed. He ran up to Jif, who stood up. "RUN!"

"Why?" questioned Jif. He knew this wasn't real, and he knew Charlie wasn't a zombie.

"TSUNAMI!" cried Vin. He grabbed Jif by the shoulders and shook him twice. "TSUNAMI!" He ran off down the common as the park emptied of life. Except for Yuzuyu. She tugged Jif's right pant leg.

"Jif, I'm scared," she whined. Jif didn't look at her.

"No, you're not. You're brave," answered Jif emphatically. He turned his head and gazed down at the beautiful little creature he so loved, but he had to hate if he had to be free. "It's just me who wants you to be scared."

"What are you saying?"

"This is not real," Jif said, gazing at the beautiful but fake surroundings. "Therefore, it's meaningless. I want meaning."

Over the landscape of Boston City Centre, Jif could make out a glimpse of blue over the buildings. Ocean blue. A huge tidal wave, just like in Frontiera Island.

"Jif!" screamed Yuzuyu's voice. He didn't respond.

He paced up to the coffin that had been dropped. The lid was loose and opened slightly. Jif kicked the lid away. The coffin was empty.

He looked back at the tsunami and sighed, with a grin.

"I know now!" he shouted. The building began to disappear beneath the water. "I can't fix everything!" He drew two more breaths as a distant roar became audible.

"And I need to let go if I'm to continue living. I need to let Charlie find his own way! And I have to let Yuzuyu grow up!"

The ground began to shake, the wave approaching at a colossal speed.

"I'M READY!" he shouted at the top of his lungs. He gazed over the green. The tidal wave gushed its way through the street below at a tremendous speed. Cars, signposts, everything was being sucked into it, tossed around, like the jaws of a tiger. The last road was gone; now it was coming over the green.

"Do it!" he snarled, bowing his head, eyes closed, and holding his hands in front of his waist. Defensive. He felt its presence approach, a splash of cold his face. At the last second, he opened his eyes. The water engulfed him like a blanket. He felt himself taking breath, and then he couldn't.

The temperature was phenomenal. From being perfectly warm to icy cold was unbearable. But he hadn't moved. The speed should have knocked him back, but he was still standing in the same place.

No light! Deep black! Except, for something red, shining from above him. He looked up. A spinning circle of dark red. The only thing to go for.

He thrust his arms down and swam up. The circle of red seemed to be approaching him as well as him approaching the circle. In no time, he was there. He reached for the tunnel, and it engulfed him. And the temperature went up again.

SIXTEEN

Jif's vision was nothing but dark red. But as he tried to move, white cogs suddenly appeared, spinning round as if to clunk his brain into drive. His eyes felt heavy and stuck. He was aware he was lying down on something soft and was covered in something light. He felt hot and sweaty.

He struggled to open his eyes, fearful of what he might see next. He'd been swimming in a black sea, and now he was lying down somewhere confined. If what he'd seen in the past several weeks was a limbo, what would be in this world?

His eyes finally pried open, sticky in the corners and sore from lack of use. He could feel the tracks of his tears.

He was looking straight up at a white ceiling, with a fluorescent light toward the end of his bed. He could see he'd been covered with an old thin blue blanket, which smelt of blood and urine. The room he was in was white brick walled but gradually turning yellow with age. Opposite him was another bed, empty, with a bedsheet and blanket neatly made over the length with a saliva-stained pillow at the head. Around him, yet more beds, some with people lying in them, asleep, hooked up to monitor and respirators.

He realized there was an intrusion in his left hand. He raised it and saw a drip feed inserted over his wrist. The plastic tube ran along his arm and up to a clear bag filled with liquid, hooked on a steel pole with a small hook at the very top. It was a look to his left that he realized someone was sitting next to him.

It was Yuzuyu.

She was asleep, head bowed, eyes closed, breathing softly through her nose. Her blonde fringe covered her eyes as she was bowed. Her hair had grown, from the base of her head, now disappearing behind her back. Dressed in a yellow puffer jacket, which made her look like a bodybuilder, unzipped, revealing a Bratz T-shirt. Lying down, he could see what leggings she had, or if there was anything there at all. He was unsure if he was still dreaming.

He reached over, painfully, with his left hand. He tried to touch her face, but he could see how far she was and kept on missing. Finally he touched her nose and got a reaction.

"Ghhhuuu!" she gasped. Her head jerked back, and her eyes jammed open in panic. Her arms appeared and folded over her chest to cover her breasts. Her eyes moved and realized who it was. Her open mouth rose to a smile. She stood up off her seat and rushed into Jif.

"JIF!" she exclaimed. She thrust her head into Jif's face, so all he could see were her eyes, now clenched shut. He felt the cold nylon of the puffer jacket force its way between the pillows his neck with a horrid scuffling noise of fabric against fabric. She held up his head slightly and connected her forehead with hers. A small tear emanated form her right eye.

"I thought I lost you," she said, pulling her head back. She panted as more tears flooded from her eyes. Jif groaned in his throat, wanting to reply, but unable to say anything he thought would have been out of taste. Yuzuyu answered for him and bowed down again, puckering her lips, delivering dozens of kisses on his forehead.

He sniffed. He liked her smell, like the scent of roses, mixed with talcum powder. He could feel her body heat and the heat and smell of her breath on his face. He finally knew this was not a dream. He wanted to bury himself into her body and forget everything that had happened, but he felt unable to move.

She pulled him up by his shoulders till he sat upright and kissed his cheeks aggressively while he tried to snuggle her neck. But as soon as it began, Yuzuyu pulled away again. She sat down again and stared, now looking serious.

"Why are you so scared?" she asked him slowly. Jif failed to understand and shook his head. "You love," she began, "you love me so much you wanna make love to me, but you're scared 'cause I'm a girl!"

Jif grunted in his throat, moving his tongue around, trying to speak. He glanced down to see the blankets had slipped down a little when he was sat up and saw he was in a pair of beige hospital pajamas. The top had no sleeves. His realized his head was light and cold, like it was missing something. He put his right hand on top of his skull and felt a blade of stubble where his hair used to be. Someone had cut his hair, like in his dream. He could finally breathe easily, so he turned to face Yuzuyu and asked his question.

"Yuzuyu," he croaked, "I know it's a bad time, but I got to ask." He drew a breath. "Is Charlie dead?"

"No, he's not," replied Yuzuyu softly with a smile.

"Then, how long have I been . . . this way?"

"Since the shooting," she replied. He drew a breath, to ask how long it had been since then, when she cut him off. "Thirty days," she said flatly, "or one month. They said you'd never pull out!" Jif panted a while before he began again.

"I saw Charlie get shot in the eye!" Jif protested, panting a little harder.

"No," replied Yuzuyu. "When the gun fired, Charlie dived out to take the bullet." She raised her hands and pointed her first finger on her right hand, rubbing it on the knuckles of her left hand. "The bullet caught the side of his head, taking his glasses." Her first finger jousted away to symbolize the bullet. "It hit your shoulder, but you were so shocked you didn't feel a thing."

Jif suddenly felt aware of something hot on his left shoulder. He raised his pajama top to see a square bandage taped to his skin, between his armpit and his nipple. Just like when he'd seen it in his dream. He looked up again and released the cloth.

"When Charlie fell, he was on his side. He was leaking blood from the gauge in his head, and it stayed in a pool in his eye socket. He'd been knocked unconscious, and his pulse was low. So you must have thought he'd been killed."

"I was living nightmare," Jif replied almost immediately. He felt a huge weight had been taken off his shoulders knowing Charlie wasn't dead. "Everyone hated me because I hired Charlie. I hated the girls next door for putting him there, and I was tearing myself apart."

"Like now," Yuzuyu cut him off again. "You had a stomach ulcer." Jif's jaw dropped. "They removed it, but that was why you passed out!"

"I didn't know," he said, looking across to the other bed, feeling stupid.

"It's because you never think of yourself!" screamed Yuzuyu suddenly, grabbing a handful of Jif's pajama top and yanking it. "You do all these good things for me and everyone else but never anything for yourself since we first met." Her voice changed to tearful mode now. "There are times when to show you love someone, you have to be selfish. You don't wanna have sex with me 'cause I'm too young. Forget about it. Just do it!"

Yuzuyu crouched down with a crack of her knees until her head was level with Jif's shoulder. Jif couldn't make eye contact. He stared at the beds and walls opposite him, panting.

"I never thought you felt that way," he grunted in a Yorkshire accent that was developing a twang of American. "You always seemed so innocent and childlike." Yuzuyu smiled again and stroked Jif's left hand. She removed the feed tube from his wrist; liquid poured out over the hand and bed, disappearing beneath the fabric. She dropped it on the floor, leaving a dripping sound.

"Uh," groaned Jif, resting back down again as strength left his back. He turned his head to face Yuzuyu.

"Everybody misses you, Jif. They don't hate you!" she said.

"Thank you."

"It's four a.m., Jif. What a time to wake up!"

"I know."

"You're under stress because I'm young, because I wear a diaper!"

Jif didn't reply. He just stared into Yuzuyu's beautiful eyes.

"Time to stop worrying, Jif. I married you because I love you. It might have been a bad wedding, but you're a good husband to me."

"Thank you!" Jif replied with a smile, his eyes beginning to burn with tears.

"Do you remember anything?"

"Like what?"

"Me talking to you? I said to how I good you were, how you changed my diaper all the time?" Jif reacted quickly.

"Yes, yes!" he said. "In my dream you were telling me that at the coroner's office."

"Coroner?" exclaimed Yuzuyu, jerking her head back.

"It's . . . a long story," he replied, flapping a hand in her direction. "I'll tell you later." As he finished talking, Yuzuyu smiled again, when something entered Jif's brain.

"Uh, one last thing!"

"What?"

"Why's my head shaved?" Yuzuyu gave an embarrassed look.

"Iffy was convinced you had a brain tumor and started getting you ready, before the doctors did the scan."

"No brain tumor?"

"No, just the stomach!" she replied. The smile came back.

"Something came whilst you were in here," she said.

"Oh!" replied Jif. Yuzuyu bent forward to the right and reached for something on the floor. She came back up, holding an old coffee-colored A3 sheet of paper with fancy black boarder and black Japanese hieroglyphs that Jif barely recognized.

"It's my birth certificate!" exclaimed Yuzuyu.

"Finally," Jif sighed, pushing his arms forward as he sat up. He'd asked for it so many times! "What's the date?"

"May 13, 1987." Yuzuyu replied without moving the paper or breaking eye contact with Jif. She'd had plenty of time to memorize the date. Her lips slowly curved upwards to pull a smile as she nodded her head forward and gazed at Jif teasingly. "Jif?"

"What?" he said, failing to understand what she was on about.

"I'm not fifteen!" she said with a small grin, exposing a millimeter of her two front teeth. "I'm eighteen."

Jif's mouth dropped. She was no longer a child but a woman.

"So long," he murmured. "You just didn't look . . ."

"I was in the freezer, remember!" retorted Yuzuyu. "I didn't age for three years!" She placed the birth certificate on the bed, on top of where Jif's knees were. She stood out of her chair slowly and cupped Jif's left hand into her own. "You don't have to be scared anymore." She moved her head a little closer. "We can do whatever we want."

Jif realized what she meant. She was no longer a minor. And she WAS his wife! He should love her right! The way she deserved! A proper woman!

"Yuzuyu," he groaned, shuffling in his bed. He leaned as far as he could, and Yuzuyu's face filled his sight. He made the first move, puckering his lips, cupping them around the girl's mouth, suckling gently. After one smooch, she opened her mouth a little, invitingly. He jutted his tongue forward and explored her mouth. His whole mouth enclosed her own while gazing into her eyes. Her pupil's had gone wide, reflecting the shine of the light and his face. His heart was racing! She began to use her tongue, and they twisted their heads for a better feel. Jif suddenly pulled back, breaking off the kiss. He looked into Yuzuyu, waiting for a reaction. She had her mouth open, panting lightly, caught between a smile and a frown.

"Different," she complimented. "I liked it!" She then said with a smile, "It's just, your taste." Jif then caught on what she meant. He'd been fed through a tube for a month and hadn't had his teeth brushed. He glanced around and struggled with his right arm; it felt like it had been wired with lead and the joints were flexed with wood. He held his hand in front of his face. He breathed on the back of his right hand and sniffed it. Smelled of burnt toast.

"Would you like some water?" asked Yuzuyu politely. She was pointing to a white porcelain jug about a foot high and a small glass sitting next to it, on the bedside table.

"That would be good, please," replied Jif. As he sat up a little straighter, Yuzuyu handled the jug, pouring clear mineral water into the shallow glass. When it was full, she placed the jug back and carefully handed it to Jif, who had held out his hand. He drank it all in one gulp.

"Thank you," he said, holding out the glass. Yuzuyu took it from him and placed the glass down on the table before rubbing her right arm behind his head and leaning in close to him until her breast touched his chest. She puckered up and kissed his forehead, before giving him another smile.

SEVENTEEN

Jif stared through the tinted window of the old Chrysler limousine that had picked him up. Traffic was quiet, and any pedestrians who were out at that time did not notice him. He could be sure this was not a dream.

It was dark outside since it was 2:00 a.m., and the fluorescent light inside the car had turned the window into an imperfect mirror. It reflected back a picture of emptiness, and there he was in the middle of it. His reflection was quite chalky in the hard-edged glare of the lights, and he wondered what everyone else would be doing at this time of night. And what anyone would have thought when they saw. Because he couldn't see them!

He'd spent another night in the hospital before being discharged. He'd been given an old white T-shirt, some jogging pants, and a Lime.Inc green fleece, courtesy of Vin. In that time, lots of things started to make sense. The hospital janitor was the "mophead" suit in his dream. His doctor was the bald suit. The hospital lift had glass doors, like the chamber in the embassy in his dream. He'd never been inside the embassy in real life. Clearly, things around him were subconsciously picked up and implanted in his coma.

Jif had been given a mobile and quickly got a lowdown off Vincent. A summary of what had happened since the shooting. He didn't react much.

Yuzuyu was clearly happy, sitting on Jif's lap, her head against his shoulder, hugging him closely. He could feel her smile through the clothing. He could only hug her back as he was still in shock. Everything was so real.

"What are you thinking of?" asked Yuzuyu.

"Nothing really," he replied, "just, everything seems so small." He was still fixated out of the window.

"Everybody's been gathered up at the building!" she said. "They all want to see you!"

"I love you, honey!" Jif suddenly said, roaming his hands over her shoulder. Yuzuyu smiled back and looked into his eyes.

"Love you too," she replied as she leaned up and kissed him.

"I love holding you and talking to you and being able to clean you!"

"Yea," she interrupted.

"But I got to ask, Yuzuyu."

"What?"

"Do you want to get out of diapers?"

"No." She smiled, stroking Jif's chin. "I like it this way. I'm too lazy."

And with that, Jif threw his head into her shoulder and started bawling.

The car made a turn, and they were at Lime.Inc. Panget stood at the front as the gates opened for the first time, in a yellow reflective jacket. He waved the car in, and as it passed by, Jif could feel the warmth of the Sikh's welcoming in his eyes behind his glasses.

They'd never parked in the garage before, but today they did. The garage door opened as they entered the gates, a three-meter-high plastic roll-up, shutter-type door. The motor was drowned out by the sound of plastic sections creaking against each other as it was rolled up. Coasting through the opening, the car went down an incline where a huge concrete layout greeted them. There were no road markings, no signs. The six or seven industrial lights flickered as the car cruised up to an extending block at the end of the garage. The two steel sliding doors told Jif it was the elevator.

Jif wiped his eyes and rode to the elevator to floor 3. The girl still held on to the man's arm, almost propping him up. He penguin walked into his office and, with stiff arm, reached for the light switch. The office was bathed in tea-coloured illumination.

"It hasn't changed a bit!" exclaimed Jif.

"No, it hasn't," replied Yuzuyu. "I made sure no one touched anything."

Jif continued his shuffle to the fire exit door. He pulled his left hand from Yuzuyu's grip and leaned it against the door. With his right arm, he reached up, with an agonizing look on his face, and pushed his fingers into the gap in the shiny tin box next to the alarm. He yanked his hand down, and a wire emerged from the gap.

"Why don't you want them to know you're coming in?" asked Yuzuyu.

"Anybody can set off an alarm," replied Jif, "but there's only one person's voice." He jabbed the push bar, and the door swung open, silently.

The corridor was dark, like in his dream. He could make out the stairs next to the door and a couple of the rooms, but that was it. He heard a hum of a man's voice from below him. Charlie must have been there. He wanted to run downstairs and tell him he was back, but his legs felt like lead. He crouched down with a crack of his knees and hugged Yuzuyu. She turned her head to face his profile.

"I think I . . . ," he began. He didn't finish his sentence. He drew a deep breath and closed his eyes. "HELLO?"

There was a smacking of wood and creaking as someone ran up the stairs. Charlie appeared, his mouth wide open in disbelief. A pair of horn-rimmed glasses on, his emergency pair. Black combat pants and white T-shirt, bare feet.

Charlie swayed up the stairs, and Jif could make out the scar. A deep gash on the right temple. The skin was lined and rippled, as if it had been burnt. And he could sigh in relief, when he saw both Charlie's eyes blink. THEY WERE BOTH THERE! He wasn't shot in the eye!

At the top of the stairs, Charlie staggered towards Jif, arms out. And Jif leaned forward, his eyes burning. They collapsed into each other and broke down simultaneously, sobbing into each other's shoulder.

"I thought you were dead!" yelled Charlie. "I thought you were dead!"

"I'm sorry," said Jif automatically. Charlie's shaky hands moved from Jif back to his chest, and the boy eased himself from the fat man.

"For what?" he spluttered through a sob.

"For putting you through all this," Jif replied. It was as if he'd been rehearsing lines for a play. "I knew the risks, and I didn't tell you." Jif raised his head slightly as he dropped a tear and spluttered a breath. "And I know you love Naomi, and I have been sticking my nose in when it's not may place to do so."

"Jif," began Charlie as he took off his glasses and wiped his eyes.

"I don't hate her. I just hate what she does to you, but you are your own man, and I'm not ya dad, so I gotta let you do what ya have to."

"You . . . ," Charlie began again. "You thought I was dead?"

"I thought you were dead! That's why I've been in that coma for long. I was blaming myself for it all!" Charlie was shaking his head.

"Not me," stated Charlie. "Iffy's dead!" Charlie suddenly clipped. Jif didn't react immediately. He swallowed and held his hands in front of his crotch.

"When?"

"Two days after you were in hospital. They think it was a broken heart 'coz he couldn't do his job."

Jif nodded in agreement.

"That was always Iffy, always needed to do what he was good at. Did Vin take him?"

"Yea. Didn't say where. I didn't get to see him. I didn't get to thank him. He put the towel to my head after you passed out."

"How long were you out? Ya see . . . I . . . couldn't find a pulse! I believed you were dead!"

"Well, when I woke up, I could hear bells ringing in my head. I felt drunk! I thought I'd been sleeping. And then Naomi held me."

"She did? I never thought a hard girl like that would . . ."

"She kissed me too. In the ambulance. But I didn't kiss her back. I was too shocked!" He looked up again. "I felt as though I'd failed again. I'd hurt myself trying, but I couldn't stop a bullet. I could do what I had to."

"I think, felt failure," stated Jif. "I think, every man in that room felt failure. Vin lost his deal. The guy who shot didn't kill me. I guess, no one wins."

"Nicely put."

"Did . . . did you get my package?"

"Yea, they paid me."

"No . . . did you get the information? About the girl? The reason you wanted to go to MIT?"

"Oh! Yea! Yea, I got it. A shocker!"

"I know. Too bad! At least, you don't have heartbreak, now that you're in love with Naomi."

"To think that I wanted to fuck my own sister. Well, half sister. But I can't believe that no one ever told me! Not even my parents! I couldn't even remember!"

"Well, now you know."

"I met her, you know. She came over. She didn't go to MIT after all. She's at Harvard. Gonna be a lawyer."

"What you wanted to be?" joked Jif.

"Shut up, man." He chuckled.

"Anyway, I'll let you get on with—" There was a creak of the stairs as Naomi appeared. She was dressed in a pink negligee. Pretty. Chelsea was behind her, and the rest of the Babylon Zoo residents appeared round the corner of the stairs.

"I thought you wouldn't pull out," Naomi sighed in a sad, weak voice. *She is glad to see me because it is good for Charlie.* At last, she was a human being. She did love and care for Charlie.

"I say, never quit. You know, I tried to kill you twice, in my dream."

"Kill me! Why?"

"I blamed you for Charlie's death! It felt so real too. I gunned everyone in this house. I could even smell the gunpowder! But all I can say now is I'm glad I didn't."

"Jif," stated the girl, "I myself have killed people, and I am glad you didn't do what you did in reality because when a man commits murder, he will never forget it, and he will never be the same person again." She came close to Charlie and held the boy's hand. She smiled. She was in love him. Jif nodded in agreement and acceptance.

"Quite right. Rock is the perfect example."

"Who's Rock?" asked Charlie, confused.

"The dead Jap. He hated Yuzuyu!"

"That's why?" they both exclaimed.

"Yep." Jif stopped and looked down at his watch. "Come on, guys. It's 2:00 am. We all gotta go work in the morning, ain't we?"

"Some of us," replied Foxy. The residents started to depart along the stairs.

"Goodnight, Jif," lilted Rajah.

"And don't sleep too long," stated Naomi.

"Or you won't wake up for thirty days," joked Charlie. And all the girls giggled their way down the stairs.

"Come on, Jif," coaxed Yuzuyu, "I'll fix you." They stumbled into the bedroom. She tried to pull off his fleece. He got hold of her shoulders and sat her on the bed. Her puffer slipped off her shoulders easily but got bunched up around her wrists. She hastily pulled them off while Jif undressed his top half. She pulled on his trousers toward herself and pulled him onto the bed. Trousers were pulled off, along with underwear. She kissed him repeatedly on his chest, before removing her black jeans. She paused and then shuffled closer to him, so that her hips were level with his face. She placed his hands on the side of the diaper and made a tugging motion.

"Pull off my diaper, Jif," she said with a smile. Jif scooped her clothes that were on the bed and dropped them in a pile next to the bedside table that he completely forgot about. They straddle each other for the first time, playing with each other's sex organs.

"I want you to be dominant," he said, placing her onto him. They continued until they got tired and couldn't continue anymore. They finished in a film of sweat. She was still onto him, in a kneeling position. Both satisfied and relaxed.

"Daski," she whispered in Japanese. Jif knew what she was saying, but she spoke it in English anyway. "I love you, Jif," mumbled Yuzuyu as she cupped his head in her hands. She kissed his lips again and started crying, pushing her head into his shoulder. Jif wrapped her body again with his arms and squeezed her closer to him. "I'm so happy," she blubbered.

Jif felt himself becoming weaker and weaker. He didn't want to sleep after making love; it would be so wrong! But he just couldn't keep his eyes open.

"Yuzuyu," he called, "I can't stay awake. I'm fallin' asleep!"

"It's OK," reassured Yuzuyu, pulling her head from his shoulder and kissing his cheek. "It's OK. I'm tired too."

"Uh . . . ," he groaned. "Thank you." And with that, Jif closed his eyes and let slumber consume his body.

EIGHTEEN

Jif opened his eyes again as the morning sun tried to fight its way through the curtains. He pondered if this was reality. Had he been dreaming all this time? Was this a dream now? Then she kissed him. And he smiled as he knew this was reality.

THE END

GLOSSARY

BG = Bodyguard

Black and white = police car

EST = Eastern Standard Time

GMT = Greenwich Mean Time

Head shed = nickname for anyone with authority

JST = Japanese Standard time

Sit rep = Situation Report

Slime = Intelligence Corps